Praise for Karen Kincy's
Other

"This who-done-it is an unusual blend of mystery and fantasy, starring original characters not often featured in modern urban fantasy for teens. I really enjoyed it."
—Annette Curtis Klause,
author of *Blood and Chocolate*

"*Other* has it all: love, shifters, pookas, and nail-biting action. What's even better, Kincy's characters are vibrant, real, and lovable. This is a debut that leaves you aching for more."
—Carrie Jones, *New York Times*
bestselling author of *Need* and *Captivate*

"Gwen is extremely likable as the impulsive, conflicted heroine…[and the] romance is a dynamic counterpoint to the suspenseful mystery."
—*Booklist*

"The emotional turmoil of the characters is evident and will appeal to readers who have felt misunderstood or as if they don't belong."
—*School Library Journal*

Praise for Karen Kincy's
Bloodborn

"With *Bloodborn*, Karen Kincy opens a frightening new chapter in the werewolf legacy. Brilliant, dark, and filled with haunting images. Highly recommended."

—Jonathan Maberry, *New York Times*
bestselling author of *Rot & Ruin*
and *The King of Plagues*

"A bridge between paranormals and boys' realism about thugs and delinquents, reminiscent of Neal Shusterman's *Dark Fusion: Red Rider's Hood.*"

—*Kirkus Reviews*

"Teens will enjoy this alternate-reality story of a young man trying to come to terms with what he is."

—*VOYA*

Foxfire

Also by Karen Kincy

Other
Bloodborn

Foxfire

karen kincy

flux
™
Woodbury, Minnesota

First Edition
First Printing, 2012

Book format by Bob Gaul
Cover design by Lisa Novak
Cover image © Fox statue: Keren Su/Photodisc/PunchStock
             Man: eyedear/Shutterstock Images
             Pagoda: MIXA Co. Ltd./PunchStock
             Red fox: iStockphoto.com/Eric Isselée

Flux, an imprint of Llewellyn Worldwide Ltd.

Library of Congress Cataloging-in-Publication Data
Kincy, Karen, 1986–
  Foxfire/Karen Kincy.—1st ed.
     p. cm.—(Other; #3)
  Summary: At age six, Tavian Kimura was abandonned by his mother —a kitsune, or Japanese fox-spirit. Now he's back in Tokyo, with girl-friend Gwen by his side. Pursued by a faceless ghost and a gang of fierce dog-spirits, and made ill by his untrained magic, Tavian realizes that finding his mother might be the only way to get answers before it's too late.—Provided by publisher.
  ISBN 978-0-7387-3057-8
  [1. Shapeshifting—Fiction. 2. Supernatural—Fiction. 3. Magic—Fiction.] I. Title.
  PZ7.K5656Fox 2012
  [Fic]—dc23

                                2012019102
Flux
Llewellyn Worldwide Ltd.
2143 Wooddale Drive
Woodbury, MN 55125-2989
www.fluxnow.com

Printed in the United States of America

To Mad and Ellie, my sisters and first fans,
for the nights we howled at the moon

one

Cold.

Bitter, bone-deep cold, the kind that gnaws at your toes and nose. Your tail, too, when you have one, and right now I do. Its white tip brushes along the snow, flicking pine needles away as I skulk after my mother, my pawprints in hers, our ears pricked for any sound of humans. We don't belong here, so close to the fields. But the scent of cooking tofu on the wind makes my stomach ache harder than any cold could.

My mother freezes, one paw raised, then coughs. *Hide.*

I dart beneath a low bush and crouch, shivering.

The longer I hold still, the more I freeze. I'm just a kit fox, and my fur hasn't grown as thick as my mother's. She sniffs the air, then glances at me, her orange eyes sparkling.

Voices. Heavy boots, tamping down the snow. Two boys walk down the path, talking.

My mother sits and rubs her tail with her forepaws. Her fur crackles, the tiny sparks melting into a white ball of light. *Kitsune-bi.* Foxfire. A smile curls my lips, and I poke my nose farther out from the leaves.

The boys stop. "Look," the fat one says. "Pawprints."

The skinny one squats over the snow, then shudders. "Foxes?"

"Maybe. We should get out of here."

My mother rears onto her hind legs and tosses the ball of foxfire down the slope. It rolls like a white apple, right under the nose of the fat boy. His gaze latches onto it, and he starts to trot after it—he can't help himself. The foxfire rolls into a dark tangle of forest, and the fat boy crashes after it in his clumsy hunger.

"Daisuke!" the skinny boy shouts. "Daisuke, stop!"

My mother flicks her ear at me. Time to go. I climb out from under the bush and shake myself off, careful not to let the boys see. We flit through the shadows. The snow-burdened farmhouse stands ahead, just through the trees. Golden light spills from a kitchen window, along with the scent of tofu. I nearly whimper.

"Daisuke!" The skinny boy's voice sounds shrill with panic.

I glance back. I hope we haven't hurt them…but no, we trick, not kill.

The skinny boy whistles, then waves his arm as if calling a pet to come. I sniff with laughter. That won't help.

Then three dogs streak from behind the farmhouse. Their breath steams the air as they pant, their black-spotted tongues lolling, their tightly curled tails held high. *Hokkaido-inu*, a breed with a fierce hatred of foxes.

My mother flattens herself to the ground, but it's too late. Barking, the dogs spin toward her, their paws kicking mud into the snow.

The skinny boy laughs. "Found the fox, Daisuke!"

My mother's muzzle twists into a snarl. The dogs hurtle toward her as if she's nothing more than a scrap of meat to be snatched up. My heartbeat drums against my chest, and my legs lock into stiff logs.

A dog leaps upon my mother and drives its jaws toward her neck. She twists nimbly out of the way and sprints for the trees. The dogs tear after her, their teeth snapping inches from her bushy tail. She dodges between roots and brambles, a zigzagging streak of orange, then vanishes into the darkness of the night.

Daisuke stumbles back onto the path, blinking. "What happened?"

"You fell for foxfire," the other boy says. "But I set the dogs on the little *kitsune* bitch."

They don't know I'm here. Quivering, I sink down into the snow and hide in the white. Wind shakes new snow like salt onto Japan. It blankets the black trees as the boys walk toward the farmhouse. It piles thick on my back as I wait for my mother. Soon I have to blink to see, then shake myself to not be buried alive. I dig a little den beneath the gnarled toes of a tree, then settle down for the night.

She will come back. She's never left me alone before, not for long.

Fear drifts down inside me, settling higher and higher.

She will come back.

"Seriously, Tavian. What were you dreaming about?" Gwen asks.

We're crammed in the sardine-tight rows of economy airline seating. Outside the tiny porthole window, dark sky and equally dark water stream by. I rest my forehead against the cool glass and squeeze my sleep-fogged eyes shut.

"Nothing spectacular," I lie.

"You were making these weird noises," she says, and I glance at her. "Whimpers." She narrows her eyes at me. They gleam amber in the dim light, and I know she knows I'm not telling the whole truth. Or even a smidgen of it.

There's no point in arguing about it, and I don't want her eyes to get any brighter, not with a plane full of humans. I slip my fingers between hers.

4

"I'll tell you later," I whisper. "All right?"

"Okay." Her mouth twists in that wry smile of hers. Snarky, she calls it. "With interest."

I arch an eyebrow. "Interest?"

"Well, if you're withholding interesting information from me now," she says, "you'd better make it extra juicy later."

Her hot breath in my ear distracts me, but I keep a straight face. "Yes, ma'am."

Gwen's smile relaxes into something realer. "You ready?"

"For what?"

"Japan."

I laugh to mask my dread. "I'd better be."

She squeezes my hand, then leans against my shoulder and shuts her eyes.

I don't keep track of time. I'm lost in the sameness of the stale air and humming of the plane. My eyelids keep slipping down, but whenever I close them, all I see is the white of snow. I don't want to return to that dream. I already know what happens next, when that winter night blurred into an eternity. Frigid fear still seeps through me now, like I never closed the door on that part of my life. Believe me, I've tried.

My mother left me to the snow and the dogs. I was six years old.

Dawn strengthens and takes hold, a gorgeous cherry-blossom pink that makes my fingers itch for a paintbrush. We land in Narita International Airport at around noon. The polished floors and exposed steel ceilings reflect the human swarms and the gleam of artificial light. By the time we get through customs, Gwen's famished. She keeps groaning dramatically whenever we walk past vending machines, which stand like an army of robots with a tidy rainbow of snacks and drinks in their glass bellies.

"They have everything here," she says. "Jasmine tea, ice cream, ramen noodle soup—"

"Schoolgirl panties," I say.

Gwen wrinkles her nose. "Tavian!"

"It's true," I say, grinning. "It's a fetish around here. Businessmen pay tons of yen for—"

"Are those your grandparents over there?" She lowers her voice. "Because I'm not sure they're interested in panties."

My heartbeat stumbles. "Where?"

I've only met them once, when I was seven, and that was the day before I left Japan. My memory of them is more than a little moth-eaten, and I have to fill in their faces with the photos in our family album.

Gwen laughs. "I'm kidding! Wow, don't have a heart attack."

I make a noise between a growl and a sigh. I have no idea how she's so hyper on so little sleep. Then again, that's Gwen for you.

She inhales sharply. "Holy crap. Is that a Bigness Burger?"

Ahead, a fast-food joint with a blaring, mustard-yellow sign beckons. Some desperate guy in a grinning fox suit is hopping around and waving like he's walking on hot coals. I wince and walk faster past this travesty.

"Look!" Gwen says. "Isn't that their kitsune mascot? Ki-chan?"

"Yes," I mutter. "But that *thing* is not a kitsune."

I happen to know a thing or two about the subject, being the genuine article myself.

She rolls her eyes. "Oh, you're just biased."

"I'm biased toward fast-food chains not making an idiot out of me."

Gwen arches her eyebrows. "Well, I think it's cute."

"Japan can be a cute overdose." I pretend to squeal like an anime girl. "Oh, so *kawaii!*"

"Admit it. Ki-chan is cool." She pokes me. "In America you'd never see anybody using an Other as a mascot."

"Because it's not politically correct. How would you feel if McDonald's made up Perky the Pooka to sell fries?"

Gwen snorts. "That might be kind of nice. You know, if people thought pookas weren't evil rampaging demon horses."

I shrug. I guess she knows a thing or two about that.

Ki-chan hears us speaking English and zeros in on us. He squats before Gwen—the most obvious sales-pitch target—and scoops air with both hands. Maybe he thinks he can literally reel us in with the sheer force of his craziness. He even makes a little yipping noise that makes me bite back a smile.

"Come on," Gwen says, "aren't you hungry? I read in the guidebook that Bigness Burger makes fabulous barbecued eel."

I stare at her. "You're actually interested in eating barbecued eel?"

"We're in Japan!" She throws her arms into the air and dances, almost crashing into my suitcase. "Aren't you excited?"

I catch her by the wrist and tug her to face me. She leans against me, her face flushed, her hair already wild, and kisses me quickly.

"This isn't my first time here," I say.

Her smile fades. "Bad memories?"

I shrug again. She's only heard the quick and dirty version of my life in Japan.

Her eyes get big. "Grandparents. Three o'clock."

"My three o'clock or yours?"

"Mine. See? They have a red umbrella."

Sure enough, a silver-haired man in a crisp ivory suit strolls along with a red umbrella held high—that's our signal. A woman about his age follows at his heels, chattering a million miles an hour in Japanese. She's wearing grey plaid pants pulled up way too high at the waist. She's got to be what, four foot six? Maybe? Granted, I'm only five foot four, but I could get used to this whole actually-being-taller-than-somebody thing.

I squint. Are they really Tsuyoshi and Michiko, my *ojīsan* and *obāsan*?

The woman glances in our direction. Her nut-brown skin is wrinkled in a thousand folds. She sucks in her breath, then seizes her husband's arm. He swivels toward us, his face statuesque. He's carrying her black and pink purse, which kind of destroys his stony I'm-your-elder-so-you'd-better-respect-me look.

His gaze moves from me to Gwen—specifically, Gwen's coppery curls.

She tries out a smile. "Are you Tavian's grandparents?"

The man's brows descend and he adjusts his square glasses. "Octavian?"

"Yes." I hold out my hand so he can shake it. "I'm your grandson?"

He grabs my hand like he wants to pulverize it and gives it a brisk up-and-down shake. "My name is Kimura Tsuyoshi. I am your grandfather." Talking with him over the telephone didn't do justice to his deep, Darth Vader voice. He's only a few inches taller than me, so I have no clue why he gets to sound so imposing.

"And this is your grandmother," he says, "Kimura Michiko."

Michiko nods with a polite smile, and I bow back.

"Obāsan," I say. "Good to finally see you."

She straightens, her mouth all puckered up like she's sucking on a straw and getting only air. Of course she's staring at Gwen, who's blushing red-hot and towering over everybody like a giantess.

"Yes," Michiko says, "good to see you."

"Thanks so much for inviting me and Tavian to come visit for the holidays!" Gwen says, shaking Tsuyoshi's hand. "I've never traveled abroad before. I mean, I know this isn't just travel, and I'm really looking forward to getting to know you better." She clutches my hand. "I know you mean a lot to Tavian."

Tsuyoshi and Michiko both nod, turtle-slow. They both speak English well, according to Mom and Dad, but Gwen does have a tendency to rattle off words when she gets nervous. I squeeze Gwen's hand and try to communicate through eyebrows alone that she should talk slowly and simply. Also, not keel over dead under the force of Tsuyoshi's scrutiny.

"Let's go," Tsuyoshi says.

He folds the red umbrella and marches away. Michiko follows him, so Gwen and I have no choice but to lug our luggage and try to keep up.

"I thought they were fluent in English?" Gwen whispers in my ear.

"They are." I smirk. "But don't worry, I bought you that phrase book."

She sighs. "I can't learn Japanese in three weeks."

I arch an eyebrow. "You'd be surprised what you can pick up when forced to communicate like a Neanderthal."

Or when you can't communicate at all, and your growls and yips brand you a crazy boy.

We file out of the airport and head for the parking garage. Tsuyoshi takes a key fob from his pocket and clicks the button. A silver Audi sedan flashes its lights. I arch my eyebrows. Nice! And also pretty damn expensive. We all pile into the Audi and the engine starts with a tiger's purr. Gwen glances at me and squeezes my hand.

"Buckle down," Michiko says.

I think she means "buckle up," but I fasten my seat belt anyway—and just in time. Tsuyoshi peels rubber as he whips the Audi into reverse, drifts sideways, then shifts into drive and zooms out of the parking garage. We hit the road, and Michiko rattles off something in Japanese. Tsuyoshi mutters back and I don't catch any of it.

Gwen looks at me and mouths, "What did they say?"

I shrug and shake my head.

Frost ices the black trees along the highway, and the blank sky hints at snow. It's the twenty-first of December: the first day of winter. I know it's stupid, but I wish I could have returned to Japan in the summer. Winter feels unlucky. When I joked about this with my parents back home, Mom told me not to worry, and Dad said it was important to Tsuyoshi and Michiko that I was visiting them for *Shōgatsu*—New Year's—which is a huge deal in Japan.

I guess they're right.

The highway from Narita to Tokyo is lined by ugly concrete clone buildings and construction, but Gwen still presses her nose against the glass, soaking up every glimpse of Japan. The hum of tires on pavement starts to lull me asleep.

The car window reflects my spiky hair and the shadows under my eyes. In the corner of the glass, an eggshell-white oval drifts nearer. A face, but it has no eyes, no nose, no mouth. Faceless. Blank skin stretched tight over a hairless skull. When I blink, it's gone, and the hairs on my arms are standing on end.

Either my brain is glitching, or I'm being haunted.

two

Akasaka, Tokyo: a neighborhood in the Minato ward, in the heart of the metropolis. Tsuyoshi screeches to a halt in front of an imposing skyscraper—maybe his resumé includes stunt driver—and tosses a valet his keys. The rest of us climb out at a more reasonable pace, faintly carsick in my case. Gwen peers up at the glass-and-steel tower, squinting as the wind blows snowflakes into her eyes. I feel conspicuously shabby as we enter the polished granite lobby. Uniformed men and women bow smartly as we pass.

We take the elevator up to the thirty-eighth floor, near the top of the skyscraper. Michiko unlocks the door and I resist the urge to gawk. Outside, Tokyo glitters beyond vast windows. Inside, everything glistens in hardwood, eggshell white, and bits of glossy black. The condo looks as elegant and well-balanced as a calligraphy scroll.

I knew they were well-off, but I hadn't actually seen it until now.

We all take off our shoes and step into house slippers. Tracking any dirt past the *genkan*, or entryway, would be an enormous no-no. I'm about to walk onto the raised floor of the living room when I freeze in midstep, inches away from a faux pas. I'm *tebura*, empty-handed. I unzip my bag and pull out a collectible tin of Aplets and Cotlets. I bought the fruit candies at the airport in Seattle, after Gwen reminded me I didn't have a gift for my hosts.

Holding the Aplets and Cotlets in both hands, I offer them to my grandparents with a slight bow. "*Tsumaranai mono desu ga, dōzo.*" My very rough translation: I'm afraid this isn't much of a gift; please accept this boring thing.

Tsuyoshi and Michiko both incline their heads. "*Arigatō gozaimasu.*" Thank you.

"*Dōitashimashite.*" You're welcome.

My face heats. I'm sure my Japanese sounds awful, or I've forgotten something vital about gift-giving and now look like an ungrateful idiot. But Michiko takes the tin from me with a small smile, then squirrels it away in the kitchen.

Tsuyoshi turns to me. "Leave your things here," he says in Japanese.

I nod, the rusty language gears clicking in my brain. Michiko starts to lug my huge suitcase away, despite the fact that it's almost taller than she is, and I say, "Please," also in Japanese. "Let me help."

"Oh, no, you should prepare for dinner."

Frowning, Gwen taps me on the shoulder. "Tavian?" she whispers.

"Sorry," I say to her. "We're eating soon, so it's time to get ready."

"You could have said that in English," she mutters, her cheeks red.

In the bathroom, I'm confronted by a ridiculously high-tech toilet that looks like it might either start self-replicating or eat my butt. I try a button, and I get a flushing noise but nothing more. One of those modesty sound effects for those embarrassed by certain—ahem—noises. After some fiddling, I flush the stupid thing.

Bathroom conquered, I discover Gwen lingering in the hallway. She glances back and forth between the doorways of the two guest bedrooms, each furnished with a tiny bed and a tiny window that looks out onto falling snow.

"Did you call dibs on a bedroom yet?" I say.

She shrugs. "They're more like closets. I'm not sure I'll fit."

I roll my eyes. "I'll take the right-hand one."

I toss my jacket onto my bed, but it looks too sloppy

in the pristine black-and-white aesthetic of the room, so I fold it neatly.

Gwen arches her eyebrows. "You okay?" she says in a low voice.

"What do you mean?"

"Well, you don't normally fold clothes. Your bedroom floor at home doesn't have a square inch of visible carpet."

I try to laugh, but it sounds fake.

Gwen furrows her brow. "No, seriously. You look sick."

"I'm exhausted," I say. "Aren't you?"

"Hopefully you didn't catch some germs from that nasty recycled air on the plane."

Of course, the plane wasn't the problem. I can't stop thinking about the car ride here and what I saw in the window. I *am* exhausted. Maybe I'm hallucinating.

I meet Gwen's eyes. "This is going to sound really dumb."

"Tavian. Just tell me."

"I can't tell you, exactly." I blow out my breath. "I don't know what it was. When we were in the car, I saw this sort of white oval reflected in the window, like a face, only it didn't have any face on it. No eyes, no nose, no mouth, no anything."

"A faceless face? Isn't that impossible?" There's still more snark than worry in her voice.

"I swear, that's what it looked like. Blank skin stretched over bone. Smooth as an egg."

Gwen shivers. "You really saw this?"

I nod.

"Are there any Others here like that?"

I hesitate. "I didn't think of that. I thought I was dreaming."

"Was that what you were dreaming about on the plane?"

"No." I swallow, trying to wet my parched mouth. "That was about my mother."

"Oh." Gwen starts to say something more, then stops herself.

There's a little cough. I glance back. Michiko stands in the doorway, wearing a blue dress patterned with either cloudy flowers or flowery clouds.

"Dinnertime," she says.

Tsuyoshi and Michiko have a fairly traditional dining room, with a low table and pillows for kneeling. Dinner itself is delicious, a stew simmering in a hotpot on the table: beef, tofu, thick *udon* noodles, and tender *shitake* mushrooms. The hot *miso* broth slides down my throat and settles in my belly, filling me with a warm, dozy feeling.

For dessert, Michiko makes a big show out of opening the tin of Aplets and Cotlets, exclaiming over each sugar-powdered candy as if it's precious. I can't stop smiling, and for the first time today, Japan feels a little like home.

After dinner, Gwen calls her parents and I guiltily snatch up my cell phone, remembering I promised to tell

Mom and Dad whether I'd crashed into the Pacific or not.

I stand by the window and dial. "Hey, this is Tavian—"

"Tavian?" Mom says. "Wait a second, let me get your father." Without waiting for me to reply, I hear some muffled movement. "Kazuki! It's Tavian!"

My dad joins on the other line. "Was your flight delayed?" is the first thing out his mouth.

"No," I say. "Sorry, I meant to call sooner—"

"I knew he would be okay," Mom says.

Dad grunts.

"How are Ojīsan and Obāsan?" Mom talks rapid-fire, like she's afraid Dad will butt in. "I hope you've been nothing but polite to them."

"Yes, Mom. It's great to finally meet them."

"And your Japanese?" Dad says.

I frown and slide one finger down the cool glass of the window. "Not too horrific."

"Your grandparents don't like English," Dad says, for the eight hundred billionth time. "You should respect them by speaking their language."

I clench my jaw. "I'm trying."

"Octavian." Dad sounds like he's getting pissed.

"Kazuki," Mom says. "I'm sure Tavian is doing just fine. And I'm sure your parents are more than *under-standing*." I can imagine her glaring at Dad while she says that.

They know my Japanese is childish at best. I spent the first six years of my life mostly as a fox. At the orphanage, they taught me how to behave like a good little boy, and I learned fast to avoid the sting of a textbook to the head. But Mom and Dad took me to America when I was seven, and Japanese was no longer a necessity.

"What are you planning to visit tomorrow?" Mom says, her voice falsely chipper. "Which district of Tokyo?"

"Not sure yet. I'm guessing Gwen will love Shibuya. Especially Harajuku."

"Harajuku?" Dad grumbles. "Full of punks and hipsters."

Dad grew up in Tokyo, unlike Mom, who's second-generation Japanese-American. This doesn't stop Mom from making an exaggerated sigh, like my dad is totally uncultured.

"Octavian, ignore your father."

I swallow a yawn. "Anyway, it's almost eleven here. It must be really early over there."

"Nearly six a.m.," Mom says.

"And your mother still hasn't had her coffee yet," Dad mutters. "She needs it."

I laugh, imagining their joking bickering.

After saying goodbye, I tiptoe into Gwen's guest bedroom. She's still on the phone with her parents, talking in an excited murmur. She smiles when I blow her a kiss goodnight. I sneak back into my own bedroom before I'm caught.

I'm so tired I pass out the moment I hit my bed.

In my dreams, I'm no longer in Tokyo, but Hokkaido, the wild northernmost island. I'm walking naked through the snow, and for some reason I can't turn into a fox, no matter how hard I strain for the transformation.

In the snow, there is only me, alone, lost. I don't belong here.

Cold scrapes every bit of warmth from my skin. Above the howling wind, I hear a woman's scream. The sound cuts straight to my bone. The wind shifts, and she screams again. Not a woman—a vixen's cry. I run, stumbling, numb, until I trip sprawling in the snow. Flurries descend on me, burying me. My teeth chatter so hard they hurt.

Before me, a geisha-pale woman stands in the snow. Her hair flies like a ragged black banner flecked with snow. She wears a gleaming white kimono—the color of a bride, or of the dead. She lifts her arms to me, beckoning. Her red lips part, and she screams again. The call of a vixen who has lost her kit.

"*Okāsan,*" I say. Mother.

A tear slides down her cheek. "*Kogitsune.*" Little Fox.

"Why are you here?" I say.

"Come with me," she says, her eyes as beautiful and hard as amber.

I climb to my feet, shivering, my skin icy. "Where?"
"Home."

The snowy landscape shimmers, and for a second I see the deep green forests of Washington. The face of my mother blinks into Mom—the woman who raised me—then back into my mother.

Dread worms its way into my heart. "I can't."

"Kogitsune." Okāsan sounds faraway. "Come with me before it is too late."

I step toward her, to touch her, to know that she's real.

But there's a man standing before me, and he has no face. The snow doesn't even touch his dark suit, just falls right through. He's thin, like rice paper. Like a ghost.

The faceless man raises both of his hands to me, palms out, as if I'm a child about to fall from a high place and he'll catch me. Okāsan's face twists, her teeth sharpening into fangs, her ears pointing into black tips.

Her voice vibrates with a growl. "You're dead."

The faceless man reaches into his jacket and draws a gun.

Okāsan's eyes narrow, and she laughs.

He pulls the trigger; the dream shatters. Red blooms on white, spattering the snow, soaking the kimono as she falls.

I wake with a gasp, a piercing pain radiating from the scar above my heart. With every heartbeat, fresh pain makes me double over in agony. I feel like I might vomit. I stagger to my feet and lurch to the bathroom.

In the hall, I nearly crash into Tsuyoshi, who's standing there with a glass of water.

"Tavian!" he says.

I lean against the wall and try to stand up straight. "Sorry. Excuse me."

"What is the matter?"

I shut my eyes. The pain is making me sweat. My mouth fills with saliva, and I swallow until the urge to retch fades. "I don't know what my parents told you, but several months ago there were murders in my hometown...somebody was killing Others like me...I got shot, and..."

Tsuyoshi points to my chest. "There?"

I nod. "Above my heart."

"And it pains you?"

"Sometimes. I don't know why. They took the bullet out." Slowly, the throbbing starts to feel less raw. "It's getting better now...I need to rest."

Tsuyoshi frowns. "Do you need a doctor?"

Believe me, I've asked doctors, and put up with endless tests, but they can't find anything wrong, physically. They told me it was predictable angina, which means I get chest pains periodically. They told me to take aspirin for it, but that hasn't helped. Not that it's ever been this bad before. This is pain in another league.

"I'm fine," I say.

Which is what I've been telling everybody, including Gwen, so they would let me travel.

Something shifts on Tsuyoshi's face, as if he understands me now. "I know of a temple," he says, "where they can help you."

I frown. I don't know what he means.

Tsuyoshi takes off his glasses and polishes them meticulously on his shirt. "Human doctors may not know how to treat people like you." Which I guess is a polite way of saying, treat Others. "We will need to talk to the *myobu.*"

Myobu, temple foxes. Servants of the rice god Inari. Also known as celestial kitsune, considered by humans to be far more sophisticated and trustworthy than the petty, devilish *nogitsune*—that is, field foxes like my mother. And me, of course. Somehow, I don't think they're going to bestow any blessings on me.

"My mother was a nogitsune," I say flatly.

Tsuyoshi's face creases into a frown. "That is why you must speak to the myobu."

Why? So they can try to sell me some overpriced mumbo jumbo?

I bite the inside of my cheek. I don't want to be disrespectful to Tsuyoshi. "All right. I will think about it. Thank you."

He is silent for a very long time. "Sleep."

I nod, return to my bedroom, and lie down.

His face blank, Tsuyoshi shuts the door behind me. His shadow lingers for a moment. When I'm sure he's gone, I sneak over to Gwen's bedroom. The blinds on the window by her bed are open, the light of Tokyo casting an amber glow on her face. One arm lies flung above her head, and her sheets twist around her legs.

"Gwen?" I whisper.

She remains peaceful, sleeping. I could leave her this way. I should leave her this way. But I need to tell her about this, or I'll be tempted to chicken out later.

I shut the door, then lie on the bed beside her. She mumbles something unintelligible and scoots back against me, almost shoving me onto the floor.

"Hey," I murmur in her ear.

She blinks herself awake, and frowns. "Don't you have a bed of your own?"

"It's not as nice as yours."

"Scandalous. Your grandparents are going to kill you if they find out."

I try to smile. "Gwen, I need to tell you something."

Her frown deepens and she sits up. "What? What's going on?"

"Remember how I was dreaming on the flight here?"

"Yeah. You never really told me what that was about, though."

I swing my legs over the edge of the bed. "The night my kitsune mother left me in the snow. In Hokkaido. More of a memory, really. Tonight I dreamed about her again, but it didn't make any sense. We were in Hokkaido, but we were both human—in reality, we were pretty much always foxes in the winter, since it was so cold."

Gwen arches an eyebrow. "So you've been dreaming about her? That's not that weird."

"It gets weirder, trust me. My kitsune mother was wearing a kimono, one as white as the snow, and she was calling for me to come with her. But there was a man in a suit. He pulled out a gun and shot her. Blood soaked the snow…"

"Did you recognize the man?"

"I couldn't—he had no face."

"No face?" Gwen sucks in her breath. "Like what you saw in the car?"

"Yes. I think so? I don't know what else it could be."

She stares at me, her eyes glittering. "Tavian. Do you know what the faceless man is?"

I shake my head.

"I did some research." She flicks on the light, rummages in her bag, and lugs out a beat-up old textbook.

"So much for packing light," I say.

Her cheeks redden. "Part of my Paranormal Studies," she says. "Thought I might as well study Japanese Others while I was, you know, in Japan."

"Wow." I arch my eyebrows. "I'm impressed by your insanity."

She brushes my comment away. "If I'm majoring in this, I'd better know my shit."

"Gwen, you're half-pooka. One of the rarest Others in America. An extreme minority. Plus, you're smart.

Every college in existence is going to be fighting to admit you."

She rolls her eyes. "Your flattery will get you nothing."

"Not even a kiss?" I say, and I prove my point.

Gwen makes an impatient noise, but she kisses me back. "Anyway." She scoots sideways on the bed, so I can't keep distracting her, and flips open her book. "I read up on *yōkai*." Spirit, demon, monster. One of my names, at the orphanage. "And," she says, "I found an entry on *noppera-bō*. Faceless ghosts."

Faceless ghosts. Ice water trickles through my blood.

"Apparently," Gwen says, "the noppera-bō can mimic any human face, which it does before it wipes its features away. The book says they're harmless spirits fond of frightening humans."

"Harmless." I furrow my brow. "He shot my mother."

"Well, your biological mother isn't human."

I rake my fingers through my hair. "Then why, if I saw a noppera-bō, didn't it have a face? Why was it already faceless?"

"I don't know."

"Does the book say anything else?" I say. "Like where it comes from?"

Gwen shakes her head. "There isn't anything in here about them entering dreams, either." She tilts her head sideways and fiddles with one of her curls. "Do you think your kitsune mother was actually entering your dreams? I mean, I remember when you entered my mind, back when—you know." She presses her lips together.

And I do know. I'm never going to forget. It's how I got the scar above my heart, from the hunting rifle of the serial killer who missed his mark. In the hospital, I lay drifting in a white bed, my mind numbed by drugs, and I saw Gwen when I closed my eyes. When I slipped into her sleep, I could feel her pain—something was horribly wrong.

Gwen. You have to wake up.

Are you okay?

Don't worry about me. Worry about yourself.

"Tavian?" Gwen clutches my hand. "Are you okay?"

I shake my head to fling the memory away. "Yeah."

"Sorry, I didn't mean—"

"No worries."

She squeezes my hand, then lets go. "When it happened," she says, "I could only hear your voice. Is that how it's supposed to work? Is that what your mother did?"

"She's full kitsune," I say. "Much more powerful than me."

"If she's so powerful, then why hasn't she entered your dreams before? She's had more than a decade to do it." Gwen twists her mouth. "Or she could have picked up a phone."

"We're in Japan now."

"So she waited for you to come to her? Why didn't she come to America?"

My jaw tightens and I climb to my feet. "I don't know

why she left me. I don't know why she wants me to come with her now."

"Do you trust her?"

"Why are you so pissed about this?" I realize I'm talking way too loud, so I lower my voice to a whisper. "If your pooka father visited you, wouldn't you be excited?"

She scoffs. "I'm not pissed."

"Really? Because you definitely don't seem happy about it."

"Tavian." Gwen wraps her arms around my waist and leans against me. "It's just...something seems off. Be careful. Okay?"

"Of course."

My heart twinges, a shadow of the pain I felt before, but enough to make my stomach squirm. I breathe in deeply through my nose. Should I tell Gwen? I've been letting her believe I haven't been hurting anymore.

"I am kind of jealous," she mutters.

"Oh?"

"I have a feeling my pooka dad is too busy gallivanting around Wales to actually discover he has a daughter." Then Gwen laughs. "Not that I could afford a ticket to Wales to find out."

"Hey," I say. "Since you came with me to Japan, I'll come with you to Wales. As soon as we're rich and famous."

"Tavian, you're so sweet." She yawns. "Now go back to bed. You look like a zombie."

I wonder if I'm pale, if my circulation is poor somehow. "Right."

She stretches her arms over her head, baring the skin of her belly, then yanks her T-shirt back down and groans. "Bollocks. I have got to shapeshift. Soon. Before I go crazy. It's been this constant craving ever since the flight here, but that really wasn't the time or the place."

I arch my eyebrows. "You shapeshifted before we left. Spent a good three hours running around in the forest as a horse. That wasn't enough?"

"Apparently not," she says dryly. "Wish I could tell my pooka half to shut up, but no such luck. Maybe we could shapeshift tomorrow?"

"In the city?"

She smirks. "We can get creative."

"Sounds like a date."

We kiss goodnight, a genuine kiss on the lips this time. As I pad toward the door, Gwen mumbles something, her face smushed against her pillow.

"What was that?" I say.

"Tomorrow," she says, "we explore Tokyo."

"Definitely."

If only so I can find answers to my dreams.

three

I remember when Mom and Dad—though they weren't that to me yet—took me on the train from Sapporo, Hokkaido, to Ueno, Tokyo. I remember glass-and-steel canyons flowing with rivers of people. I remember shivering, hiding behind the woman who tried to calm me down, and baring my teeth at people.

Now, riding the Tokyo Metro, packed tight with dozens of strangers, I feel the fox inside me flattening his ears, wary. I glance from face to face, noting only blank expressions. The metro feels like a place between places, or the time between a dream and waking.

And then, we're here: Harajuku.

I grab Gwen's hand and we swell upward with the crowd, surfacing in the overcast daylight. Gwen brandishes her camera and snaps photos of Harajuku Station, a white-and-brown building that looks more like an English cottage. To the west, snow frosts the bare branches of trees in a park—Yoyogi Park. But we're really here for the pedestrian bridge, Jingu Bashi, that connects Harajuku with Yoyogi Park.

"Harajuku kids," Gwen breathes, as if unearthing a rare artifact.

She grabs my hand, her grip crushing, and drags me forward. We run along the length of the bridge and skid to a halt in the center, at the epicenter of the Harajuku kids.

Doll-like, hair-ribboned girls in Alice in Wonderland dresses—Gothic Lolitas—giggle around a girl wearing a neon rainbow sweater, striped tights, and huge star-shaped sunglasses. They're watching an androgynous kid in a black frockcoat and top hat pose next to a guy with ghostly makeup, electric-blue dreads, and pink contact lenses. Androgynous Kid and Blue-Dreads Guy make the peace sign, a tourist takes their picture, and then the Harajuku kids scatter back into the surrounding kaleidoscope of crazy clothes and crazier hair.

"I want that dress," Gwen says, clinging to my arm.

She points to a scary-cute girl wearing a Lolita kimono-dress, black and red and trimmed with copious quantities of white lace. I look at Gwen's face to see if she's joking or not, but she seems dead serious. Then again, she does have a weakness for weird fashion.

"Oh, no," I groan. "You want to buy something already?"

Gwen whacks me on the arm, then makes a beeline to the girl in the kimono-dress. "Photo?" she says.

The Harajuku girl smiles and strikes a pose. Gwen snaps a photo.

"Kawaii," the girl says, pointing at Gwen's red hair. Cute.

Gwen's cheeks redden. "Uh, thanks. Arigatō." She moves back to me and mutters, "Are they staring at *me?*"

"Well, you are an American giantess with curly red hair."

She makes a face between a grin and a grimace. "Wow."

While Gwen snaps photos, I slip a sketchpad from my backpack. I haven't been drawing much lately, mostly due to the looming threat of college and my parents breathing down my neck. *Art can be your hobby! You can still have a real career!* Yeah. But it would be a crime not to capture these Harajuku kids on paper.

I lean against the railing and start sketching the people nearby. A trio of candy-bright girls with lollipops cluster at one end of the bridge and flirt coyly with two steampunk guys in trench coats, top hats, and intricate steel arm bracers. The guys must be cosplaying, dressed up as favorite characters from an anime I vaguely remember. A girl in a schoolgirl uniform minces across the bridge, a furry black tail trailing from her skirt.

Is she yōkai? I try not to stare.

Cat ears poke from her hair, and when she smiles, she flashes sharp teeth. A bell jingles at the collar around her neck. Her eyes, lemon-yellow with slit pupils, look too flat. Contacts.

I bite back a smile and go stand by Gwen.

"Look," I whisper. "See the cat girl?"

Gwen follows my gaze. "Is she a *bakeneko*?"

I remember hearing about bakeneko when I was a kid—it literally means "monster cat," as in a really big kitty with paranormal powers. Legend says they start out as ordinary human pets, then grow bigger and bigger and become yōkai. I doubt that's true; bakeneko have a reputation for being tricksters, like nogitsune.

"No," I say. "Just a girl cosplaying as one."

A smile spreads on Gwen's face. "Really?"

The bakeneko cosplayer strolls past us and I pretend to stare at the skyline behind her.

I talk in a low voice. "It's pretty awesome that they actually would cosplay as an Other in Japan."

"I know! The closest they ever get to that in America is Halloween." Gwen rolls her eyes. "And that's usually ridiculously stereotypical, offensive crap ordered from some catalog."

I grimace. Like guys who like to smear on some gray face paint, add plastic fangs, and run around pretending to bite girls because they're "werewolves." And usually the girls who get fake-bitten are wearing sheer dresses and body glitter since they're "faeries." Never mind what real werewolves and faeries look like, or that both of those Others would kick some serious ass if they saw those costumes.

"Japan is different." I laugh. "Though this *is* Harajuku."

"True," Gwen says.

We stand side by side in silence for a while, watching the pageantry of strangeness that could exist nowhere else. Watching the Harajuku kids makes me feel claustrophobic, in a way, like all the different people—the not-normal people—in Tokyo, maybe all of Japan, are crammed onto this one bridge. They know where they belong, and it isn't with everyone else. I wonder how many of these kids take out their piercings and wash the temporary dye from their hair every night, then go work as secretaries and study at Tokyo University in the morning.

"I'm thirsty," Gwen says. "Are you?"

"Let's go find something to drink. There might be some drinking fountains in the park."

We cross the rest of the bridge and head west into Yoyogi Park. The sun peeks through ragged clouds, and frost glitters on the grass and trees. Here, people wear darker clothes and take up less space. Gwen makes a beeline for a vending machine selling drinks—the hot ones marked with red buttons, the cold ones with blue. She buys a can of jasmine tea and pops the top, releasing a puff of steam into the chilly air.

"Isn't this amazing?" she says.

I peer into the machine. "Oh, cool! Minute Maid

Hot Lemonade." I feed the vending machine some coins, wrap my numb fingers around the warm can, and take a sip of tanginess. "I remember drinking this when I was little."

"Really?" Gwen says.

She must be wondering how a half-wild fox boy could have found the money to buy anything from a vending machine.

My cheeks warm. "My kitsune mother bought it for me." I hesitate. "With fake coins. Illusions, made from her magic. So technically she didn't buy it, she stole it. But in her defense, I was a little brat who wouldn't stop whimpering for lemonade."

Gwen laughs. "I'm trying to imagine you as a little brat." She drains her jasmine tea. "I have to pee. Wait here?"

"Sure."

She jogs toward the nearest public restroom. I finish my hot lemonade, then sit on a bench outside the restroom with my sketchpad. I love how the frost looks like sugar dusted on the grass and trees. Well, it's not like that's a sight unique to Japan. I sigh and slip my sketchbook back into my pack. This trip is going to be a total artistic failure if I don't stop hearing nagging in my head.

The door creaks open behind me.

"Ready?" I say, my gaze still on the park.

"You need to go," Gwen says.

Frowning, I turn toward her. Her face looks strangely serene. "What?"

"She is coming."

"Who?"

Gwen raises her hand to brush back her hair—no, she's wiping her face, wiping her face *away*, leaving nothing but blank skin.

The noppera-bō.

The fox inside me leaps to the forefront, snarling, and I barely manage to stay human. I jump away from the noppera-bō, outside of its range. It reaches for me, its hand like Gwen's but maggot-white. I stare at it for a full second, then run. Adrenaline electrifies my muscles as I sprint though Yoyogi Park.

I hurtle though the bushes, clenching my jaw to keep myself from transforming. That would not be a good idea, in broad daylight in the middle of Tokyo.

Behind me, I hear Gwen's voice. "Wait! Come back!"

And find out whether it's really her or the noppera-bō? Unlikely.

I hightail it out of the park and dive into the heart of the shopping district, where there are more people and, hopefully, safe places to hide. I hit the sidewalk running and zigzag through girls carrying shopping bags, trying to avoid a collision. Tokyo is such a maze of medieval streets, like a rabbit warren, that it's hard to make any headway. I see some white-gloved policemen chatting on the sidewalk and I slow to a brisk walk, not wanting to look like I'm running from the law.

I could tell them I'm being stalked by a noppera-bō, but I doubt that would help.

Breath ragged, I wait at a crosswalk. A thought creeps into my mind. If the Gwen who came out of the restroom was the noppera-bō, what happened to the real Gwen? Ice solidifies in my stomach. How long have I been talking to a ghost?

Sunlight angles onto the storefront next to me so that the windows reflect the street. I can't see anything but the rush of the crowd. At my feet, the morning's rain puddles on the sidewalk, shivering slightly in the breeze. It stills, and I see myself.

The noppera-bō settles beside me in the puddle, silently, like a white petal falling.

Forget the crosswalk.

I dart down a side street, panting. There's a dead end straight ahead, so I take a left, then a right. If I twist and turn enough, maybe I'll lose the ghost. Can you actually *lose* ghosts? I mean, they aren't exactly physical. A crazy laugh swells inside me, but I don't have enough air for it; I have to keep breathing and running—damn it, my lungs are burning.

Gasping, I stumble to a halt and lean with my hands on my knees. My legs tremble when I take a step forward and my kneecaps feel wobbly. Adrenaline pulses through my bloodstream.

Where am I?

This definitely isn't Harajuku anymore. Everything is cracked, crumbling, graying. Trees with yellowed leaves strain for what little sun slips between the crowded buildings. There's a distinct stink of stale urine in the air.

I spot a tiny newsstand wedged between an abandoned apartment building and what can only be a sex shop. Maybe I can buy a map and find my way back out.

The newsstand is nothing more than a metal box stacked high with neat bundles of newspapers and magazines. Fluorescent light shines on the bald head of a man who looks like he hasn't smiled in years. He squints at me as I approach.

"Excuse me," I say. "Do you—"

"No English," he says, with a thick accent.

Why can't I remember any Japanese? I stand there like a moron, words flapping around my mind like scared chickens. Wait, don't I have a cellphone with me? I can call Gwen and—shit, dead battery. Maybe I left my charger in my backpack—

The stench of wet fur drifts on the breeze.

Dog.

Every muscle in my body tenses, and I drop into a crouch. I try not to bare my teeth. I loathe dogs, like all kitsune, primarily because dogs love running down foxes and ripping them into shreds of bloody fur. Where's that smell coming from?

I sidestep away from the newsstand and sniff the air. Nothing.

I rise from my crouch, sweating, not ready to laugh it off. Maybe somebody has a little breed in one of the apartment buildings, maybe a *shiba inu*. I should really be worrying about the noppera-bō, though I don't see anything reflective here…

A bark.

A deep bark, from a big dog.

"Oh, shit," I whisper.

Three men slink from the shadows, all of them wearing battered leather jackets and ripped T-shirts. They reek of dog, a powerful animal smell that fills my nose and makes me retch. The bleached-blond guy takes off his jacket, revealing tattooed arms—the mark of a *yakuza*, Japanese mafia. The tallest man bares yellowed canines, and the third begins to pant, his black-spotted tongue lolling.

Then I get it.

Their clothes aren't ripped by choice, but because they're shapeshifters who have to fight to stay human. And I don't need Gwen's textbook to know what kind.

Inugami.

Dog-spirits. Even more disgusting—and deadly—than dogs.

"This isn't your territory, fox," the tallest one says in Japanese, his voice chain-smoker gravelly.

Japanese returns to its rightful place in my brain, and I say, "I know."

The bleached-blond guy laughs, more of a woof, and it makes me flinch. All three of them bare their teeth in grins. When the man with the black-spotted tongue turns his head, the skin under his chin jiggles, loose like the folds on a wrinkly dog's neck.

I glance at the newspaper man, but he's gone. Not a good sign.

The tallest man advances on me. "Don't you know who I am?"

I shake my head, hard. I try not to stare at his face or the string of drool dripping from his mouth. His breath smells like rotten meat. Would he kill me slower if I suggested a dentist?

"My name is Katashi. You're on Kuro Inu land."

Kuro Inu, Black Dog. Clever. Must be the name of his gang.

For some reason, when I get scared, I get extra sarcastic. "I'm sorry," I say, "I got lost. I'm an American tourist, okay? That means I'm stupid. I wasn't trying to trespass."

A growl rumbles from Katashi's throat. "You're a nogitsune."

I don't know how he can tell, or why this matters. "So?"

"You smell like her." Katashi drives me against the wall. "Like Yukimi."

My bones bend under my skin, on the brink of changing into a fox's skeleton. "Who's Yukimi?"

A corner of Katashi's mouth twists. "An excellent reason to kill you."

Behind him, the bleached-blond guy ditches his clothes in favor of a pale yellow pelt. His face darkens into a black mask. The man with the black-spotted tongue looks like a hunchback. His spine pops as he falls to all fours, his body twisting into that of a gray mastiff.

"Run, little fox, run," Katashi singsongs.

Katashi casually slings off his jacket, unbuttons his shirt, and peels off his tight jeans. His entire body is tattooed with an image of a dog feasting on a gutted rabbit. The rabbit's blood spirals over his shoulders and arms, twisting into snakes down his legs.

Katashi shuts his eyes, then shapeshifts into a huge black dog.

I try to dredge up some kitsune magic, but I can only think of stupid illusions—a golden apple, a kite that flies itself—and each of those requires an object of some sort. But I can improvise. I spot a length of broken wood on the ground and grab it, willing it to look like a blade. It flashes along its length, and the sight of steel drives them back a step.

Pain blooms in my chest, sharp and fierce.

My heartbeat stutters. I gasp, my vision blacking, and the blade clatters on the ground, broken wood again. The pain throbs, fading, and I grimace, doubled over, one hand pressed above my ribs. It's worse than I've felt in a long time.

The yellow dog, the gray mastiff, and the black dog slink closer to me, their teeth bared, their fur spiking along their spines. My instincts are screaming at me to change into a fox and run, but my heart is going so fast it's skipping beats—and I don't want to find out what might happen if I push it. I back against the wall, my palms flat against the concrete, the world suddenly sharp with clarity.

This is all too real. I could die.

With a bellowing bark, the black dog—Katashi—lunges for me. I twist out of the way; his jaws click shut where my hand was a minute before. He growls, and barks again.

He's trying to scare me into running, so he can chase me down.

Like hell I'm going to run. I—

A hawk screams overhead. Everyone looks up.

A stone-gray streak dives from the sky. The hawk's wings snap open, slowing its plummet, and its talons slash ragged red grooves in Katashi's head. Katashi yelps and leaps, trying to bite the hawk, but the bird of prey pumps its wings hard, gaining altitude. The yellow dog scrabbles after it, his teeth inches from its feathers.

"Watch out!" I shout.

The hawk flares its tail, feathers spreading like a fan, and lands on the pavement. Doesn't it know that's suicide? The yellow dog crouches, the muscles in its hindquarters bunching.

The hawk's body shimmers like a heat wave, then shifts. Feathers to hair, talons to hooves. A black horse spins to face the dogs, tossing its wild mane, its eyes glowing golden.

Gwen.

four

Gwen rears with a fierce whinny, her hooves flashing. The gray mastiff makes the mistake of sneaking behind her, and she kicks him in the ribs. He crashes against a wall and slides down, whimpering. The yellow dog cringes, his tail between his legs. Katashi barks at him, disgust clear on his face. I grab a chunk of concrete and hurl it at the black dog. It hits him between the shoulders and he whirls, snarling.

"Leave us alone," I say.

I sound much braver than I feel. I actually want to pee myself.

Blood trickles down Katashi's face, and he blinks it

from his eyes. He stalks toward me, stiff-legged and snarling, his impressively yellow teeth bared. I circle away from him, toward the bigger and meaner pooka. Gwen huffs, her breath stirring my hair.

"We don't want to fight you," I say, "but we will."

Katashi charges, his jowls trailing ropes of drool.

My legs lock as the black dog barrels toward me. Thoughts dart through my head rapid-fire—don't let him bite Gwen—don't let him bite you—hurt him before he hurts you.

I lunge for a nearby garbage can and grab the lid like a shield. Katashi leaps, his legs tucked beneath his body, his jaws aiming for my neck. I raise the lid to meet him. His head crashes into the metal, his weight driving me to the ground. He lands on top of me; his claws dig into my stomach as he drags himself up.

A wildcat scream splits the air.

Katashi leaps from me, and I climb up in time to see a cougar crouched and ready to spring. Katashi runs for the street, his tail held low. The cougar blinks into the shape of a black horse again. Gwen lands a well-aimed kick on the dog's rear. Katashi stumbles and falls, his nose hitting the dirt, then scrabbles up and keeps running. The yellow dog follows without a backward glance, and the gray mastiff limps after them.

As they leave, Gwen snorts as if to clear the stink of the dogs from her nostrils.

"Thanks," I say. "Pooka to the rescue."

She rolls her golden eyes, then trots toward me and

shapeshifts back into a girl. I offer my jacket to her so she doesn't have to be totally naked, and she snatches it from me.

"What the *hell* happened to you?" she says. "I tried calling you—"

"My phone's battery died. Sorry."

"Why did you even run off in the first place? When I came out of the bathroom, you were already halfway across the park. I yelled at you, but you didn't stop. Did you not hear me?"

I wince. "I thought you were the noppera-bō."

Her eyebrows go sky-high. "Really? You're telling me you saw the noppera-bō again? And it looked like me?"

"Gwen." When I hold her hands, I discover they're shaking. "I'm okay."

She narrows her eyes and tries to yank away. "You're not okay. You just got into a fight with some big-ass dogs."

"Big-ass dog-spirits, to be exact," I say.

Gwen tugs my jacket closer around herself. "Inugami?"

I nod. "Apparently part of a yakuza gang."

She pales. "Some inugami gangsters just saw me shapeshifting?"

"How would they know it was you?"

"Tavian. I'm the only pooka in Japan."

"Exactly. They have no clue what a pooka is."

Gwen shivers, her arms dotted with goose bumps. "Damn it, it's freezing. Let's get out of here."

"Where are your clothes?"

She scowls at me. "Where do you think? In an alley. Ruined. I shapeshifted into a hawk as soon as I lost sight of you."

"Do you want to buy some new ones?"

Her scowl deepens. "Tavian, the nearest clothing stores are in Harajuku. I think I'll pass."

"I thought you liked that dress with the—"

"Tavian."

"So you're going to walk through Tokyo naked?"

"Of course not." She pulls off my jacket and hands it to me, which seems counterproductive. "I'm going to ride in your pocket. Put your jacket back on."

This doesn't make any sense, but I do as she says. She rolls her neck to get the kinks out, then shapeshifts into a little ferret with golden eyes.

"Oh." I hadn't seen her in this animal form before. "Ingenious."

I kneel, holding out my hands, but she climbs up my leg, her claws pricking through my jeans, and crawls into the front pocket of my jacket. I reach into my pocket to make sure she's settled all right, and she nips my finger almost hard enough to break skin.

"Okay, okay, we're going."

We manage to get on the metro without encountering anything more than salarymen at lunch hour, swarming around every station in search of yakisoba, teriyaki, sushi, and McDonald's. My stomach rumbles ominously, and I know Gwen must be starving—shapeshifting burns hundreds of calories, according to her, and she has the appetite to prove it. When I linger in front of a Bigness Burger, a little tempted by the barbecued eel sandwich, Gwen makes an impatient squeak.

"Do you want me to buy some?" I mutter, trying not to be the crazy guy talking to himself.

Gwen peers out of my pocket and nods.

I sigh. "All right."

She disappears back into my pocket, and I walk into the Bigness Burger. Inside, Ki-chan's cartoon face is plastered everywhere, grinning manically. I swallow my pride and order a "kitsune burger" with fries. I sit at a corner table and poke bits of burger into my pocket, where they disappear to the sound of sharp teeth gnashing. That should keep Gwen satisfied.

I eat the fries while glancing at my reflection in the windowpane. Every time I glimpse somebody behind me, my heartbeat goes from zero to sixty in two seconds flat. But I don't see the noppera-bō again; maybe there are too many witnesses for it to reappear.

Why is it haunting me at all?

By some stroke of amazing luck, I sneak into my grandparents' condo with the key Michiko provided earlier, and make it all the way to the bathroom with Gwen-the-ferret still riding in my jacket pocket. I lock the door and Gwen crawls out. I let her shimmy down my leg. She shapeshifts into a girl and stretches, her back cracking.

"I'm not doing that again any time soon," she says.

"I wasn't suggesting it," I mumble under my breath.

I pretend like I'm not checking her out, but she notices and rolls her eyes. She turns on the water and climbs into the shower, yelping at the heat. I exit the bathroom and look for a laundry hamper where I can drop off my jacket—it stinks like inugami.

Michiko catches me red-handed by the washing machine. "Octavian!" she says. "When did you get home? Where's Gwen?"

"She's in the shower. We just got back."

Michiko peers into the laundry hamper. "Did you enjoy Harajuku?" Something in her voice shrouds the sentence with implied meanings.

Did you get lost? Mugged?

Did you not even go to Harajuku?

Were you two fooling around?

I plaster a smile on my face. "*Hai!* It was a little crazy, though."

Michiko nods knowingly. "Tsuyoshi was worried that it might be too much for Gwen."

Too much? Before we left, Gwen ticked off a list of Japanese things she wasn't really interested in seeing: bonsai gardens, excessively stodgy museums, geisha, *ikebana* flower arrangements, tea ceremonies. She's not very good at sitting still when there are places to be explored.

If anything, running into those inugami was probably her idea of excitement.

To Michiko, I say, "Maybe we will go somewhere quieter tomorrow."

She smiles, her eyes crinkling with crow's feet. "Dinner will be at six."

"Arigatō."

I slip into Gwen's bedroom and start reading her textbook on yōkai. I stare at the entry on noppera-bō, then flip to the page on inugami. Nothing much, just stories about how dog-spirits are loyal to humans, and how they love hunting down evil field foxes.

You smell like her. Like Yukimi.

An excellent reason to kill you.

"Hey." Gwen stands in the doorway, wrapped in one towel and wringing her hair with another. "You can have the shower now."

"Thanks," I say.

She frowns. "Are you *sure* you're okay? You still look sick."

I blow out my breath through my nose. "Remember how I had those random pains? Here?" I rest my hand over my heart.

Gwen's face twists. "Tavian, you said you were better!"

"It wasn't bad enough to mention before," I say. "But since last night…it's worse."

She steps closer to me and grabs my hand, her grip

tight. "Tavian," she murmurs, "what if this has something to do with the noppera-bō?"

"'You need to go. She is coming.'"

"What does that mean?"

"It's what the noppera-bō told me when he was pretending to be you." I stare out the window, my eyes unfocused.

"But who is 'she'?" Gwen says.

But there is a man standing before me, and he has no face. The snow doesn't even touch his dark suit, just falls right through. He's thin like rice paper. Like a ghost.

"My mother?" I say, so softly I'm not sure it's audible.

Gwen's hand slides from mine. "What?"

"The noppera-bō shot my kitsune mother in my dream." I grip my hair in my hands. "Who is he? How did she know him?"

She shivers. "You don't even know if he's on your side."

"I need to find out."

Gwen takes a deep breath, then nods.

I head for the shower. Steaming water beats against my head and back. My thoughts dissolve in the heat, swirling inside my mind, until a single word floats to the surface.

Yukimi.

Yuki, snow. *Mi*, beauty. Snow beauty.

My mother's name? Does she have enough of a reputation around Tokyo that those inugami would recognize me as her son?

I only ever knew my mother as Okāsan. I never knew her kitsune name, her true name, the source of her power. She promised I would know her name when I was old enough to have a kitsune name of my own; she promised she would teach me all the magic she knew. But of course her promises are as good as dust.

I shut off the water and step into the fog. I towel off my hair, then reach to wipe the mirror clean. Before I can, my muscles lock. A thin line streaks the mirror, as if an invisible finger is trailing down the fogged glass. Faster, then, more lines appear: *kanji* characters.

The invisible finger ceases to write.

I stare at the kanji. The only character I understand is the one for "now," which could mean all sorts of things depending on the other characters. I run out of the bathroom clutching my towel, grab my Japanese-English dictionary from my bag, and sprint back. My fingers shaking, I flip through the tissue-thin pages. Kanji characters aren't alphabetical, so it takes me minutes to find the first, then the second, then the rest. When I do, I'm not sure my translation is right.

Leave now. It is almost too late.

I frown at my dictionary, double-checking the second-to-last character, then look back up at the mirror.

The noppera-bō floats in the mirror behind me, a white smudge.

I scream before I can stop myself and the noppera-bō vanishes, just like that, faster than the fog fades.

There's a knock on the door. "Octavian? What's wrong?"

Michiko.

"Nothing!" I say. "I just…I slipped coming out of the shower, and…and I almost fell…" I can't lie fast enough.

Michiko yanks open the door, and I clutch my towel. She looks only mildly alarmed about seeing me in the nude; maybe she thought I'd slipped and cracked my head open on the toilet.

"Be more careful!" she says.

"I will." I nod and hold the towel tighter.

Her gaze moves to the kanji on the mirror behind me. She looks at the dictionary, then, and her lips thin. *Leave now. It is almost too late.* Oh no. She thinks I wrote that. Does she think I was mocking their hospitality? Does she think I'm ungrateful?

"I was practicing my kanji." It sounds so pitiful that I wince. "Does it make any sense?"

Her face softens. "I can help you learn. After you get dressed, of course," she says, without a hint of sarcasm.

After Michiko shuts the door, I lower the toilet lid and sit, my legs Jell-O as the adrenaline leaves my system.

You need to go. She is coming.

Leave now. It is almost too late.

A tight thrill runs from my stomach to my chest. I can't tell if it's fear, excitement, or both.

Let her come.

All throughout dinner, Tsuyoshi asks polite questions about our day, and Gwen and I pretend like we had the most boring time in Harajuku ever. Later, my grandparents announce they are going to bed early because winter makes their bones ache. I'm secretly glad, since I'm not about to admit that I, a strapping young man, am also feeling dead tired at the ungodly hour of nine o'clock. After saying goodnight to Tsuyoshi and Michiko, I surreptitiously follow Gwen to her bedroom.

She lies on her bed and stares at me. "What happened?"

"When?"

"In the bathroom, earlier. Michiko told me something about you drawing kanji on the mirror."

"Oh." I lie beside her and put my arm around her waist. "Guess."

"Your kitsune mom?"

"No." I wrinkle my nose. "I highly doubt she's spying on me in the bathroom nowadays."

"The noppera-bō?"

"Bingo."

The muscles in Gwen's back tense beneath my touch. "What did it say?"

"'Leave now. It is almost too late.'"

"Well, that's cheerful," she says.

"I know." I'm silent for a moment. "But I'm not the type to run away. I'd rather let my kitsune mother come to me, and find out what's really going on."

Gwen says nothing, just snuggles closer to me and sighs.

We lie together, then, warm in the chill of the night. Outside, in the amber glow of the streetlights, it begins to snow. Gwen's breathing slips into the slow rhythm of sleep. I glance at the door. I know I should go back to my own bedroom, but...just a little while longer. Gwen feels so good in my arms, like a puzzle piece clicking into place.

"Tavian."

It's just a whisper, so quiet I'm not sure I heard or imagined it.

"Come to me."

A cold eel twists in my stomach. It's my kitsune mother's voice. How does she know the name that Mom and Dad gave to me?

"Tavian."

Impossibly, she sounds like she's right outside the door. I slip away from Gwen, gently so I don't wake her. My heartbeat knocks against my ribs as I cross the room. I grip the doorknob with a sweaty hand, then twist it and fling the door open.

Darkness. At the end of the hall, a white ball of light disappears around the corner. Foxfire.

"Tavian."

My whispered name echoes off the walls in a way I know defies the physics of the house. I run down the hall and come to the genkan. The foxfire glows from the crack beneath the front door. When I open the door, I see the foxfire flit into the elevator just as the doors slide shut.

Why won't she stop and face me? Why does she keep running away?

"Wait!" The stillness of the hallway swallows my voice. "Okāsan!"

The elevator dings, and the doors open with a soft clunk. It's empty. I dart into the elevator. My hand moves to the button, but one of them is already lit: 40, the top floor. The elevator ascends. In the polished steel of the walls, I can see myself reflected. The noppera-bō walks behind me, then vanishes. It's too late for him; I want to find her now, and I will.

The elevator dings, then opens.

I'm in a dark room illuminated by a bare light bulb. Before me, snow falls on a steep staircase leading to the roof. The white flecks floating in the black look like the drifting of marine decay in the deep ocean, and for a moment, I feel like I'm sinking. I grab the railing of the stairs and drag myself upward, to the roof, where the whiteness of snow surrounds me.

She is there. Standing at the edge of the building, staring out at Tokyo.

She's wearing a dark jacket and jeans, not a kimono—maybe that was my imagination—but her long hair flies behind her in the wind.

My heartbeat thuds so hard I wonder if she can hear it.

This might not be my mother. I'm terrified that when

she turns around, she'll wipe away her face. That I'll be forced to confront the noppera-bō. I open my mouth to speak, but before I can, she turns to me.

Her face is the face I remembered from eleven years ago, with the same high cheekbones and sharp chin, but I don't remember the faint lines by her eyes, or the streak of white in her hair. She stares at me with glittering, slit-pupil eyes more like those of an animal than a woman.

Was she always this wild?

"Okāsan?" I say.

She stares at me, unblinking, until my own eyes water and I have to blink. She doesn't vanish like I'd feared. Am I dreaming, or is this real?

Her eyes narrow. She steps toward me, the snow crunching beneath her boots. "You should not be here." She speaks perfect English, with only a trace of an accent.

Suddenly, I'm aware of the cold. "Why?"

"You should not exist."

"What do you mean?"

She doesn't say anything, just tilts her head to one side, her eyes reflecting the lights of Tokyo. She looks inhuman.

"What do you *mean*?" My voice is ragged, my throat raw. I walk toward her, my bare feet burning-cold in the snow. "You can't say that. You can't come back to me after eleven years, after leaving me alone in the snow. I thought maybe you died."

She sidesteps away from me as I advance on her. She holds herself low to the ground, ready to run.

"I should not exist," I continue. "Do you mean I was an accident? Is that why you left me?"

Her eyes flicker with something resembling sadness. "No."

"Then tell me!"

I reach to grab her by the shoulder, to pull her to me, but she curls her lip, baring fox fangs. Her hand darts out and closes around my chin. Her fingers are hot on my skin, almost feverish. She tugs my face downward so she can stare into my eyes—only then do I realize she's smaller than I am. She's tiny, but she holds herself with such grace and fearlessness that I thought she was taller.

"Are you still a fox?" she whispers. "Can you still change?"

I blink, disoriented. "Yes, of course."

Her face blurs as I stare at her, my eyes tearing. I retreat from her touch and peel off my T-shirt in the frigid air. I'm shaking uncontrollably. Cold stiffens my joints as I unzip my jeans. My kitsune mother stares at me as impassively as a fox regards a dead mouse, wondering if it's worth eating or not. This woman is a stranger to me. Unrecognizable.

They line the hall as I walk past, barking at me like dogs, until I want to flatten my ears against my skull—

I creep from the dormitory, my nose twitching as a mouse scratches in the wall. I'm starving. A flashlight flicks on, and I scream—

They laugh at me as I huddle in the corner. I'm shivering, my pants wet because I didn't understand how to ask for the bathroom, didn't think that I could escape the cage of this room without them punishing me—

I shut my eyes against the flashbacks, my stomach queasy.

Fox.

I can do this. This is who I am: half-kitsune. I can show her the truth. Or is the kitsune part of me dying? Is this why it feels like my ribs are clenching my heart, squeezing it tight? I strip away the rest of my clothes, prepared to become a fox.

"You are broken," she says softly, almost as if I wasn't meant to hear.

I clench my fists and jaw and stomach, then let the tension go all at once, drawing on the power inside me to push my body from human to fox. My heartbeat stutters, then stops. I gasp and stagger forward. My heartbeat stumbles back, erratic, weak, and I open my eyes. I'm on my hands and knees in the snow, naked. White snow fills my sight. My kitsune mother speaks, but her voice sounds too faraway to hear. My eyes slip shut as the pain gives away to sweet numbness.

Okāsan.

Darkness overtakes me.

five

Lying on my back, moving through a bright hallway. Strangers run beside me, their voices muffled. We stop at an elevator, and when the doors open, I see my kitsune mother standing in the corner, waiting for me. She looks at me but doesn't say a word, and no one else seems to see her. I try to reach for her, but a stranger grabs my hand and pushes it down.

I open my eyes.

I'm lying in a bed in a strange room. It's early morning, judging by the gray light outside. When I move, my clothing rustles—I'm wearing a flimsy gown. I'm in a hospital. And Gwen is sleeping in a chair nearby, a pillow wedged between her head and the wall. I cough, then wince. My ribs feel like a rhinoceros stomped on them.

"Gwen?"

She frowns in her sleep, dark circles under her eyes.

I raise my voice. "Gwen?"

She blinks herself awake, then stares at me. "Tavian!" I can tell she's been crying, and my throat tightens. "Are you okay? Do you need anything?"

I shake my head. "What happened?"

Gwen picks up her chair and moves it closer to my bed, then grips my hand as if she's afraid I might drift away without her anchoring me. "I don't know. They found you unconscious on the roof of the skyscraper, naked, in the snow—why did you go up there?"

I look away. "I was following my kitsune mother. I didn't know if it was a dream or not."

Her eyes glitter. "What did she do to you?"

"Nothing." My voice sounds hollow. "She talked to me. I tried to change into a fox, then passed out."

Gwen's jaw tightens. "Michiko tried to translate what the doctors were saying for me. She said they were afraid you'd had a heart attack, but when they did some tests, they couldn't find anything wrong. Just like the doctors back home."

My kitsune mother's voice whispers through my mind. *You are broken.*

"I don't think it's physical," I say. "I think it's paranormal. Something to do with my kitsune half. It happened when I dreamed of my kitsune mother being killed, and also when I tried to use an illusion against the Kuro Inu. Tsuyoshi wants me to go to a temple, to see if they can help me."

"Tavian." Gwen glares at me, but her voice sounds husky.

"I'm sorry I didn't tell you, I thought it was nothing to worry about; just predictable angina. Just pain."

She looks away and blows out her breath. "It's not just pain. Not if you're passing out because of it. Not if it's keeping you from becoming a fox."

"I don't know if that's why, though I haven't shape-shifted since we got here."

"Tavian … this can't be good."

"I know."

Then again, Gwen is much more of a hardcore shape-shifter than I am.

She sighs and rests her head beside mine, but I'm already looking outside the window at the drifting snow. I wonder where my mother is now. Why do I even want to find her? My stomach feels sick, like the memory I had of her soured and started rotting, twisting with worms. I should hate her, but she's the woman who gave birth to me, who raised me for the first six years of my life.

A phone buzzes—mine, on a table against the wall.

Gwen looks up. "You want me to get that?"

"Yes please."

She grabs it and answers. "Hi, this is Tavian's phone."

Her face gets a pinched look. "Ms. Kimura! Yes, he's here with me. Yes, he's awake." She hands the phone to me.

Great. Talking to my parents is definitely not going to be a picnic.

I clear my throat. "Mom? I—"

"Octavian! What possessed you to go outside alone, in the cold, with your condition?"

"I wasn't alone."

"I—what do you mean?"

I think for a moment. "Who called the paramedics?"

Mom pauses. "I don't know. Kazuki, do you know?"

"No," Dad says, and nothing more.

"Then who was it?" Mom says, her voice sharp with impatience.

There isn't a good way to phrase what I want to say next, so I plunge right in. "It must have been my kitsune mother."

Silence. For so long, I wonder if my phone died.

"Are you still there?" I say.

"Yes." Mom draws in a slow breath. "That *woman* lured you there?"

She didn't lure me. Well, there was foxfire involved, but I went of my own free will.

Out loud, I say, "I wanted to meet her."

More silence.

"Your mother is very upset," Dad says, as if I couldn't tell.

"I'm not upset," Mom says quickly. "Not about that."

But I know that every time I talk about my biological

parents—my biological mother, really—Mom laces her fingers together so tightly her knuckles turn white, and she speaks in this tight, crisp way, like she's biting off her words. I can imagine her doing it right now, and Dad putting a hand on her shoulder to comfort her.

"Octavian," Mom says, "I hope you know that your father and I will always support you when you want to learn more about your biological parents. It's perfectly natural."

That's what she always says, often enough that it sounds like a script. But in private, when I'm not supposed to be listening, she talks about things totally differently. One night, when I was maybe eight or nine, she was whispering a little too loudly in the hall.

I already tried to explain things to his teachers. He wasn't given a chance at a normal childhood. Not for the first six years of his life. That woman raised him like an animal. That woman didn't even teach him how to dress himself. If they can't recognize the consequences of such neglect and abuse, then to hell with them.

"Hello?" Mom says. "Are you all right?"

"Yes," I say. "Sorry. I was thinking about what you said."

"Tavian." Dad clears his throat. "Now would be a good time to focus on your future."

"My future?" I say, stupidly, since I already know where this is going.

"While you're in Tokyo, you should use your time to do something productive. Talk with your grandfather."

Dad's voice is brisk, like he's on an international conference call. "I already told him about your interest in graphic design, and I'm sure he would be more than willing to find a place for you in the company."

The company being the family hotel business, the reason why Dad has such a cushy job with their U.S. division.

"I will," I say, too tired to argue.

Maybe I'll be able to sit behind a desk for eight hours a day, five days a week. Maybe I can make art for a living. If creating logos and marketing pieces for a hotel counts as art...

"Oh!" Mom says. "Will you get out for Christmas Eve?"

"It's Christmas Eve?" I say dully. "I forgot. Not feeling very merry right now."

"Not until tomorrow," Dad says. "We wish you weren't in the hospital, but it's the best for your health."

"Right," I say.

"Get some sleep," Mom says. "You sound exhausted."

"Well, it looks like I'm going to be stuck in bed for a while," I say, trying to joke about it.

Mom sighs, but I can tell she's feeling slightly better.

Sure enough, I spend Christmas Eve in the hospital while the doctors find absolutely nothing new. Gwen stays with me, reading passages from her book on yōkai out loud. My head swims with visions of strange-skinned demons and beautiful women with hideous secrets. I'd forgotten about the sheer number of Others who live in

Japan, coexisting with humans for centuries, even millennia. Why do I feel like I don't belong?

They finally let me leave on Christmas night. Tsuyoshi and Michiko treat me and Gwen to dinner. We go to a restaurant wedged between two concrete buildings, totally boring on the outside, totally vibrant on the inside. Red paper lanterns cast a warm glow over low tables where people perch on cushions. The menu promises all sorts of tofu delights. Tofu is a kitsune's best friend. As evidenced, of course, by *kitsune udon*, a fantastic soup of chunky noodles loaded with deep-fried tofu. You can guess what I order.

"Better than hospital food?" Tsuyoshi says, with a deep chuckle.

I smile, but it feels like a mask. "Thank you for dinner. Merry Christmas!"

"Merry Christmas!" everyone choruses, playing their parts.

This is all too nice, like my grandparents want to counteract the bad luck of me ending up in the hospital. Like it's their fault, not mine.

A skinny waiter refills Gwen's teacup, his eyes fixed on her red hair. She's gotten nothing but stares ever since she set foot in this restaurant—and she still doesn't seem tired of it. Of course they gave her a fork, assuming a *gaijin* like her couldn't possibly handle chopsticks.

Michiko smiles at me. "We knew this was a good place for kitsune."

The waiter's eyes sharpen. "Kitsune?"

"Our grandson." Michiko nods at me. "We adopted him."

I freeze, a chopstick-load of udon noodles halfway to my mouth. Oh my god. What did she just say? Telling somebody you're Other is *not* polite dinner conversation back in the States. That's the sort of thing that can get you killed. Or at least shot.

Gwen nudges my ankle with her toes, and I unclench my fists.

The waiter gives me a big smile, his teeth bleached bright. "Do you like the kitsune udon?"

I let nothing show on my face. "I'm eating it right now."

"Another bowl, then, on the house." The waiter bows and leaves.

Michiko smiles and looks at Tsuyoshi, who nods like a bobble-head. Why are they *smiling*? Is this *okay*? I don't even know if I'm angry or scared or…happy. That might be pride on their faces, but I'm definitely not ready to be publicly announced as kitsune.

"Excuse me," I say, in my politest Japanese possible, "but that makes me uncomfortable."

Tsuyoshi's bushy eyebrows descend. "What does?"

I meet his eyes. "Telling people that I'm kitsune."

Silence. Tsuyoshi stares into his rice bowl, and Michiko busies herself rearranging the dishes in front of her. My face heats until I'm sure it must be the color of the lanterns above.

"You may have forgotten," Tsuyoshi says quietly, "the place of the kitsune in Japan."

I don't think I could ever forget my childhood.

Out loud, I say, "I remember the place of the nogit-sune."

Tsuyoshi's eyes flash. "There is no need to speak of that."

Is he asking me to pretend I'm not a field fox? To let the waiter believe that I'm actually a temple fox? That I'm good luck rather than bad? I clench my jaw, biting back my words.

Gwen keeps her head down, taking quick, quiet bites of her food. I can tell she's trying to figure out what we're saying, even though she doesn't understand very much Japanese.

The waiter returns with a giant smile on his face and a steaming-hot bowl of kitsune udon.

"Thank you," I say, since it seems like the safest thing to do.

"Enjoy your dinner." The waiter bows again, then leaves.

I stare at the ghosts of steam dancing above my bowl. My stomach feels hollow, but I'm not hungry anymore. Still, I force myself to drink every last drop of broth, if only to see Michiko smile again. Tsuyoshi won't meet my eyes for the rest of dinner.

When I go to the restroom before we leave, Tsuyoshi meets me by the sinks. I look at him in the mirror; his face looks gray and whole decade older. "We will see the myobu tomorrow."

I concentrate on washing my hands. "I'm not one of them."

He closes the distance between us, his face so close I could count every wrinkle. "There is no need for your birth mother to bring disgrace to the Kimura name. *Shiranu ga hotoke.*"

Shiranu ga hotoke. Not knowing is Buddha. Ignorance is bliss.

Tsuyoshi's voice is low yet intense, like the distant roar of a waterfall. "You have a duty to this family. You will leave behind your past. You will speak to the myobu."

My hands stop moving. I keep my head down and stare into the sink. Then I nod, because I know I have to.

Tsuyoshi wakes me at sunrise. He's wearing an expensive suit and carrying a briefcase. In silence, we take the elevator down and drive to Ueno Park. Dawn tints the sky cherry-blossom pink over gray branches of trees famous for their flowers in springtime. Frost sparkles on the grass, turning the vast lawn into a galaxy.

"Be careful," Tsuyoshi mutters, as he parks the car, "and don't meet strangers in the eye."

"Why?" I say. "Isn't it safe around here?"

Tsuyoshi shakes his head. "Homeless people." He unbuckles his seat belt and slides out. "*Bakemono.*"

Bakemono. Changed thing, as in yōkai who shape-shift, or those whose bodies were once human but are now supernaturally, irreversibly changed. The word has overtones of the monstrous—like the scary stories kids at the orphanage told, after the lights went out and they thought I couldn't hear their whispers.

So are there are both homeless people and bake-mono in the park? Or are the bakemono homeless?

"There," Tsuyoshi murmurs.

At the other end of the path, a stunted old man hobbles nearer, leaning on a blue umbrella like a walk-ing stick. He's wearing a muddy gray tracksuit and bat-tered running shoes. His gray beard probably hasn't seen a comb in ages. He keeps his gaze lowered politely as he passes us, or maybe he's looking for fallen change.

"No," Tsuyoshi whispers. "Not a bakemono. A man."

I don't bother pointing out that as shapeshifters, kit-sune are bakemono too—even those myobu we're going to see. Of course, myobu are too *respectable* to be mon-sters, and I suspect Tsuyoshi would smack me if I called them "bakemono" to their faces.

"Another one," Tsuyoshi says.

"Where?" I whisper.

I'm getting a sick little thrill from spotting the homeless

and worrying that they might be dangerous, might be Other. This time, it's a woman squatting by a garbage can, picking through a take-out box of noodles with chopsticks. She's wearing nothing but rags, and her long black hair curtains her face, hiding her features. A man jogs past, and she cranes her neck toward him in a fluid, boneless motion.

Tsuyoshi sucks in his breath. "Bakemono."

"How can you tell?"

The woman answers my question when her neck snakes longer and longer, like silly putty, even while her body stays motionless. She arches her neck high over the jogger, keeping pace with him, as if she's going to sink fangs into his back. What is she? The word dances around the edges of my memory. I swear Gwen just told me, that there was a picture of this particular yōkai in her textbook.

"*Rokurokubi*," Tsuyoshi whispers. "Long neck woman."

The rokurokubi sighs and withdraws from the jogger, her neck retracting into itself. She spots us and blinks her doe eyes.

"*Ohayō gozaimasu*," she says. Good morning.

I bow to her, just because it's better to err on the side of polite.

The rokurokubi loops her neck toward Tsuyoshi to get a better look. "I am very hungry," she says in English, her voice breathy. "I would love a bite to eat."

Don't rokurokubi prey on men? Or is that a myth?

Tsuyoshi stares the rokurokubi in the eye. "I'm sorry, but we don't have any food."

The rokurokubi drifts close to me. "If you could spare a few yen…"

Oh. Oh! She's begging for change, that's all. I dig out a five hundred yen coin from my pocket.

"Take this," I tell the rokurokubi.

Her body shuffles forward to meet her head, until her neck looks nearly normal. She cups her hands and I give her the coin. Our fingers brush for a second—her skin feels chapped from the cold, but nothing odd. Normal.

"*Arigatō gozaimasu*," she says. Thank you very much. She shuffles away into the darkness, her head bowed, her hair swaying in the wind.

Tsuyoshi blows out his breath in a plume of white. "That was brave."

God, I feel like such a jerk. Assuming she was going to mug us, or worse, just because she's Other.

To my grandfather, I shrug. "It was the right thing to do."

He arches his eyebrows but says nothing.

We wind along a road through the trees as sleepy birds chirp in the canopy. A woman jogs past us, her black ponytail bobbing, her running shoes crunching the snow. At a bend in the road, an iron fence opens to a moss-streaked stone *torii*, an arched gate marking the boundary between the mundane and the sacred.

Beyond this torii, framed by its tall columns, rows of smaller torii—wooden, painted persimmon-red and black—stand in orderly ranks, guiding a path between their posts.

"Almost there," Tsuyoshi says.

We pass through the torii, the stone steps beneath our feet worn by thousands before us. The vivid red of the gates looks stark against the frosted leaves of bamboo. The path ends at a shrine to Inari, its sweeping roof hung with white paper lanterns, red banners, and straw ropes—all the traditional Shinto trappings. A pair of snarling stone foxes, both wearing red bibs, stand guard on either side.

"Kitsune," I say, the word a cloudy whisper.

Something white and delicate drifts before my face. I hold out my hand. Not a snowflake—a cherry blossom. An ancient, gnarled tree shades the shrine, laden with flowers.

A shiver crawls down my back, and not because of the cold.

Cherry blossoms, *sakura*, are cherished for the way they fall in their prime, a beautiful death, a reminder of mortality. To have an ever-blooming tree, with sakura untouched by winter—it makes the hair on my arms bristle. The air reeks of yōkai magic.

"Illusions," I say. "The blossoms, maybe the entire tree."

Someone coughs quietly.

Tsuyoshi dips into a low bow. I do the same, to be safe, and peek up through the fringes of my hair. Silk rustles like wind through leaves. Indigo, shot with gold, slithers along the flagstones—a kimono, worn by a woman. A twelve-layered kimono, exactly like those worn by court ladies a thousand years ago. Her eyes glitter like slivers of amber, and a sleek white tail peeks coyly from the folds of her garment. A jolt of recognition travels my spine. She smells, very faintly, of fox.

six

"May I help you?" she says, her voice silky.

Tsuyoshi slips a silver case from an inner jacket pocket, flips it open, and slides out a *meishi,* or business card, with a calculated slickness that can come only from decades of practice. I know from Dad that Tsuyoshi only half-retired so he could keep the honorary title of Chairman and the prestigious meishi that go with it. The temple fox murmurs her thanks, then whips out a meishi of her own from her kimono.

Clearly they mean business.

I glance at the myobu's meishi. It's elegantly printed in gold on fine rice paper. Her name: Shizuka. Her rank:

some Japanese I can't entirely read, but I recognize the characters for *miko*, shrine maiden.

The two of them bow again, and then Tsuyoshi looks at me. His cheeks darken. "And this is my grandson, Octavian Kimura. I spoke of him earlier."

Despite being a meishi-less embarrassment, I try a charming smile.

"Yes." Shizuka blinks, her thick eyelashes like black wings. "Follow me."

She glides beyond the Inari shrine and opens a small gate. Behind the gate, a narrow path winds through the bamboo. I follow close behind her, trying not to sniff the air, wondering if she can tell that I'm also a kitsune.

We reach a greenhouse topped by a high-arching glass dome. Shizuka unlocks the door and waves for us to enter before her. Inside, the air is the perfect temperature of a May morning, thick with the sweet scent of citrus leaves and the musk of earth. Shizuka slips off her shoes, and we do the same, moss squishing beneath our feet. A jade pool glimmers beneath the apex of the dome, shaded by an exquisitely gnarled lime tree no taller than I am, but likely five times as old.

"Please, sit." Shizuka settles on a mossy boulder by the pool.

Tsuyoshi pinches his trousers at the knees and tugs them up as he sits on another boulder. His posture is ramrod straight, the briefcase still clutched in his hand, but his forehead is slightly creased, like this is improper somehow. I'm left with the floor itself.

Shizuka looks at me, her eyes half-closed. "Your mother or your father?"

"Excuse me?" I say.

"Who was human?" she says.

"His father." Tsuyoshi says. "His mother was a nog-itsune."

"Ah." Shizuka's face remains calm, but in that one little word there's a delicate touch of scorn. "May I see the papers?"

Tsuyoshi slips an envelope from his briefcase and hands it to Shizuka. When she opens the envelope, I glimpse the word "orphanage" clear across the front. Blood rushes into my face. My adoption papers. If this myobu wants to know my pedigree, she's going to be disappointed. My parents didn't leave much of a trace.

Shizuka squints as she reads. "Hokkaido. Few kitsune live there."

I shrug. "I met one or two when I was young."

She glances at me over the top of the paper. "Do you have any recollection of your mother's name?"

"No."

"Your father's?"

"No. I never met him."

This is sounding really bad, isn't it? Poor little kit-fox Tavian, raised like a wild thing by a delinquent field fox mother who was crazy enough to live in the frigid north.

I keep my face carefully empty. "She promised to tell me her true name once I had one of my own."

"I see." Shizuka's eyes glimmer brighter. "You are nameless."

I press my fingernails into the palms of my hands. I don't need her to tell me this is bad. Like faeries, kitsune guard their true names zealously. A true name unlocks a kitsune's innermost power, and can be used to control the kitsune itself. That's all I know, humiliatingly enough.

"Octavian," she says, like she can tell my mind is wandering.

"Yes?"

"Watch."

Shizuka flicks back the long sleeves of her kimono, all twelve layers, and dips her fingers into the jade pool. She lifts a fallen lime leaf, glossy with water, in the palm of her hand. With a sideways glance at me, she flexes her fingers ever so slightly. The leaf shimmers in her hand, its emerald color lightening to silver. A coin.

Tsuyoshi grunts appreciatively. "Beautiful."

Beautiful? A simple illusion. Though I'd rather not tell them how my kitsune mother tricked vending machines, or how I copied her once I found out counterfeit coins could pay for street food, as long as I ran fast enough after the silver faded away.

"Now you," Shizuka says.

She drops the coin into the pool, and it sinks for a second before bobbing back to the surface, a leaf once more. I fish out the leaf from the water and hold it in my hand.

I concentrate on the color of the leaf, imagining how the greenness will bleed away, baring gleaming silver.

And the shape of the leaf…that will ripple like molten metal, reforming into a circle. One, two, three seconds pass. Sweat breaks out on my forehead. A little air hisses from between my lips, and at last the illusion takes hold.

Shizuka looks first at the coin, then at my face. "Fascinating."

"It normally doesn't take so long." I toss the coin into the pool. The moment it's no longer touching my skin, it returns to a leaf. "Illusions have been harder since…my sickness." I assume Tsuyoshi already told her.

Shizuka studies my face, then reaches into the pool and pinches the water between her fingertips. She lifts the water, shaping it into a fine silver chain that sways and flashes. Not silver—the links *are* water. She drapes the chain over my hand, and I feel its cool slipperiness before it dissolves into a trickle of liquid a second later.

"Try that," she says.

I nod, but my mouth fills with the metallic taste of fear. I've never even seen that before, and working with nothing but water looks impossible. What does she want to prove? That I'm a half-breed nogitsune upstart who can't compete with her myobu talent?

I clench my jaw and dip my fingers into the pool. I focus on the water clinging to my skin, dripping into perfect tiny links…interlocking links…my chest tightens with pain. I glare at the pool, blood flaming in my face.

Damn it. I'm not this weak. I can do this.

Darkness edges my eyesight. My face goes cold as

the blood drains away. My heartbeat flops inside my ribs and I slump, my limbs as limp as jellyfish tentacles.

"Octavian!" Tsuyoshi grips my shoulder.

Shizuka's hand descends upon my wrist and warmth flashes through my skin. Slowly, my heartbeat returns to its normal rhythm.

"That is enough," she says, her voice low.

I clench and unclench my jaw. "I know I could have done it, before ..."

"It is amazing," she says with an arched eyebrow, "that you have managed to do so much with so little. You are a half-breed, and undoubtedly completely untrained."

I guess that's a compliment? "Thank you," I say.

"Are you aware," she says, "of how rare half-breed kitsune are?"

Tsuyoshi shakes his head. "We know of no others like Octavian."

Shizuka folds her hands in her lap, her gaze downcast. "That is because the others are dead."

A jolt of alarm gives my bones a bit more solidity. "Dead?"

"A human body is simply too weak to contain a kitsune's power. A half-breed such as yourself lives on the brink between surviving and being consumed by the magic within."

Consumed. When I close my eyes, I see maggots of electricity worming inside me. So I came all the way to Japan to get a diagnosis from temple fox, and it's fatal. Fantastic.

You should not exist.

Tsuyoshi stares into the pool as if it holds the future. "But why now?"

"He has grown beyond the foxfire of a kit."

I furrow my brow. "Foxfire? Do you mean the white balls of light?"

Shizuka's smile bares sharp teeth. "One might consider those a manifestation of a kitsune's magic. There is much to learn."

I could let myself be insulted, but she's right.

Shizuka stands, her kimono slithering itself straight around her. She clasps her hands demurely. "Unfortunately, we are out of time, and another visitor awaits me."

Tsuyoshi climbs to his feet somewhat stiffly and clears his throat. "Thank you. We are most indebted to you and would greatly appreciate any future assistance."

I unfold from my cross-legged position, wincing at my stiff muscles. Shizuka bows, and Tsuyoshi bows deeper in return. Is that it? We're leaving? My grandfather glances at me, and I also bow, though perhaps not deeply enough to be polite.

"Excuse me for leaving," Shizuka murmurs, "and take care."

Take care? Take *care?* Maybe I'm losing my mind, but I see a gleam in the myobu's eyes as she shows us to the greenhouse door.

And people think nogitsune are the evil ones.

I grit my teeth as I step out, determined to show no sign of weakness. You know what, I'm not even sure I believe her nice little theory about my kitsune magic eating away my human body. If half-breeds are so incredibly rare, how does she even know how they died? Maybe kitsune hardly ever have children with humans. Or they make such terrible mothers that their kits die off quickly enough to be forgotten.

Wow, aren't we bitter?

Are you still a kitsune? Can you still change?

Did my kitsune mother know I was doomed? Is that why she left me?

I realize I'm walking alone. "Ojīsan?"

I glance back to see Tsuyoshi handing a small envelope to Shizuka with a bow. "A token of our appreciation."

Shizuka smiles, her face sweet. "Thank you."

Tsuyoshi returns to me, his expression betraying nothing.

"A token of our appreciation?" I repeat.

"A gift," he says, "for the restoration of the shrine."

I glance at the perfectly trimmed shrubbery and spotlessly painted shrine buildings. Doesn't look like this place needs much restoration, though I doubt Shizuka would turn up her nose at a check—which is vastly superior to the traditional offering of tofu decorated with a red maple leaf. Those twelve-layered kimonos aren't cheap.

"Well, that was … interesting," I say, choosing my words carefully. "That's the first time I heard any of that about kitsune, half-breeds, and foxfire. I'm not sure what to think."

Tsuyoshi thins his lips. "Do you doubt Shizuka?"

Did I sound that sarcastic?

"I would rather not believe that I'm going to drop dead."

"This is serious," he says, his voice cutting. "We need her help."

"It didn't seem like she wanted to help." My throat clenches. "Or could."

Tsuyoshi marches down the path. "We will see."

Maybe he has more faith in his "gift" than I do.

Tourists and visitors cluster around the shrine to Inari, chatting, laughing, and posing for photos by the kitsune statues—for luck. If only they knew who walked between them, dragging misfortune behind him like a tangle of dark seaweed pulling him down.

We return to the condo at noon, to the sound of laughter in the kitchen—Gwen and Michiko. Gwen is red-faced, her curls tamed into a ponytail, and wearing a too-small apron. Michiko stands beside her, guiding the wicked knife in Gwen's hand. Chopped veggies sit in neat heaps on the granite counter.

"Tavian!" Gwen says, glancing up.

"Watch your fingers," Michiko says.

Gwen's face gets even redder, and she sets down the

knife before looking back up at me. "We're making *bento*. Aren't they cute?" She holds out a lacquered lunchbox.

I'm mildly horrified that Gwen is showing such an interest in making adorable pandas out of sticky rice and seaweed, nestled in a forest of broccoli trees. Back home, her idea of cooking encompassed sandwiches and boxed mac and cheese. Japan is definitely corrupting her, making her more girly-girl. Not that it's a bad thing.

When I don't smile big enough, Gwen's eyes narrow. "What happened? What did the myobu tell you?"

Tsuyoshi clears his throat. "It was helpful."

Michiko looks at her husband, and he nods slightly. She purses her lips. I have no idea what they just communicated.

"Lunch is nearly ready," Michiko says.

Tsuyoshi and I both wash our hands, then wait at the table. I plaster a hopeful, happy smile on my face for Gwen's benefit, though I have a suspicion it looks more like the death grin of a cadaver.

Gwen sits beside me. "You okay?" she whispers.

I nod.

Michiko sets bento boxes in front of each of us, then takes her place at the table. I get the cute pandas Gwen made; Tsuyoshi chuckles at the smiley boiled eggs in his bento. We eat in silence. Try as I might, my tongue can't taste any of the food, but I pretend it's delicious. What a waste.

Afterward, Gwen drags me to my bedroom.

"All right," she says, shutting the door halfway. "Tell me."

I stand by the window, open my mouth, and shut it again. I roll back my shoulders to stretch my spine, then sit cross-legged on the floor. There's a tiny hole in the bottom of my sock, and I poke at it.

"What do you want to know?" I say in a low voice.

"Everything."

Well, shit. I have to talk now, don't I?

My gaze still on the hole in my sock, or the window, or anywhere but Gwen, I give her a recap of what Shizuka told me. Ending with, "So that means I'm really screwed up. Though a temple fox would never put it in such a crude way."

Gwen says nothing.

I poke at the sock-hole again. "I need new socks," I mutter.

"Tavian." Her voice sounds steely. "So they didn't help you at all?"

I shrug. "Now I know what's wrong with me."

I glance sideways at her. She's working her jaw like she's grinding words between her teeth. Her eyes glimmer gold.

"We're going to fix this," she says.

I laugh an empty laugh. "Got any ideas?"

"I'm *thinking*."

This time I laugh a real laugh, but it comes out kind of scratchy. "Gwen." I climb to my feet and take both of her hands. "Come here."

She lets me hug her, but her muscles stiffen beneath my touch. "I'm pissed."

"I can tell."

"Aren't you?" She looks into my eyes. "At your kitsune mother? At everything?"

"How can I be pissed when I have happy pandas in my stomach?"

"Tavian," she says, resting her head on my chest. "Be serious."

I sigh. "I'm not sure being pissed makes a difference. But I'm not going to just roll over and give up. Hell no."

"Good," she says, her voice muffled.

I squeeze her gently, trying to make us both feel better, when all I really feel like doing is running away. She leans back to look at me, then kisses me on the lips. I slide my fingers up her back and into her hair, freeing her curls from her ponytail.

"I'm not leaving you," I whisper.

She holds me tighter in reply.

As we stand together, our breathing slows to the same rhythm and I feel her heartbeat against my chest.

"I've been worrying a lot," she says. "About you."

I sit on the edge of my bed and draw Gwen down to sit next to me. Her cheeks look red and splotchy, and I know she's trying not to cry. I kiss her, softly at first, then harder. The tension in her muscles melts, and she lies back on the bed. I slide my hands into the back pockets of her jeans, my blood burning hotter.

"What are you attempting to do?" she murmurs, half-smiling.

"I'm not attempting to do anything," I say. "I'm already succeeding."

She scoffs, but she's smiling. "You wish."

I wiggle my eyebrows, over-the-top suggestive, and start kissing up her arm like a deranged Casanova. She laughs.

"That's more like it," I say.

"Naughty fox boy," she whispers, "you know we can't do anything."

"Consider it a promise for the future," I say, and I bend down to kiss her on the lips.

seven

That afternoon, we head out to Shinjuku Gyoen National Garden, which is surprisingly big for a garden in the middle of Tokyo, and surprisingly popular for the middle of winter. Scattered crowds stroll and chat beneath snow-dusted evergreens, while the late sun paints everything gold. An icy wind numbs my fingers and face.

"Tavian," Gwen says, "someone is following us."

I walk closer to her and our arms bump. We aren't holding hands—that's too mushy for public in Japan. "Is it the noppera-bō?" I whisper. "With all these people?"

"No." She glances back over her shoulder. "Take a look."

She stops at a park bench and tugs me to sit beside her. I pretend to be interested in pines farther down the path.

The gray mastiff.

It's too massive for anything but an inugami. Passersby are shying away from the beast, maybe because it's wearing a leather-studded collar but no leash—illegal, I saw the signs. Or maybe they're shying away from the equally massive thug walking around with unconcealed tattoos on his arms. Reflective sunglasses hide his eyes, and his black hair hangs long and loose down his back. I don't know who he is, but I'd rather not introduce myself.

"The Kuro Inu," I say out of the corner of my mouth.

"Who?" Gwen says.

"Oh, that's the name of their little yakuza gang."

"Tavian? Gwen?" Michiko is waiting for us, farther along the path.

I saunter over to my grandmother, slowly, so it doesn't look like I've seen anything alarming.

"It's a pity the roses aren't blooming at this time of year," Michiko says, determined to be our tour guide. "But the French Formal Garden is still quite lovely. Now, onward to the traditional Japanese garden. In the spring, there are wonderful cherry blossoms. In the fall, the chrysanthemums bring crowds equal to their beauty."

Behind us, I can hear the gray mastiff panting heavily.

"Gwen would love to see the Japanese garden," I say. "And the teahouse there. Could we have some tea?"

Gwen nods, her eyes brightening at the lie.

Maybe if we go indoors, the inugami won't follow us. The gray mastiff won't be allowed in, and most places frown upon yakuza flaunting their tattoos—at least, that's what our guidebook says. I doubt that etiquette will stop a drooling brute of a dog-spirit from having his revenge. But it'll be better than being out here.

"An excellent idea!" Michiko chirps. She swivels around, trying to spot her wayward husband, and discovers him standing beneath a tree, his high-tech binoculars pointed upward.

I groan. Now is not the time to be bird-watching.

"Tsuyoshi!" Michiko calls.

He pretends not to hear. Or else he's actually hard of hearing.

Would he be deaf to the sound of an inugami's nails clicking closer on the pavement?

Dread seizes me and I run to my grandfather. "Ojīsan!"

A tiny brown bird zips from the tree, and Tsuyoshi follows it with his binoculars until it's lost from sight. Then he lowers his binoculars and frowns at me.

"We want to go to the teahouse," I say.

"Then go," Tsuyoshi says. "There are many fascinating birds here."

"But you—"

"Tavian?" Gwen calls.

I whirl around. The tattooed thug advances on Michiko.

He towers over her, his muscles rippling like lean pythons beneath his inked skin. My grandmother grips the handle of her umbrella. I sprint to them, my legs slow, like I'm running through water or a nightmare. The fox paces inside me, ready to take over, but I force myself to calm down. Keeling over wouldn't accomplish anything.

"Excuse me." The thug has a soft voice with a slight rasp in it, like claws snagged in velvet. "Are you Michiko Kimura?"

Clearly the inugami have been doing their homework.

"Yes." Michiko thins her lips. "I don't believe we've met."

"My name is Yuta." He slips off his sunglasses and actually *bows* to her—are even the yakuza polite to old ladies?

My gaze drifts to the tattoos on Yuta's arms, and I can't help staring. A red-horned black dragon, twisting, serpentine, breathes fire and dissolves into curls of its own smoke.

"Can we help you with something?" Michiko asks politely.

Yuta nods, his eyes slivers of obsidian. "Oh, I think you can."

The mastiff pants, his jowls parting like he's smiling at us. He creeps closer to Gwen, his head held low. I grab her wrist; her hazel eyes have a gleam in them that means they're seconds away from glowing.

"Do you speak English?" Gwen says to Yuta.

"Yes, I do," he says, with an upper-crust British accent.

"Take your dog away," she says, tacking on a semi-sincere, "Please."

Yuta's lips curl into a crooked smile. "His name is Ushio. You can pet him if you like." He says "pet" with an upward flick of his eyebrows, as if he's inviting Gwen to do something filthy with the gray mastiff.

"No thank you," Gwen says, her voice icy, her face flaming.

The gray mastiff—Ushio—jabs his muzzle against her hand and drags his slimy tongue along her fingers. She shudders.

Yuta meets my gaze. "Tavian, come walk with us."

"Why?" I say.

"My brother, Katashi, wants to talk to you again."

Let me guess. He wants to have a little chat with torture on the side.

I clench my hands at my sides. "I'd rather not."

"You blunt Americans never fail to amuse me," Yuta says, still smiling. "Our next invitation will not be nearly so polite."

I stare coldly at him. "It's crowded here, don't you think?"

Yuta's smile widens. "You can't hide in crowds forever, fox." He slips his sunglasses back on, then turns to Gwen. "Did Ushio lick you? My apologies. I must say, you are remarkable. Katashi says you are like nothing he has seen before, Miss…"

"Gwen," she says, nonchalantly. "And I prefer not to be called 'Miss.'"

Yuta peers at her over his sunglasses. "And what *are* you, Gwen?"

Her eyes burn gold. "Guess."

Yuta laughs huskily. "I'm not familiar with American yōkai."

I grab Gwen's wrist and shake my head. Snarkiness won't help. I can tell she wants to give those inugami another dose of pooka medicine, but we're in enough trouble already.

She exhales. "I'm a pooka."

"Pooka." Yuta says the word slowly, like he's rolling a hard candy around his mouth, tasting it. "Katashi was determined to discover the identity of what he saw earlier. A word of advice: my brother and his friends are easily insulted, and not so easily ignored. Don't trespass on Kuro Inu territory again if you can help it."

Michiko's hand clamps around my wrist. "Excellent advice," she tells Yuta. "Thank you. Now we really must hurry to the teahouse before it becomes too crowded and we can't get a table." She says all this in rapid-fire Japanese, then glances at Gwen's uncomprehending face and sighs. "Tea," she says in English. "Now."

"Enjoy your tea," Yuta says. "See you around."

He saunters away. Ushio lingers, staring at me—trying to prove he's dominant, or something else primitive and disgusting like that. I bare my teeth; the dog growls. A trickle of drool slips from his jowls and lands on my shoe.

"Disgusting," I say.

Ushio barks and I leap back, my heart pounding.

"Leave him alone," Gwen says, her shoulders rigid.

Yuta glances back. "Ushio!" he calls.

The mastiff trudges away, with a backward glance and a growl. Yuta and Ushio turn a corner and disappear.

I shudder. Is that it? They just threaten us and leave?

"Tsuyoshi!" Michiko marches over to her husband.

My grandfather still has his eyes glued to his binoculars, looking beyond the trees at a road. A powerful engine rumbles, and a sleek black Jaguar luxury sedan slides past. I don't need binoculars to glimpse the shadowy man in a suit sitting the back.

He's watching us.

The reflective window slides shut, and the Jaguar speeds away.

"Octavian." Tsuyoshi turns to me. "That was Zenjiro Matsuzawa."

"Who?" I say.

"A very powerful man." He speaks with hushed awe, like Zenjiro is a celebrity.

"We shouldn't wait outside," Michiko says.

"Hai," Tsuyoshi says.

She marches toward the teahouse and we all follow her. The teahouse looks gorgeous, with upswept roofs reflected in a pond beside evergreens pruned into pillowy shapes. But I don't have more than a second to admire it before Michiko pulls and Gwen pushes me into the teahouse. We kneel on tatami mats around a low table.

"Are you certain it was Zenjiro Matsuzawa?" Michiko murmurs.

Tsuyoshi meets her eyes and nods.

"I see." Michiko's nostrils flare. "Then those were his dogs."

I stare at them. "Is Zenjiro the head of the Kuro Inu?"

Tsuyoshi laughs bleakly. "The Kuro Inu? No, the inugami are mere henchmen, nothing more than hunting dogs. Zenjiro is human. The lower ranks of yakuza may include yōkai, but the yakuza bosses are all human."

"So he's a yakuza boss?"

"Of course. The Matsuzawa family is infamous."

Michiko stares down at her hands. "Why was Zenjiro watching us? Did we do something wrong, something to anger him?"

"Nothing that I know," Tsuyoshi says. "Perhaps Zenjiro was evaluating his men."

Gwen and I share a secret glance. Was our back-alley fight with a handful of inugami really enough to catch their boss's eye?

Then Michiko squints at me. "You are familiar with the Kuro Inu?"

Guilty as charged. But what I am going to say?

"Yes," I say slowly. "It was—"

A waitress brings us bowls of green tea. We thank her and sip our tea. I try not to scald my mouth. The tea house is relatively empty, with only a few tourists in the corner snapping photos. I would definitely see if there were any inugami here.

Michiko lowers her voice to barely above a murmur. "How did you meet the Kuro Inu?"

I clear my throat. "I trespassed on their territory in Harajuku. They smelled that I was a kitsune, and they got aggressive about it. Gwen found me and saved me from them."

Michiko's eyebrows go sky-high. "By shapeshifting?"

Gwen blushes. "Yes."

Tsuyoshi steeples his hands on the table, his face solemn, his eyes stormy. "It is very shameful for a yakuza to be defeated by a woman. Even if that woman is a foreign yōkai; maybe especially so. They will fight viciously to regain their honor. And the yakuza who are inugami hold a deep hatred of kitsune."

"Of course," I say.

Gwen twists her mouth. "So how will they try to regain their honor? A fight to the death?" Embers of anger smolder in her eyes, like she'd love to kick their asses.

"Possibly. They will try to humiliate you in a way that warns others away from trespassing on their territory." The way he says *humiliate* implies everything leading up to and including death. "You should never fight an inugami. Not because you will always lose, but because their pride will be so wounded they will be honor-bound to fight back."

For some bizarre reason, there's what looks like a glimmer of pride in my grandfather's eyes as he looks at Gwen. Does he think I'm incapable of fighting? Just because my kitsune magic is apparently out of control and might randomly kill me doesn't make me an invalid. I could have figured out a way to fight the inugami alone.

And then I feel stupid for being jealous of Gwen.

"Understand?" Tsuyoshi says.

I nod like a puppet.

"Octavian Kimura?" the waitress says, her voice so feathery that I almost don't hear it. She looks between our faces.

"Yes?" I say.

With a slight bow, she hands me an envelope. When I take it, a hair drifts to the table—long and black.

I open it slowly, my fingers clumsy. It's handwritten in English.

Last time was not enough. Do not look for me. I will come for you.

It doesn't have a signature.

"Tavian?" Michiko says. "What is it?"

I swallow, my mouth dry. "I...I don't know."

I hand the letter over to her. She reads its quickly, her dark eyes sharp, then gives it to Tsuyoshi.

"What does it say?" Gwen says, her voice taut with impatience.

Tsuyoshi slides it over to her.

"Who is this from?" Michiko asks.

"One of the Kuro Inu?" I furrow my brow. "But why

would they need to repeat what they already said to me in person?"

Tsuyoshi shakes his head, and oddly, he looks triumphant. "No."

"Then who?" I say.

"Shizuka. I knew she would want to speak with you again."

Michiko purses her lips. "Rather impolite for a temple maiden…"

But Tsuyoshi is still smiling. "Finally, some good news." He toasts with his bowl of tea, then takes a swig.

Gwen glances sideways at me, her eyes questioning.

I look at the long black hair that fell from the letter, pinch it between two fingers, and lift it to my face.

Would it be stupid to hope it came from my kitsune mother?

Dinner feels like a ritual of normalcy, where everyone takes their prearranged places and swallows their anxieties before starting to eat the feast Michiko has cooked. I can almost taste my grandmother's concern simmered in her soup, mingled with her hope that everything will be all right.

I crunch a rice cracker seasoned with sea salt and sugar. "These are delicious."

"Arigatō," Michiko says, and she's very good at almost making her smile touch her eyes.

Later in the evening, Michiko and Tsuyoshi wind down, their movements slower and stiffer. I can see their masks slipping, revealing their true age. I sneak into the kitchen on the pretense of snatching another rice cracker, but really I'm hoping I'll be caught by Michiko so she can scold me and I can crack some bad joke to see her smile, this time for real.

But the kitchen remains empty and bare beneath the flat fluorescent lights, and the cracker tastes like sawdust in my mouth. With a sigh, I head to the living room, where the TV plays with the sound muted. Tsuyoshi snores, slumped low in a leather easy chair, his chin propped on his chest. I slip the remote from his hand before it can clatter onto the floor and wake him.

His snoring stops and I wince, hoping I'm not being too loud.

Tsuyoshi turns toward me, his eyes still shut. "Tavian," he says, without stirring. His voice sounds hollow and sleep-roughened. "You have spoken to her."

The hairs on my arms prickle. "I don't know what you mean."

"I warned you," he says, "that she would come."

He rubs his eyes with a clumsy hand, and his face smudges, revealing the blank skin underneath.

The return of the noppera-bō.

"I thought you went on vacation," I mutter, trying to barricade my fear behind humor.

The fake Tsuyoshi lies in his chair, blank-faced, his chest moving as if he's breathing through his nonexistent mouth and nose. Thoroughly creeped out, I back away and hurry to the guest bedroom, shutting the door behind me. Wait. Should I have talked to the ghost? Interrogated it?

The doorknob turns behind me, and I leap away from the door.

Gwen enters the room, finished with her shower, wrapped in a towel. She's carrying another towel, but she's not using it to dry her hair, which drips all over the carpet.

"Gwen," I say, shutting the door behind her.

She stands by the window and stares out at the brooding clouds, their underbellies glowing orange by the light of Tokyo. Her hair keeps dripping.

"The noppera-bō is here," I whisper. "Pretending to be Tsuyoshi."

She turns toward me, her eyes distant. "I need to talk to you." Her voice sounds hollow.

And I know it's the noppera-bō.

This time, I say, "Then talk."

The noppera-bō lets Gwen's hands go limp. The towel slips from her body, leaving her pale and naked against the black night outside the window.

"We do not have much time," she says, her mouth barely moving. "She is keeping me out."

"Who?"

"Her name must not be spoken."

"Is she Yukimi?"

The noppera-bō shushes me with a hiss like wind racing through grass. "She is watching you."

I advance on this ghost-as-Gwen. "Who are you?" I take another step. "Tell me the truth."

"You will know when you find my face."

I frown. "Why can't you show it to me?"

"I am dead." Gwen's head lists to the left and stays at an unnatural tilt. "You must learn my name."

I clench my hands into fists and step even closer. "Have you forgotten it?"

She shakes her head, then opens her mouth to speak again.

There's a whisper in my head. *Do not speak to him.*

Yukimi's voice.

My thoughts feel sludgy, like they're swimming in muck. The muscles in my legs twitch as if activated by electricity, and they move by themselves. I walk stiffly toward the ghost masquerading as Gwen.

Fear flickers, briefly, in the noppera-bō's borrowed eyes. "Wait."

I back Gwen against the window, my arms drifting upward, my hands pressing on the icy glass on either side of her head. I'm trapping her, but I don't want to.

"Let me speak," Gwen says.

No, Yukimi says in my head.

My hands move to unlatch the window and fling it wide open, to grab Gwen by the shoulders and push her out into the frigid air. But she fights against me, clinging to my arms, clawing at my skin, snowflakes sticking to her wet hair.

She cries, "Tavian!"

I know that the noppera-bō might not be imitating her—it might be possessing her body, and I could throw the real Gwen out the window to plummet to the pavement below. But *I* am possessed, by Yukimi, who has crawled into my brain and is making my muscles move.

I strain against the force puppeting me from within, but Yukimi's grip upon my mind is ironclad.

I lunge and shove Gwen through the window.

To fall thirty-eight stories down.

eight

A scream trapped in my throat, I grip the edge of the windowsill and lean into the night, watching as Gwen plummets from the skyscraper, bringing her hand to her mouth to stifle a shriek. As she falls, her fingers smooth away her face, leaving only blankness; her body drifts apart into mist, disappearing into blackness.

It wasn't really her.

But try telling that to my heart, which is beating so hard and fast it's skipping beats. I fall to my knees, clutching my forehead, fighting Yukimi's grip on my mind.

I snarl at myself. "Get out of my head!"

No need to shout, she whispers.

With a sudden relief of pressure inside my skull, Yukimi leaves me. I crouch, panting, a splitting headache thudding behind my temples. Snow swirls into the bedroom on the wind, carrying a wisp of mist that may or may not be a piece of the defeated ghost. I hold my breath, waiting for it to reappear or leave me forever.

The door opens.

Gwen walks in, wrapped in a towel, and I scramble away from her. But this time she's wringing her hair dry, not letting it drip everywhere like she just doesn't care.

"Shut the window!" she says. "It's freezing in here. Are you trying to turn my hair into icicles?"

I exhale in a shuddering breath. "I thought you were the noppera-bō. Again. It came inside, pretending to be you…"

"Tavian!" Gwen latches the window. "Are you okay?"

"Yes, I'm okay…" I stop and squint at her. "What's the best place to get pizza in Klikamuks?"

"The Olivescent," she says, without skipping a beat.

"And what were you eating the first time we met there?"

"Calzones." She sighs. "Tavian, I don't think the ghost would have answered the first question correctly, you know." And she sounds snarky enough that I know she's real.

I turn up the thermostat and grab a blanket. We huddle together on my bed for warmth. Shivering, I tell her what happened, how Yukimi entered my mind while I was awake.

Gwen rubs the goose bumps on her arms. "She can do that?"

"I didn't know."

"This is bad, Tavian. Really bad. Maybe you should ask for help."

"From who?" I'm too tired to muster any sarcasm. "The myobu?"

"Maybe."

I squeeze Gwen's hand. "I don't understand what Yukimi wants from me. Or who the noppera-bō *is*—was."

She twists a curl around her finger. "We're going to have to find out."

"He could be anybody. At least, anybody who was an enemy of Yukimi, or who hated her enough to stay after death. Maybe he thinks Yukimi is so evil she'd hurt her own son." I rub my pounding head. "She already has."

Gwen hugs me, and I hug her back even though she's getting water all over me from her hair. "I'm sure there's a story behind this, Tavian. An explanation. We're going to find out."

I wish I shared her confidence. I grimace. "I hope I didn't wake my grandparents."

"I don't think they heard you," Gwen says. "Michiko was already snoring when I walked past their room, and that alone would drown out anything under one hundred decibels."

"Hey," I say, mustering some pretend outrage, "she's my grandmother."

"Your loud grandmother," Gwen says. "I'm glad I'm sleeping next to you."

"In your own bedroom," I say.

She arches her eyebrows. "I wasn't suggesting anything inappropriate."

I can't help smiling. "Sure. After we get home, you're in big trouble."

"That's more like it." She snuggles against me and shuts her eyes.

I hold her close, maybe a little closer than I need to, trying to erase the image of her falling from my mind.

Twilight in the forest. I crawl from my den and yawn, my tongue curling. The sweet loamy scent of earth clings to my fur. It's a fine evening to be a fox. I tilt my head back to look at the stars winking into being between gaps in the lacy canopy. Wind ruffles my red fur, carrying a delicious perfume—a delicate spice over a deeper, musky smell.

Nose held high, I trot deeper between the trees.

Fireflies light my path, floating around me in a scattering of glow. A yip breaks the stillness of the air. I cock my head toward the sound. Another yip—a vixen.

I slink closer, poking my face between a tangle of vines.

A pure white fox stands in a grove of apricot trees, her eyes as golden as the ripening fruits. She walks nearer on slender legs, her sleek tail trailing behind her. We touch noses. I inhale the spicy-musky perfume, and I realize it's the vixen's scent.

I dance back with a yip, inviting her to come run with me. The vixen narrows her eyes and gives me a short growl. I whine questioningly and tilt my head to one side. Why doesn't she feel like slipping between the shadows, trotting beneath fences into farms, and maybe finding a nice plump chicken for dinner?

Tavian. Now is not the time to think with your stomach.

The whisper echoes in my head, paradoxically loud. I skitter back, my ears flattened against my skull. I know that voice.

Shizuka?

The white fox smiles, the corners of her lips curling. *Yes.*

Around me, the forest ripples as if it were only ever a reflection. I blink and stagger back, swimming in the melting green. This is a dream. Shizuka has entered my dream.

Tail bristling, fur spiking along my spine, I growl.

Calm down, Shizuka says. *No need to wake yet.*

The white fox walks to me and rests her muzzle on my shoulder. The forest quiets, settling back into the illusion my imagination has created for me. But now I'm totally lucid, and I'm not sure I like the idea of a myobu creeping into my mind at night.

Shizuka sniffs, a miffed, whistling sound. *I won't stay for long.*

And she can read my thoughts now. Great.

Why are you here?

She sits and wraps her tail daintily around her paws. *You would do well to return to the shrine in the morning.* She pauses to sniff the air, then glances back at me. *Alone.*

I prick my ears. Why?

There is much left unsaid.

So the myobu didn't think I was a total—I force my mind to swerve from those thoughts. Must be polite.

Shizuka laughs silently, a chiming sound in my head.

Wait. So if she didn't send the unsigned letter…

Letter?

Never mind. I'll figure that out later.

Shizuka tilts her head. *Goodbye, Tavian.*

Her fur shimmers at the edges, twinkling like sun on snow. The brightness sweeps over her body until she's nothing but a fox-shaped glow. With a blinding flash, she blinks out.

And I'm left alone in the forest of my dreams.

Over a breakfast of seaweed-sprinkled rice, fried tofu, and corn puffs—the last one's for Gwen, who had a craving for cereal—I break the news to my grandparents.

"The letter wasn't from Shizuka," I say.

Tsuyoshi frowns over the top of his newspaper. "Oh?"

"I had a dream about her, last night." I wrinkle my nose. "Technically, she entered my dreams."

Gwen crunches some corn puffs. "What did she say?"

"Shizuka asked me to come back to the shrine, this morning. She wants to talk to me."

"Then you must go at once," Michiko says, pouring herself more tea. "It wouldn't be very polite to keep a high-ranking myobu such as Shizuka waiting, especially after she took the trouble of inviting you personally."

Tsuyoshi frowns. "Shizuka didn't send you the letter at the teahouse?"

Last time was not enough. Do not look for me. I will come for you.

"No." I remember the long black hair that drifted from the letter. "It might be from one of the Kuro Inu. Another threat."

Tsuyoshi's face hardens. "I will come with you to the shrine."

"Shizuka asked me to come alone," I say.

"Oh," Tsuyoshi says, with a tinge of disappointment. "Why?"

"She didn't say."

Michiko nods at my bowl of food. "Finish your breakfast and find out."

It's hard to swallow with a stomach that feels like it's already full of eels, but I scrape the last grains of rice into my mouth, excuse myself, and hurry to get ready.

At the door, Gwen kisses me on the cheek. "Good luck."

I can see in her eyes that she's not content staying at home, waiting for the news I'll bring back. I can only hope she won't do something *too* adventurous to make up for it.

As I board the metro, the eel-feeling worsens in my stomach. Sure, it'll be really *nice* if Shizuka has some sort of magic pill for me, or maybe a secret recipe. But why wait to tell me?

I can see my reflection in the subway window, and it looks pretty sarcastic. Better wipe that smirk off my face before I get to Ueno.

A prerecorded female voice announces, first in Japanese, then English, "The next station is Ueno."

I climb to my feet, grabbing a pole to hold myself steady. People trickle from the subway doors, joining the greater flow of crowds navigating the stairs. Aboveground, in Ueno Station, weak winter sun trickles through a roof of glass. On the wall nearby, a poster catches my eye. It's nothing special, artistically speaking: a super-cute snowman standing in front of a snowy castle. It's an advertisement for the upcoming Sapporo Snow Festival.

In, of course, Hokkaido.

I could buy a ticket and melt into the crowd, wait patiently for the train to my birthplace, so close and so far away. But what would be waiting for me in Hokkaido? The orphanage? I shudder, the hairs on my arms bristling. No way in hell am I going back.

I hurry out of Ueno Station, walking up the escalator. In Ueno Park I break into a jog, too edgy just to walk. By the time I get to the Inari shrine, it's hard to make myself stop moving. A line of visitors all wait their turn to speak to the myobu—a girl I don't recognize, sitting behind a persimmon-red table at the front of the shrine. I fidget behind everyone else, trying to catch her eye, hoping the flat air will carry my scent to her so she realizes I'm a kitsune and lets me bypass the wait. I'm not even here to pray.

Finally, I'm second in line, standing behind a guy in a black school uniform. He bows really low to the miko, his hair flopping over his eyes, and I can see his ears flush. He starts mumbling about how he's so sorry for taking up her exceedingly valuable time, but he would very much appreciate her blessing for good luck on his examinations, especially for admission into the prestigious Tokyo University…

I curl my toes inside my shoes, resisting the urge to step around him or maybe gently kick him to finish up. How long is this student going to blather? I don't have time for this.

The shrine maiden nods politely as she listens. She bends over the red table, her fingers moving as nimbly as a spider's legs around a bug caught in a web. She's folding a yellow square of paper into some sort of origami shape. Luckily for me, she's quick at it.

I tilt my head to get a better look at the miko. She's small, maybe even microscopic. Pink plastic butterfly

110

barrettes hold back her bangs. With her round cheeks and big black eyes, she looks maybe ten, eleven tops. What if she's new here and no one told her I'm meeting with Shizuka?

The flustered student finally stops blathering.

"Done," says the miko. "May this bring you good fortune."

She adds a last crease to her paper, then brings it to her lips and blows. The origami sculpture flares into the shape of a fat fish. With a shimmer, the paper ripples into golden scales. A perfect little paper koi—Japanese carp—not more than two inches long.

Nice. The origami-illusion even wriggles like a real fish.

"*Arigatō gozaimasu!*" The student takes the koi with a deep, deep bow.

The miko bows in return, and smiles as he slips an envelope into a box for shrine donations. Her gaze moves to me. "How may I help you?" If she knows I'm kitsune, she isn't showing it.

Maybe I underestimated this girl. Her illusions are spot-on.

I let myself smile a little. "That was impressive."

A blush blooms in her cheeks. "Excuse me?"

"The origami koi illusion. How much do they cost?"

"They are not for sale," she murmurs, in hesitating English.

Right. Even though the student just made a "donation" in return for her illusory good luck charm.

I decide to switch to English, since she's speaking it, and it will give my brain cells a rest. "I'm Tavian Kimura."

She dips her head in a brief bow. "My name is Junko. Come with me."

Junko hurries away from the shrine, her sandals scuffing on the stones, her red skirt trailing behind her. She unlatches the gate to the path fringed with bamboo trees, lets me slip through, then locks it behind her.

My arm accidentally knocks against hers. "Sorry."

Her ears redden and she walks faster, looking anywhere but at me. "Shizuka is waiting for you."

"Do you happen to know why?" I give her a smile, as if that will help pry some information out of her.

"No."

I follow Junko down the bamboo path, through a doorway I don't recognize, and into a labyrinth of hallways. The shrine complex has a tight, winding feel, like a fox den. Well, a very elegant, aboveground den.

"Did she say anything about me?"

"No." She hesitates. "Just that you were the American kitsune."

I detect curiosity in her voice. "I'm from Klikamuks, Washington."

Junko perks up. "By the White House?"

"No." I can't help but laugh. "Not Washington D.C., Washington State. In the west?"

She stares at me.

"North of California? Seattle is the nearest city to Klikamuks."

Her voice falls to a mumble. "I have never heard of Klikamuks. But I am a poor student of geography."

"Don't worry," I say. "Most people haven't heard of Klikamuks."

Junko's voice gets even more mumbly. "Are you...were you born there?" She glances coyly at me.

"No, I was born here. In Hokkaido, not Tokyo. But I was adopted."

She nods, with a quiet "mmm."

We stop outside a door with Shizuka's name on it.

"I would like to hear your story," Junko murmurs, looking at me with a sudden spark in her eyes.

I scratch behind my ear, not sure we'll meet again. "Sure!" Might as well play the part of friendly American.

"Arigatō," Junko whispers, shy again. She raps on Shizuka's door, bows her goodbye, and leaves me alone.

The door sweeps open. Shizuka stands, tall and graceful, in a red kimono decorated with golden koi brocade. I wish for an irrational second that I could paint her portrait. Then I see her white tail peeking through her kimono and I come to my senses.

"I thought you might arrive at this time," she says. "Please, sit."

Her office is a study in white and black, with splashes of color here and there: a scroll of a kitsune wedding procession, an arrangement of red twigs in a vase, an apricot in a wooden bowl.

Shizuka pours us each a cup of jasmine tea. The steam rising to my nose carries the fragrance of night-blooming flowers and yōkai magic. I sip it too quickly and burn my mouth.

"So," I say, "why did you call me back here?"

Shizuka looks at me with heavy-lidded eyes. "I know of your mother."

She says it so softly I'm not sure I heard her right. "Yukimi?"

"Her name is spoken quite often in certain circles."

"Which circles?"

Shizuka sips her tea, then swallows, her slender throat moving gracefully. "*Mizu shōbai*. The water trade."

I set my teacup down. "You mean—?"

"Yes."

The water trade is a euphemism for the business of the underworld—what goes on in the grimy underbelly of Tokyo. Under all the glitter and lights, there are bodies for sale, deaths that go unnoticed, illegal trades made in the shadows.

My guts tighten as if clenched in an invisible fist. Has my mother resorted to prostitution?

Shizuka seems to read my eyes, because she leans forward in her chair. "Yukimi would not have earned such a reputation as one of *those* women. She is one of the Sisters."

"I've never heard of them."

Shizuka crosses her ankles. "That is unsurprising.

114

They are secretive, and an American would certainly not know of them. But they are kitsune, and so the myobu are aware of their dealings. We would not like to be adversely affected."

"What do you mean by 'adversely affected'?"

"The Sisters are a gang of nogitsune who operate in the underworld. They engage in practices and behaviors that tarnish the reputation of kitsune as a whole." She says this very primly, then sits with her lips pursed as if her tea is sour.

I pick up my cup again, so that my hands have something to do. My fingers are shaking slightly. "The Sisters are yakuza?"

Shizuka laughs without humor. "No. Yakuza do not allow women among their ranks. They consider females only good for childbearing and for pleasure. The Sisters, however, make themselves out to be champions of downtrodden women. Unsurprisingly, the two factions have been bitter enemies for decades now."

I let some tea slide down my throat. "What else can you tell me about Yukimi?"

"That she is considered one of the more dangerous Sisters."

"And?"

"That is all."

"Do you know where to find her?"

Shizuka's eyes gleam amber. "No."

I bite the inside of my cheek. "But I need to find her."

"Yes." She refills her teacup. "You do."

I narrow my eyes. "You know more than you're telling me."

"Tea?" Shizuka still holds the teapot aloft.

I shake my head.

She sighs and sets the teapot down. "Octavian, you may try your best to control your foxfire, but there is only so much that can be done while you are nameless. You need to be named. Only then can you save yourself."

"How?" I rub my forehead, my head starting to ache. "I don't know very much about it—nobody ever told me much, or wrote anything down—but I thought I needed my parents to name me. My biological parents, which is a long shot."

Shizuka lowers her voice. "You need only their names, and their blood."

I'm silent for a moment. "From both of my biological parents?"

"Yes."

"But I don't know who my father is. Or was. He might not even be alive."

"Ah," she says, her voice even softer. "Without his blood, you may use his bones."

A shiver crawls down my spine and my stomach feels icy despite all the tea I drank. "And then I will be named?"

"Yes."

"By who?"

A shadow of a smile touches her lips. "Me."

nine

I take the metro home in a daze, Shizuka's words swarming around my head. The Sisters. My true name. The blood of my mother, the blood—or bones—of my father. If I find Yukimi, she can tell me about my father. And then I can be named.

Only then can you save yourself.

My phone buzzes in my pocket. A text from Gwen:

Come home now.

That's it.

Dread pulses through my veins. Why didn't she call me?

At the stop for Akasaka, I wedge myself through the crowds on the platform and take the stairs two at a time. I jog down the street, slowing to a brisk walk when I reach my grandparents' building. The doorman narrows his eyes when he sees me puffing, and I try not to skid on the marble floors in the lobby.

The elevator, predictably, takes several eternities to make it to the thirty-eighth floor. Finally, I burst out and sprint the last distance to the apartment. My hands sweaty, I fumble with the keys, then unlock the door and burst inside.

The living room is empty.

"Hello?" I kick off my shoes. "Is anybody home?"

Then, from the bathroom, I hear Gwen call, "Tavian?"

I force myself to walk at a normal pace and to keep my face somewhat calm, just in case I'm grossly overreacting. Gwen meets me in the doorway, her face pinched. There's a little blood on her hands. My stomach ties itself into a tight knot.

"Come in here," she says, "and talk to your grandmother."

"It's nothing to worry about!" Michiko says.

Gwen steps aside so I can see into the bathroom. Michiko is standing by the sink, the medicine cabinet open, her arm under the faucet. Red water swirls down the drain. She's washing a wound on her arm, deep red holes in a crescent on her soft old skin—a bite mark, big enough to be a dog's. Sourness rises in my throat.

"Inugami." Gwen's voice is husky, like she's been screaming.

"What happened?" I say.

"A dog bit me," Michiko says, matter-of-factly. "But I know how to bandage myself. My father was a doctor, and my mother was a nurse. There's no need to go to the hospital."

Gwen heaves a growling sigh. "It's going to get infected. Tavian, don't you agree?"

I ball my hands into fists. "What *happened*?"

"They attacked us." Gwen's eyes flash gold. "They must have started stalking us the moment we stepped out the door. On the way back from grocery shopping, on this little back street, we hear a dog's nails clicking on the pavement. There's nobody else around. We look back and Ushio's charging at us. He knocks Michiko over, and—"

"A lot of perfectly good pickles wasted," Michiko muses, daubing antiseptic on her arm. "Smashed all over the sidewalk."

"Obāsan!" I say. "I don't care about pickles. I care about you. You're hurt. Gwen is right, you need to go to the doctor."

Michiko actually rolls her eyes at me. "Unnecessary."

Gwen sighs. "Do you want to know what happened or not?"

"Sorry," I say.

"So Michiko is on the sidewalk," Gwen says, "and Ushio is growling and slobbering in her face. I grab the inugami by his collar and try to yank him off her, but he's too heavy. He snaps at me, then bites Michiko on the arm. Of course this makes me really angry, because he just won't let go, no matter how much I hurt him."

"He is a rather strong dog." Michiko unwraps a gauze bandage.

"Here," I say, "let me help you with that."

My grandmother glances at me. "Do you know how?"

"Well, no, but I can still help."

Behind Michiko's head, Gwen mouths, "Impossible."

Michiko holds out her arm. "Wrap it tight enough to stop the bleeding, but not too tight or it will restrict circulation." She speaks in a brisk, I-have-medical-savvy way.

As I follow her instructions, I glance at Gwen. I can see now that she's wearing her shirt inside-out, which means she must have shapeshifted completely, but I'm still trying to figure out how she fought off the inugami single-handedly and protected my grandmother.

I cough. "So how did you beat Ushio?"

Gwen rubs the back of her neck. "I bit him."

"As a snake," Michiko adds.

"Not a venomous one," Gwen says quickly. "Well, not very…"

I raise my eyebrows. "Seriously?"

"Tavian!" Gwen says. "It's shapeshifting, not science. I don't know exactly what kind of snake I was. I don't always have a particular *species* in mind when I visualize the animal I want to become."

"Ushio staggered away," Michiko says. "He was alive when we left."

"You've never turned into a snake before," I say to Gwen.

"So?" she says, her eyes flashing.

"Fascinating." Michiko says.

"Yeah, fascinating," I say. "But Obāsan, you really should see a doctor. Just to be on the safe side."

My grandmother scoffs. "Inugami aren't like those werewolves you have in America. One little bite won't change me into a dog-spirit. Your grandfather doesn't need to worry."

"You're not going to tell him?" I say.

"I will tell him that a dog bit me, because a dog did bite me." Michiko meets my eyes. "There is not much else we can do without provoking the inugami. We don't need this in the news."

I clench and unclench my fists. "So this was their way of humiliating us? To bite an elderly woman in the street?"

"I don't think so," Gwen says.

"Was it a crime of opportunity?" I say. "Why was Ushio alone?"

Gwen thins her lips, suspiciously quiet.

I narrow my eyes. "Tell me."

"After I shapeshifted back," she says, "I helped Michiko up and started getting dressed. Then we heard somebody laughing. Yuta and Katashi came down the street. Katashi looked furious, baring his fangs and snarling, but Yuta was laughing and holding him back. Ushio slunk up to them, whimpering, and Katashi kicked him. Yuta laughed harder and pointed to me. They were talking in Japanese; I couldn't understand them."

Michiko clears her throat. "Later, I translated for her. Katashi didn't say very much that I would like to repeat—profanity, mostly. Yuta, however, was telling his brother that Gwen was an unusual specimen, despite being a girl, and they might find her useful."

Gwen grimaces. "They let us walk away. Like it was all a test."

I curse mentally, for Michiko's sake. "Well, at least I know why they want *me* dead."

"What, because you're a kitsune?"

"Worse. Yukimi is one of the Sisters, a gang of nogitsune women. Bitter enemies with the yakuza. And apparently everybody knows I'm her son."

Night falls like a cloth of black velvet dropped over the lights of Tokyo. I hide in my bedroom with Gwen, trying not to overhear my grandparents arguing. Michiko clatters around in the kitchen, supposedly cooking dinner, but I think she's making too much noise for that.

Tsuyoshi's voice rumbles low, then rises to a shout until Michiko shushes him.

I lean back on my bed and sigh. "We're doomed."

"I'm sure your grandpa will cool down," Gwen says. "Besides, it wasn't your fault Michiko got bitten."

"It wasn't yours, either. And I was talking about the inugami."

She chews on a hangnail. "Tavian, we're not staying in Japan forever. I highly doubt Katashi is going to hop on the next flight to Seattle just to hunt us down. We can't be that important to him and his drooling companions."

"And until then?" I say. "Are we supposed to stay inside?"

Gwen glowers at me. "No. I don't care if they consider all of Tokyo their territory. I'm not going to let some disgustingly stupid dog-spirits hurt any of us. Or their creepy yakuza boss. They can go screw themselves."

I sigh. "You want to be a badass super ninja pooka, don't you?"

This isn't the first time I've called her that. Or the first time I've worried that she thinks shapeshifting makes her more indestructible than the average girl.

Gwen's cheeks redden, but she smiles.

"I didn't mean that as a compliment," I mutter.

She hits me with a pillow. "I saved your butt. You owe me."

"Yes, I do. But I don't want to have to save your butt

in return because you decide to tangle with the inugami again, on purpose, just because you feel like it."

She sniffs. "I'm not stupid. I'm not asking for trouble."

"Gwen, we've both had one too many near-death experiences. Let's not collect the whole set."

"Oh, come on." She pretends to cuff me on the head. "You don't have to worry about me, Tavian. And since when were you ever the voice of caution?"

"Now." I keep a straight face. "We didn't both survive a serial killer so we could get our asses handed to us by some dog-spirits. It's not worth it."

Her eyes glimmer. "What makes you think we'll lose?"

I open my mouth to reply, but there's a knock on the door.

"Come in!" I call.

Tsuyoshi sweeps open the door, his face shadowed. "We're going to the hospital. You can come, or stay."

"We're coming," I say.

We descend to the parking garage and climb into the silver Audi. Tsuyoshi hits the winding streets. Silence congeals the air until it's hard to breathe normally. I glance at Tsuyoshi in the rear-view mirror. Beneath the sheen of passing streetlights, his eyes betray pain. Michiko looks out her window, cradling her bitten arm.

"What happened," Tsuyoshi says, "with Shizuka?"

I swallow hard, but my mouth still feels dry. "Well,

she had more to tell me. About my kitsune mother, Yukimi. She's one of the Sisters."

Silence returns.

"The Sisters are—"

"We know who they are." Tsuyoshi's voice is taut, strained. He's driving a little too fast, passing other cars when he doesn't need to. "Do your parents know about this?"

I glance at him in the rear-view mirror again, but he isn't looking at me anymore. "Mom and Dad didn't know anything about my birth parents when they adopted me."

Tsuyoshi makes an impatient noise. "Have you told them?"

"No."

He eases up on the gas. "Things should remain that way."

I clench my hands. "Are you asking me not to tell them?"

"Tavian." Michiko twists back to look at me, her face softer. "The knowledge would be heartbreaking to them. They want to believe that they have raised a good son."

My face flames. "So I'm a bad son? Because of Yukimi?"

Michiko purses her lips. "Many have overcome the misfortune of a shameful past."

"I know you want me to keep this a secret," I say, my eyes stinging, "but I'm not like Yukimi. She's not my family. She's just the woman who gave birth to me."

Just. Can I really say that?

"There is no need to speak of this further." Tsuyoshi

brakes at an intersection and glowers at the pedestrians crossing the road. "Was that all Shizuka told you?"

"No." I exhale. "She told me that with my true name, I'll be able to control my kitsune magic and save myself. But I'm going to need the names and the blood of my parents first."

"Well, that's … good," Tsuyoshi says, with a glance at Michiko.

"Yes," Michiko says more confidently. "Our support is with you."

Our support—to bury your past so deep no one will ever find it.

The hospital appears ahead, a smallish tower shadowed by its neighbors. We descend into the underground, and Tsuyoshi parks in a garage lit by sickly yellow halogen. Gwen catches my arm as she climbs out, and gives it a squeeze.

"Relax," she whispers.

I realize I'm grinding my teeth, and I take a deep breath. The parking garage smells like stale, exhaust-laden air and mold-slicked concrete. I wrinkle my nose. There's an animal smell down here, too, a vague furry aroma I can't identify.

My shoulders stiffen. Would the inugami follow us here?

The Audi chirps as Tsuyoshi locks its doors, and I flinch at the noise. My grandfather escorts my grandmother to the elevator and I follow them, my hand in Gwen's.

In the shadows, amber eyes glint. Watching me.

I swing my head toward the eyes, my legs tense. The eyes blink out of sight. I shudder and walk faster, passing between pools of halogen light. In the darkness, I glimpse a woman, silhouetted against a ramp leading deeper into the garage. Her mane of hair stirs slightly in a subterranean breeze. She looks at me, her eyes glowing.

"Yukimi?" I whisper.

Gwen tugs me onward. "Come on. What are you looking at?"

I look away for a second, then back—but of course the woman is gone. The fox inside me creeps to the forefront of my eyes, sharpening my night vision. When the doors to the elevator swish open, the light within blinds me. Eyes watering, I follow Tsuyoshi, Michiko, and Gwen, with a backward glance into the black.

The elevator ascends to the level of the hospital's ER. Tsuyoshi ushers Michiko to the reception desk and starts speaking in rapid Japanese, too fast for me to catch much at all. Or maybe it's because my head is muddled from the smell of the parking garage, or the whispers of Yukimi in my mind.

A nurse takes Michiko to a bed where they unwrap her homemade bandage and daub antiseptic on the glistening red punctures in her arm. The temperature in my face drops by several degrees and I have to look away.

"Octavian," Tsuyoshi says gruffly, "why don't you and Gwen find something to eat?"

"Good idea," Gwen says.

She doesn't look as pale as I'm sure I do right now, but I'd bet twenty bucks she's ravenous from her shape-shifting.

Michiko twists her mouth and stares at the nurse working on her arm. "How much longer will this take? I was halfway through preparing fried rice for dinner."

The nurse shakes her head. "You need stitches."

"Oh?" Michiko says. "The wounds seemed fairly shallow when I first examined them."

"Michiko," Tsuyoshi says, his voice rumbling.

They start arguing again, and I slip away with Gwen. I lead the way back down the hall to an elevator. Luckily, the buttons are labeled in English as well as Japanese.

"Cafeteria sounds like our best bet," I say.

Gwen grimaces. "Hospital food." A growl escapes her belly.

"Your stomach thinks otherwise," I say.

She laughs, and I try to smile, but there's a strange prickling along my spine—something is off.

Turns out hospital cafeterias in Tokyo are like those pretty much anywhere else: clean, boring, and smelling a little too much like antiseptic for your appetite to survive. Gwen loads up a tray with a bowl of rice, tofu, fish, seaweed, and so on, while I linger behind her, trying to figure out where that uneasy feeling is coming from.

"I'll check out the vending machines," I say, as an excuse.

"Sure," Gwen says. "I'll snag that table in the corner. Oh, no, that lady is walking toward it..." She scrambles to load food on her tray, which would be comical any other time.

I meander over to the vending machines, keeping my pace carefully casual, pretending to be only mildly interested in my surroundings. There's no one unusual in the cafeteria, no one Other, but then why is the scent of yōkai magic still tingling in my nose?

I rummage in my wallet for some coins, not really caring whether I buy seaweed crackers or instant soup. I glance up, yen in hand, and see myself reflected in the glass belly of the vending machine.

Ah. Of course.

My face looks a lot calmer than I feel. Inside my rib cage, my heart is drumming a frantic beat. The noppera-bō slides into place beside me, a white faceless oval that looks almost ordinary overlaid against the cheery colors of the food in the machine.

"You can't speak without a mouth, can you?" I say.

The noppera-bō's blank face ripples like an invisible hand is sculpting features from a blob of white clay.

"Tavian." Gwen touches my elbow. "Ready?"

I blink, and the ghost is gone.

I growl under my breath. "You scared off the noppera-bō. It was going to tell me something, something important. In the reflection of the vending machine—didn't you see it?"

Gwen stares at me, her eyebrows raised. "No." Her eyebrows descend. "Here?"

"Yes!" I'm sweating now, for some reason.

"Tavian, there are a ton of people here." She glances at the vending machine again, then forces a smile. "Aren't you hungry? I tried some of the tofu here, it's pretty good. Kind of squishy, and I know you don't like silken tofu, but—"

"Gwen." I rub my forehead, my palms slick. "I'm not hungry."

She shakes her head. "You need to eat. This is dinner."

"Fine."

I jam a few coins into the vending machine and buy some cheap ramen. At the hot water dispenser, I scald my hand and swear. Gwen frowns at me from her table; she hasn't touched any of her food yet. I sigh and bring my ramen to her.

"Eat," I mutter. "Don't mind me. I'm just going crazy."

"You're not." She rolls her eyes. "If you want to talk to the noppera-bō, maybe you should do it somewhere less busy than here. And besides, I've never even seen it before, so …"

"So I must be crazy."

"No." She lowers her voice. "So it must be trying to talk to you and nobody else."

I grit my teeth. "I wish I knew what it wanted to tell me."

Gwen shakes her head and hands me a pair of disposable chopsticks. "Eat. Your brain needs food, you know." She digs into her bowl of broccoli and rice. "Even if it's bad food."

I force myself to consume the ramen—consume, because it's too mechanical and tasteless to be called eating. Then I sit and wait for Gwen to eat her tray of food. I rest my arms on the table and stare at my clenched hands, trying not to crack my knuckles. Finally, Gwen finishes her dinner and we head upstairs to Michiko.

I trail behind Gwen, glancing at windows with open curtains. What would happen if I went to the bathroom alone, and stood by one of the mirrors? Would the noppera-bō return?

A woman walks ahead of me, her black mane of hair swaying against the back of her lavender scrubs. Why would a nurse or a doctor leave her hair loose? Unless it's just a quick disguise.

I run after the woman and catch her by the wrist. "Yukimi!"

She faces me, frowning. "Excuse me?"

Not Yukimi.

My cheeks burn. "Sorry, I thought you were someone else."

The woman gives me a hesitant smile, the kind you give a patient who has a few screws loose, then twists her hair into a ponytail and walks briskly away, back to work.

Michiko and Tsuyoshi stand by a bed, staring at me.

"Tavian?" Gwen takes me by the elbow. "What was *that*?"

I shrug. "I don't know. Sorry. I made a mistake. Are we ready to go?"

Michiko has her purse, so she must be. "Are you all right?"

"Yes." But cold sweat dots my skin and a strange hollow feeling of dread has taken residence in my stomach.

"You haven't been," Gwen says, her voice quiet.

Tsuyoshi clears his throat. "We are already at the hospital. Perhaps you should see a doctor—"

"No, I didn't mean to worry you." Damn, how am I going to talk my way out of this one? I paste a smile on my face. "I'm tired, that's all. The sooner we get home, the better. I should go to bed early."

Tsuyoshi nods slowly, his eyes guarded.

The four of us leave the hospital together. I'm the last to exit the elevator to the parking garage, despite the tight, stale, claustrophobic air inside, because I keep glancing at the reflective steel walls. Michiko leans over to Tsuyoshi and whispers something in his ear, in Japanese, but one of the words slips on the air to me.

Sick.

And I do feel sick, feverish, my head throbbing with a migraine that must be thanks to the tug-of-war between Yukimi and the noppera-bō fighting for control of my thoughts. I wince at the pain and try not to stagger against the elevator's walls. Why are my arms and legs shaking like this? Am I about to be puppeted again?

Tsuyoshi hesitates to unlock the Audi. "What's wrong, Tavian?"

I bite the inside of my cheek. I can't tell them that I've been haunted by the noppera-bō and that Yukimi has been clawing her way inside my skull. They'd think I'm crazy for sure, or at least definitely damaged, if they don't already think that.

Damn it, damn it, damn it. Keep it together.

"Can we go home?" I say, playing the part of the good little long-suffering grandson. "Please?"

Gwen looks sideways at me, and I know she's tempted to talk.

"Yes," Michiko says. "I'm tired, Tsuyoshi. Let's go home."

I thank her with my eyes.

In the cool leather-scented air of the Audi, my mind clears a little and I feel stronger leaning against the steel of the door. I rest my sweaty forehead on the window. Tsuyoshi flicks on the headlights and pulls out of the parking garage, ascending to the street. My heart squeezes, and I twist back to look into the parking garage.

Yukimi stands, stark in a cone of light, watching me go.

I suck in my breath and force myself to shut my eyes. When I open them again, she's gone, and we're traveling along the streets of Tokyo, blending into the city's glittering flow.

ten

The moon peers at me through the window as I lie awake in bed. Sweat glues my skin together in places I'd rather not think about. My blanket feels like it's roasting me alive. I toss it off, then pad across the room to turn down the thermostat, and frown at the snow outside.

Maybe I'm feverish. Maybe this is kitsune magic burning me to ashes.

Foxfire.

I've never summoned a ball of illusory white light. And I'd never known foxfire could be anything more than that. What didn't Yukimi tell me? Where is she now? Can she save me?

I sprawl on my bed and shut my eyes.

Night air steeps in the scent of rain on hot asphalt. Cars hiss along the wet street. I open my eyes, bringing the world into sharp focus. I'm crouching in a dark alley, my nose held low, my whiskers damp in the steam rising from a manhole cover. A feral cat slouches past me, intent on a dish of day-old octopus outside a restaurant. The rich fried-batter smell of tempura saturates the breeze.

Instinctively, I know I'm waiting for something else. Someone else.

A woman's heels click on the pavement. She's wearing a cobwebby gray dress and black boots best suited for a nightclub or bar. She walks briskly, her eyes fixed on the street ahead, though she doesn't carry herself like a woman afraid of the dark. She tosses a glance over her shoulder, her long black hair fanning, and I see her face.

High cheekbones, glittering amber eyes. It's her.

"Yukimi!" calls a second woman, hurrying to join her. "Is she—?"

"Yes," Yukimi says.

The second woman's short-cropped hair reveals pointed fox ears. My ears prick. Another kitsune. I press myself low to the ground, hiding in the shadows, hoping they won't catch my scent among the odors thick in the steamy night.

"Where are the others?" Yukimi asks.

"Late," the other woman says. "We need to go, now."

Yukimi nods, and unsheathes two knives from her belt. "Aoi. Cover me."

The woman—Aoi—nods, then moves her hands as if rubbing an invisible ball. The air between her fingers begins to glow white, coalescing into foxfire. My fur stands on end.

Yukimi strides down the alley, the knives held at her sides. I skulk along the wall, following in her shadow. She pauses outside a doorway and cocks her head. I can hear a woman sobbing, faintly. A man's low voice rumbles, and the woman cries out. There's a deep bark, followed by a rumbling snarl, and the woman quiets. Yukimi curls her lip, then marches up to the door and knocks.

My heartbeat races as the door sweeps open.

A bleached-blond man with tattooed arms bares his fangs in a grin. "You have no business with the Kuro Inu, bitch."

Inugami. Recognition sweeps through me.

I've seen him before, but in the winter, not the summer, and I shouldn't even be a fox—is this a dream? Everything around me shimmers and distorts like I'm walking in front of a movie projector, and I don't belong in this movie.

This can't be *my* dream.

"Move," Yukimi says.

The blond man sniffs her, drool glistening down his chin. His gaze dips down her neckline. Yukimi snarls, and one of her knives flashes. The blond man yelps, his hand darting to his face. Blood trickles between his fingers.

"Bad dog," Yukimi says.

A bark thunders from the blond man's throat, and he lunges for her. In a blink, Yukimi twists, driving her other knife into his arm. He yanks out the blade, his face contorted, his limbs warping as he transforms into a dog. Aoi hurls her ball of foxfire at him and it shatters on his face, breaking into stinging centipedes. The inugami whines, flinging his head back and forth, scrabbling back.

Yukimi darts past him; inside the room, a naked woman hunches, bruised and battered, her arms tied to a chair. With her last knife, Yukimi cuts the woman loose and helps her to her feet.

A gunshot.

The naked woman screams, her arms flinching to cover her face.

Katashi walks into the room from a side door, a gun in his hand. He aims it directly between Yukimi's eyes. "Let go of my wife," he snarls, his voice guttural and growling.

Cornered by a man with a gun, Yukimi smiles. "Unlikely."

She doesn't see the two massive dogs creeping behind her, their muscles bunched and ready to spring. The woman in her arms whimpers.

This is Yukimi's nightmare. Nothing more.

My body ripples into its human form, and I step forward. "Yukimi."

Katashi bark-laughs. "The Sisters use little boys now?"

Yukimi cocks her head, a mixture of confusion and recognition in her eyes. She lowers her knife and walks toward me, her body held low, as if ready to dart away.

Aoi stands taut in the corner of the room. "Who is he?" she shouts.

Yukimi frowns. My vision fades in and out of focus, and I blink fast—she must be close to waking up.

"Fucking crazy foxes," Katashi says, almost lazily.

The inugami sights down the barrel of his gun, his finger twitching on the trigger. Yukimi throws up her hand like she's going to catch the bullet, stop it with her flesh—

Freeze.

The bullet hovers in front of Katashi's twisted face; Aoi lingers in midair as she leaps closer; Katashi's wife gasps, unblinking. It's like Yukimi hit the pause button on her dream.

Yukimi lowers her hand and turns to me. "You ignored my letter."

Do not look for me. I will come for you.

My throat tightens. "You've been following me. Why won't you come out of the shadows and talk?"

Her face remains expressionless, doll-beautiful. "There may be a safe place for us to meet tonight."

"Where?"

"The Sleepless Town." Her lips twitch. "Kabukicho."

I narrow my eyes. "The red-light district is safe?"

She shrugs.

"Where in Kabukicho?" I say, my voice rough.

"Near the south entrance," she says, "a small *yakisoba* stand stays open all night. Wait there. If you hurry, you won't miss the metro. The last train leaves Akasaka at midnight."

"How will I get home?"

She says nothing.

I grit my teeth. Why is she so damn frustrating to talk to? Where is the woman behind that blank-faced mask?

"So we're going to have a chat over some yakisoba. Great."

She opens her mouth to respond, then sucks in her breath.

Footsteps echo in the hollow silence of the dream. A man in dark suit enters the room. He has no face.

Yukimi snarls, a feral sound in the back of her throat. "Get out."

The noppera-bō turns to me. He stretches out his hands like he's beckoning me into his arms.

I step toward him. "Who—"

Yukimi drives her knife into the noppera-bō's back. He falls forward and tears into tatters of mist.

I stand with my hands useless at my sides. "Why did you do that?"

Yukimi wipes her blade on her sleeve. "He should not be here."

"But who *is* he?"

"No one."

"You're lying." I square my shoulders. "He's in your dream, not just mine. He knows you. Knew you."

She sheathes her blade without a word.

"Did you kill him?"

Flames blaze to life in her eyes. "Go."

She flings her hand out at me like she's throwing a piece of garbage away. I'm flung through the air. The world ripples and darkens around me as if I've plunged into a deep pool. Slowly, slowly, I rise to the surface—or am I sinking? My lungs burn, and panic builds inside my chest. I can't breathe. I kick hard, thrashing against the tangling feeling of a mind trapped between sleeping and waking.

Finally, I stop trying to fight it and just let go.

I blink myself awake. I'm lying on my bed. It's snowing outside, and I'm alone. I pinch the bridge of my nose, my head starting to throb. I'm not used to entering dreams.

The digital clock by my bed blinks to a new time: 11:46 p.m.

I have a train to catch.

It's easy to straighten my spine and let bravado steel my veins. But in reality, guilt crawls like a maggot through me, because I know that what I'm doing is stupidly dangerous. If I want to keep those I love safe, I should leave Japan and go home. But then I might as well give up—because then I would be dead.

Maybe I could live like a human. Pretend like I was never half-kitsune to begin with, and crumple my magic into a tight ball so it sits inside me, rotting away, until I'm okay.

Is it selfish to want to save yourself?

I'm alone in my train car as I take the metro from Akasaka to Shibuya. From there, I can walk to Kabukicho. I keep staring at my reflection in the windows with gritty eyes, waiting for the noppera-bō, but he never comes.

The metro glides to a halt, brakes whining, and a homeless man climbs on. He stinks of sour milk and sickness, his coat patched with duct tape. He holds out his hands to me, begging, but I shake my head. I don't have any change. If it weren't so cold out, I'd crack open the top window to breathe.

At the next stop, two women in neon clothes and three-inch heels clamber on. They stagger as the metro accelerates, then fall into the seat beside me, kicking up their feet and giggling far too loud. They stink like liquor and cigarettes. I scoot away from them, my eyes fixed on the window.

"Why are you out so late?" the woman in pink coos.

I pretend not to understand. But then what would a tourist be doing out at midnight? Well, visiting the red-light district, obviously. These women probably work in the water trade. Do they work for the yakuza? Have they seen the Sisters?

"Cute boy!" The woman in pink snaps flamingo-colored nails in my face. "Don't be rude."

This sends the woman in green into hysterics of laughter.

I look at them blankly. In slow, loud, English, I say, "Sorry, I don't speak Japanese."

"I speak English!" chirps the woman wearing green.

I grit my teeth and try to ignore them. I should have brought my MP3 player and some headphones. Of course, I might as well tape a sign to my forehead saying, "Mug me!"

"Hello," she says, in halting English. "My name is Kiko."

The woman in pink hoots and cuffs her on the shoulder.

"Would you like some fun?" Kiko manages to strike a sexy pose while slumped against her seat.

"No, no, no!" Her friend lurches to her feet, grabs a pole, and starts pole-dancing. "Like this!"

Kiko collapses, giggling, her hand over her mouth.

My face burns. I feel bad for them, making fools of themselves while the homeless man watches with a look in his eyes that's even filthier than his sour-milk smell.

The metro slows. "The next station is Shibuya."

I jump to my feet.

Kiko hauls herself upright. "Hurry, Candy! Stop dancing!"

The woman in pink—Candy—spins around the pole and leaps outside the train, amazingly nimble in her heels. I wince, imagining her falling onto the electrified tracks instead.

Not making eye contact with them, I stride down the street.

"We made it!" I hear Kiko say breathlessly. "I'm so hungry."

"You're always hungry," Candy says.

Great. They're following me.

I quicken my pace until I'm almost jogging. I slip my guidebook out of my pack to double-check the map. Yes, I should be heading toward Kabukicho. Though I could just follow Kiko and Candy, come to think of it.

Once beyond the businesslike skyscrapers of Shibuya, I spot a lightbulb-adorned arch gaudy enough for Las Vegas. Glowing billboards and marquees compete for space on the buildings crowding the narrow street, like a snapshot of a Tetris game. A steady steam of traffic passes under the arch, more people going in than out. Midnight must be prime-time for Kabukicho.

A hand grabs me by the shoulder.

I whirl around, my teeth bared. "Let go of me!"

It's Kiko.

Her eyes widen. "You do speak Japanese."

I let my teeth sharpen into fangs, then twist away from her touch. "I'm not interested."

Candy trips closer to us. "You're—you're a kitsune!"

"Like Yukimi," Kiko says.

I freeze. "Yukimi? You know her?"

Suddenly, Kiko and Candy aren't laughing anymore. They share an uneasy glance. Kiko clutches Candy's arm and mutters something in her ear. The two of them walk quickly toward the arch to Kabukicho, glancing backward at me.

"Wait!" I jog after them. "I'm looking for Yukimi."

Candy whirls at me, her long earrings tangling in her hair. "You won't find her." She half-snarls the words.

"I'm her son. I'm here to meet her."

Kiko laughs. "She doesn't have a son."

"What do you know about her?" I say.

Candy grabs Kiko's arm. "We're drunk, not stupid. Go find some other women to screw around with."

The two of them march away, their heels clicking in time.

I follow them through the arch to Kabukicho. They glance back at me, then put on a spurt of speed, dodge down a side street, and disappear into the crowd.

Two women in the water trade know about Yukimi, but they won't tell me anything. Were they protecting her? Did they think I was a spy sent by the inugami?

People eddy around me as I stand in the middle of the street. A motorbike honks at me, and I jump onto the sidewalk. I glance at my watch: 12:39 a.m. I walk back toward the glowing arch. I brush elbows with red-faced drunks, women wearing too much makeup and too little clothes, and men with expensive suits and trendy chestnut hair flirting with anything that moves.

I let the fox out a little, to sharpen my nose.

Perfume barely masking old sweat…urine-soaked snow…cigarette smoke on the wind…alcohol on the breath. The stench makes me want to retch. Over it all, there's a greasy, starchy smell, kind of like carnival food. Stir-fried noodles.

Yakisoba.

My heartbeat thudding, I zigzag through the crowd. A yakisoba stand, both brightly lit and dingy, stands near a street-corner FamilyMart convenience store—ironic, considering why I'm here. Inside the stand, a sweaty-faced woman tosses noodles, broccoli, and beef in a wok, then dumps the finished product onto paper plates. Nearby, there's an empty stool.

I hesitate. Am I supposed to sit? But that means I have to buy some of that questionable yakisoba, and besides, I don't have any cash on me. I don't see Yukimi anywhere. I grit my teeth and walk up to the yakisoba stand.

The woman tugs her hairnet straight. "Ready to order?"

I shake my head. "I'm waiting for my mother."

"Your mother?" She squints at me. "Aren't you too young to be out here so late?"

"I'm seventeen."

I don't know why I'm telling her this. Maybe it's

because she has this sort of all-purpose, industrial-strength motherly aura around her. There's real worry in her eyes.

"You hungry?" says the yakisoba woman. "You look skinny."

I shrug, but take a seat on the stool.

"Eat." The yakisoba woman pushes a paper plate toward me.

"I don't have any money," I say. "Sorry."

I'm taking up space where a real customer would sit. I should at least eat what's on the plate. But that yakisoba looks greasy and suspicious—even though the woman is nice—

"We have to go." A voice in my ear.

I almost fall off my stool. She's standing right next to me, in sunglasses and a leather coat, her hair twisted back.

"Yukimi!"

The yakisoba woman watches us, squinting.

"I have a motorcycle." Yukimi grabs my wrist, her hand hot. "We can outrun them."

"Who?"

Her lip curls. "The inugami."

eleven

W e're not going to wait for those dogs." Yukimi looks
over her sunglasses at me, her eyes glowing amber.
"Can't you smell them coming?"

I can't, actually, not over the incredible stink of Kabukicho.

Her hand tightens on my wrist, and she bolts. I run
to keep up, half-dragged through the crowd. A muscular
black-and-red motorcycle idles by a lamppost. Yukimi
climbs on and revs the engine; it rumbles like a warning
growl.

"Get on," she says.

I hesitate. Over the hubbub, I hear barking.

The fox half of me takes over and I jump onto the motorcycle behind Yukimi. She guns the engine, and I hold onto her waist to keep myself from falling. We cut through the crowd, people shrinking back from us. Behind us, the barking grows louder, followed by startled shouts. I twist back to look.

A pack of dogs pounds down the street, bellowing and baying, their breath steaming the air, their noses trained on our scent. In the lead, a black dog—Katashi.

Yukimi takes a hard left, slush spraying behind the motorcycle's tires. I tighten the muscles in my torso and thighs, straining against the force of the turn. The wind stings my eyes as we race beneath the electric glow of signs and lights. A drag queen in feathers and towering heels strays into our path, then leaps aside with a screamed insult.

"Hold on!" Yukimi shouts.

She swerves into a U-turn, dragging her heel along the pavement, clipping the edge of a booth. Kinky knick-knacks tumble to the ground and roll onto the street.

We drive straight down the street toward the pack of inugami. Yukimi raises her right hand into the air, steering with her left. A white light leaks from her clenched fist. Foxfire. A thrill sweeps down my spine.

The dogs charge toward us, barking ferociously—but Katashi skids to a halt and stares at us, one paw raised. We hurtle close enough to see the whites of his eyes. Katashi flattens his ears against his skull and woofs.

Yukimi tosses the ball of foxfire. It arcs high above

the inugami, like a meteor streaking across the sky, and the dogs turn their heads to follow its parabola above them. The foxfire trails white-hot sparks in its wake, sizzling through the air. It splatters in the middle of the pack and the dogs burst into flame.

The street erupts into screams and yelping.

Yukimi drives straight into the inferno as burning inugami stagger and flee around us. Heat lashes against my skin. I hold my breath, not wanting to singe my lungs or inhale the smell of burning fur and flesh. The flames whip over us, scorching hot, then close behind us as we break free.

Unharmed. I stare at Yukimi's hair and clothes.

"Was that an illusion?" I shout over the noise.

"Yes," Yukimi says, "but they feel the pain."

I glance back and see Katashi rolling in the snow, trying and failing to extinguish imaginary flames. The rest of his pack doesn't seem to be interested in following us. Yukimi accelerates smoothly away from the scene. We leave the inugami behind, and hear the sound of sirens.

"Won't they send firefighters?" I say.

"The illusion will vanish soon. Which is why we have to hurry."

Yukimi gives the motorcycle some more gas and we race deeper into the heart of Kabukicho. The giant smiles of girls on billboards flash by. Yukimi threads between the tangle of people and vehicles with an expertise that can come only from years of high-speed driving. We pass through another glitzy archway, leaving Kabukicho, the Sleepless City, behind.

I relax a little and lean against Yukimi.

I can't believe I'm touching her, that my kitsune mother is real and *here*. And she's taking me with her. I shut my eyes and inhale deeply. Now that we've left the stink of Kabukicho behind for the plain exhaust-and-asphalt smell of the rest of Tokyo, I can actually catch a whiff of Yukimi's own scent.

A sweetness that vanishes quickly, like the perfume of a peach, over the stronger smells of leather, smoke, and fox. Nothing like the delicate scent of Shizuka.

Nothing like the scent I remembered.

But I was a kit-fox then, back when I thought of my mother as a warm, furry creature that would curl around me and play with me and lick my nose when I whimpered. Not this woman with sinewy muscles running beneath her jacket, leaning forward on a motorcycle, plunging deeper into the city.

Words pile up inside my throat, choking me. I don't know how to say what I have to say. The whooshing of speed is too loud for me to speak, anyway. We curve along a long road, the lights of Tokyo blurring in my wind-stung eyes.

"Almost there," she says, at an intersection.

"Where?"

"Home."

A wind picks up, shaking rain from the sky. Yukimi maneuvers her motorcycle down smaller and smaller alleys until we approach a dead end, nothing more than a cracked concrete wall with a vertical garden of weeds. She doesn't slow down, just drives straight at it, her head down like she's going to ram the wall.

At the last second, I squeeze my eyes shut.

A slippery, slick feeling passes over my face and arms, like wet leaves dragging along my skin. It coats my eyelids and nose and mouth with a thin film, and I accidentally inhale some of it—and it tastes like yōkai magic. Coughing, I open my eyes. We're past the wall, and in an overgrown courtyard. The cracked concrete was nothing more than an illusion.

I laugh. "Like Diagon Alley."

"Diagon Alley?" Yukimi sounds confused.

"*Harry Potter*." I laugh again, lightheaded. This feels unreal.

Yukimi makes a neutral noise in the back of her throat. "Time for you to get off." She parks the motorcycle beneath an overhanging roof. "If you can manage."

I swing one leg over the motorcycle and stagger off, my muscles stiff. Yukimi kills the motorcycle's engine, and the headlight goes off, plunging us into gloom.

I blink to help my night vision come quicker. "This is it?"

"The Lair," Yukimi says.

She strides to a red-painted door and knocks.

After a long pause, there's a scuffling inside. "Who is that with you?" A woman's muffled voice.

Yukimi clears her throat. "A guest."

Ah. I was half-expecting her to say, "My son." Stupid of me?

Still the door doesn't open.

Yukimi growl-sighs. "Let us in. I'm exhausted. I had an encounter with Katashi's runts."

At last, the door opens.

Standing inside is Aoi. I recognize her from Yukimi's dream, though her hair has grown to her chin now and has obviously been dyed a reddish-brown color. She's wearing a flimsy silk nightgown printed all over with butterflies.

"How old is he?" Aoi looks me up and down. "Yukimi, I'm not okay with you bringing minors in here. He looks like he's never had a drink. Or a girlfriend."

My face flushes, but I fake a smile. "Looks can be deceiving."

Aoi laughs. "He can speak? But that accent..." She grimaces.

Wordlessly, Yukimi slips past Aoi, leaving me standing in the doorway. I try to follow her, but Aoi leans her arm against the wall, her silk sleeve flapping in my face.

"You have a name?" she says.

"I did think Yukimi was going to introduce us," I mutter.

Aoi snorts. "He has a sense of humor, at least!" She yells this backward, like an announcement.

From inside, Yukimi yells back, "Let him in already!"

I catch Aoi's eye. "My name is Tavian."

She arches an eyebrow. "I'm Aoi."

"I already knew."

"Oh, really?" Aoi steps aside to let me pass.

I'm in a cluttered, dimly lit house, which looks like it's been abandoned and halfway renovated at least once or twice. From the hallway, I can see a kitchen with dishes in the sink, a dark bedroom, and a living room lit by the kaleidoscope lights of a TV. I step into the living room.

Yukimi slumps on a couch, her boots on a coffee table, her head tilted back. With a groan, she rubs her forehead. She takes a medicine bottle from the table, screws it open, and pops a white pill into her mouth. She follows that with a swig of water from a wine glass.

"Yukimi?" I say.

Her eyes flash in my direction. "You're safe now. Go to bed."

"That's ridiculous," I mutter. "You can't abduct somebody and then tell them good night." My stomach twists as I remember something. "I've got to make a call."

She sits up straighter. "Why?"

I ignore her and slide my phone from my pocket. I didn't leave a note for Gwen, mostly because I didn't have the time to think of anything coherent, and because I stupidly assumed I would be back to my bed before dawn. Very stupidly.

Yukimi narrows her eyes. "Who are you calling?"

"Gwen. My girlfriend." I lift the phone to my ear.

In a flash of movement, Yukimi lunges from the couch and rips my phone from my hand.

"Give it back!" I say.

"Don't call anyone from this location," Yukimi says. "Ever."

I meet her eyes. "Oh, so I'm supposed to let everyone think that I'm dead? Because I randomly vanished?"

Something flickers in her eyes.

"Give it back," I say.

Yukimi drops my cellphone on the floor and stomps on it, grinding it beneath her heel.

Who the hell does she think she is? My *mother*?

"You know what?" I say, my voice level. "That's great. Because once they find out that I'm missing, they're going to come looking for me. Because they actually care whether I'm safe or lying dead on the side of the road somewhere."

Yukimi's face is an iron mask. "They won't find you."

"But you did," I say, my voice sounding calmer and calmer. "You cared so much that you came all this way to pick me up and bring me home. What I don't understand, though, is why you took *eleven years* to do it. Was it that fucking hard?"

She says nothing, but her pupils narrow to slits.

"I only wanted to find you again," I say, "because I need your true name, and your blood. Give those to me, and then I can leave. And I'll never have to look at your face again."

Yukimi exhales, a short hissing sound, and looks away. "Go."

"Go where?" I say. "Back to Akasaka?"

"No," she says. "Go away and grow up a little. I'm not in the mood for the yipping of a kit-fox."

"In case you haven't noticed," I say, "I grew up without you."

I leave the room before my rage boils over.

"Hey." Aoi catches my arm in the hallway. "How do you know Yukimi, anyway?"

I clench and unclench my jaw, and resist the urge to punch the wall. Should I tell Aoi the truth? Or would Yukimi like it better if I remained her shameful secret?

I meet her eyes. "I knew her a long time ago."

Aoi scrunches her eyebrows with a wry smile. "Excuse me for saying so, but you don't look old enough to have known Yukimi a long time ago. And why would she have anything to do with a boy like you?" She coughs. "No offense."

"I don't know." I shrug. "She gave birth to me?"

Aoi laughs. "You're a sarcastic little kit, aren't you?"

I lean against the wall and slide to the floor. I'm finally feeling that it's after midnight, all the exhaustion of the day piling on me like snow on a roof ready to collapse.

Aoi's laughter dies. "You aren't joking, are you? You're Yukimi's son?"

"Yes."

She crouches next to me, her fingers splayed on the floor. Her eyes look dark and huge in the shadows. "You rode here on Yukimi's motorcycle. That's why you smell like her."

I rub my eyes with the heels of my hands. "Sure."

Aoi backs away from me, still crouching like a wary animal. She mutters something to herself, but I climb to my feet.

Yukimi won't let me waltz out of here. Not while she's trying to keep me "safe" by essentially abducting me. But I'm not going to cower in a den while the inugami hunt my grandparents and Gwen. When I close my eyes, I can still picture the naked, bruised, and bound woman in Yukimi's dream. I'd rather kill those dogs myself than let them hurt Gwen like that.

I climb to my feet and stride back down the hall to the door.

"Where are you going?" Aoi says, behind me.

"Outside." I pause. "For some air."

I shut the door a little harder than necessary, my muscles still tight with unspent energy. I grip the door-knob in my hand, watching my fingernails darken to black claws. Anger is one of the fastest ways to bring out the fox in me.

I peel my fingers from the doorknob and turn to the darkness of the courtyard. Out here, alone, I can hear the muffled rumble of traffic, the distant whoop of a police siren, and the wails of an insomniac baby in one of the nearby buildings.

I glance at my watch: 2:10 a.m.

Gwen must still be sleeping. If I can find a way out, then all I need to do next is get Yukimi's true name and some of her blood.

All I need to do. That's an understatement.

I spread my fingers on the secret doorway in the cracked concrete wall. Rough, unyielding concrete. I grit my teeth and shove, my shoulders straining. I brace myself on the slick ground and throw my entire weight on the wall. My left foot slips out from under me and I bang my knee on the ground.

"Shit," I hiss.

Of course it won't open for me. Yukimi probably handcrafted this illusion herself. Maybe it only works for people who aren't pissed off at her. That would be perfect.

I pace along the perimeter of the courtyard, brushing the grit and snow from my stinging hands. There's another door, but it's locked. I stare at the fire escape above my head, curious, then jump and grab the bottom rung of the ladder. My hands slip on the icy iron bar and I fall back down.

Times like this, I wish I could fly. Gwen has it easy.

Down on my hands and knees, I discover a missing brick in the wall across the corner from the fire escape. I kick at the weak section until more bricks crumble away. Through the ragged-edged hole, light from a faraway street lamp leaks through.

"Excellent." I rub my frigid hands together.

Now, if only I could fit through. Well, a fox could.

But that's a transformation I haven't made in Japan since I was seven years old. I swallow hard and stare at the freedom beyond. I'm afraid of what will happen if I push it. Afraid of the way my heartbeat is erratic right now. Afraid that if I fall, no one will hear me.

It's damn cold out here. I'm starting to shiver uncontrollably.

"Well, a little fur would help that," I whisper.

I roll my shoulders to get the kinks out, then flex my fingers. The bones in my hands ache as they rearrange into paws. I pant, my breath steaming the air, and run my tongue over my sharpening teeth. Pain shivers through my nerves.

This isn't supposed to hurt. Should I keep going?

I force myself to breathe steadily and focus on the transformation. There's a prickling along my arms as red fur shadows my skin, but no pelt sweeping over me in a fraction of a second. My skeleton aches, resistant to the change, and I clench my muscles, willing it to shrink into fox bones.

A snarl rips through the air. I swing my head around. Yukimi.

"Stop," she says.

I bare my teeth at her. "Leave me alone."

"This is not the way you need to do this," she says.

My teeth itch as they retreat to their human bluntness. I wrap my arms tight around my chest, fighting the urge to whine against the sharp pain inside me.

"Eat this," she says.

She crouches beside me, a fruit cradled in her hand. An apricot, almost, but it's too small for that. The strange fruit's skin shimmers the color of honey on cream.

Shivering, I stare at it. "What is it?" My voice sounds raspy.

Her eyes burn like embers. "It will help you get better."

I laugh, a short bark. "So you know there's something wrong with me. That I'm going to die." My voice snags on the words. "That's why you left me in Hokkaido, isn't it?"

Yukimi's face betrays no emotions.

I take the fruit. It feels warm and oddly light in my hand, its skin covered with a delicate fuzz. I bring it to my nose and sniff. Jasmine-almond-nectar-syrup, an intoxicating confusion that tingles in my nose and hovers in the back of my throat.

"This is an illusion," I say. "Isn't it?"

"No," Yukimi says. "Eat it. Trust me."

I force my stiff legs to straighten, and stand. "Trusting you is the last thing I want to do right now." But I'm still clutching the fruit in the palm of my sweaty hand.

Yukimi crouches with her arms resting on her thighs, her hands hanging near her knees. A wind whistles through the courtyard and spreads her hair behind her.

"This isn't going to work." I force the words past my tight throat. "I know half-breeds like myself aren't strong enough to control a kitsune's magic. The myobu told me."

"The myobu?" She flashes her fangs. "They know nothing."

"You said yourself that I was broken."

Yukimi looks me in the eye. "Broken things can be mended."

Anger reignites in me, and heat spreads through my skin like wildfire. I hate how she's speaking so calmly, like this is nothing important and I'm nothing to her.

"There's a lot you're never going to mend," I say.

I fling the fruit from my hand. It bounces against the wall and rolls across the snow. Yukimi stares at it, can't even look me in the eye. I'm done with this, done with her.

I turn my back on her and walk away.

"Kogitsune," she says. Little Fox.

The word hits me in the back like an arrow. I stop, my spine stiffening. "What did you call me?"

"Kogitsune, eat the fruit."

twelve

As I stand with my back to Yukimi, I suck in the icy night air to steady myself and freeze the blurring in my eyes. Once I'm sure my voice won't betray me, I speak.

"My name is Octavian Kimura," I say. "You never named me."

There's a long silence. I turn back, and she's standing there looking at me with her head tilted to one side.

"And you never told me your true name," I add.

"Very few have ever known it," she says.

"I'm your son." I swallow past the burning tightness in my throat. "Or did you think I was just a pet?"

She seems unimpressed by my jab. "You were a kit-fox."

"I'm not a kit-fox anymore."

"I can see that."

I circle closer to her. "When were you planning on naming me? And telling me the truth about why we were in Hokkaido, and who my father was? Why can't you tell me now?"

"You tell me," she says, "why you need my name. And my blood."

I take a slow breath and let it out again. "Shizuka, the myobu, said that's what she needed for my naming ceremony. Along with the name and the blood of my father."

Yukimi folds her arms. "And you trust this idiot Shizuka?"

I shrug. "Despite being a myobu, she's tried to help me much more than you ever have." But I think of the donation Tsuyoshi gave to the shrine, and I grimace.

"You know nearly nothing," Yukimi says calmly.

"Through no fault of my own," I say.

I glance at the fruit on the ground, then pick it out of the snow. It's bruised but unbroken.

"Tell me what this is," I say, "at least."

"Anburojia."

I blink. "Ambrosia?"

"That's what we call it. I'm sure scientists have given it some other name, something Latin, but they haven't discovered what we have." A smile touches Yukimi's eyes.

"The anburojia fruit tastes incredibly bitter to everyone who does not have magic. For those who do, it's a sweet delicacy that enhances our power."

"Enhances." I grimace. "I don't do drugs."

"It isn't illegal, and it isn't poisonous."

She has no reason to give me anything dangerous. Does she?

Yukimi curls her hand around mine, closing my fingers around the fruit. Her eyes meet mine, and beneath their phosphorescent glow, a confusion of emotions tangle.

"Will you try it?" she says.

She isn't crawling into my head and puppeting me to eat the fruit. She's just…asking.

A frigid wind gusts through the air, blowing her hair across her face like black ink across white paper. My eyes stinging, I raise the anburojia to my lips and take a bite.

Flavor floods my mouth. Anburojia tastes the way harps sound, glimmering on my tongue like gold. I shut my eyes and hear a groan escape me. I suck the juice from my fingers and bite deeper into the anburojia. My teeth hit the pit of the fruit and I gnaw away its red flesh, devouring every last shred of it.

"Delicious," Yukimi says, "isn't it?"

I nod and swallow again, the taste of the anburojia lingering on my tongue. "I don't feel any different."

She laughs, then, and it catches me so off-guard I flinch.

"Maybe I need to eat more," I say, my taste buds aching.

Yukimi shakes her head and takes the anburojia pit from my fingers. She tucks it into her pocket. "I have no more with me. These fruits can be difficult to obtain."

I frown. "You said they weren't illegal."

"And they aren't." She turns away from me, and starts walking. "Let's go. There's a lot of night left."

"Where?"

Yukimi throws a glance back at me. "Nowhere and everywhere."

I run after her, excitement shivering through me. Her ears have sharpened into foxy points, peeking through her disheveled hair. She seizes my wrist and marches through the illusory wall. This time, I pass through without a hitch.

"I have a favorite alley," she says.

I arch my eyebrows. "For shapeshifting?"

Yukimi says nothing, but when she looks away, I glimpse what might be a smile. She lets go of my wrist and strides ahead without looking back, like she's not afraid of me running away—or she's so confident that I will follow her.

Of course I do.

Her favorite alley smells strongly like mold and rodents, but it's only a few twists and turns away from the Sisters' Lair. An old wooden cask stands in the corner of the alley, smelling faintly of sake. Yukimi slides the top aside, removes her leather jacket, and tosses it into the cask. She starts kicking off her boots.

"Wait," I say.

"Wait?" She drops her boots into the cask. "Don't worry. Nobody but kitsune even know this cask exists. The most you have to worry about is rats nibbling at my illusion."

A twisting has taken residence in my stomach, and I clench my hands to keep them from trembling. "I haven't done this since I came to Japan. Shapeshifting, I mean."

Yukimi looks back at me with fox eyes. "You are a kitsune."

"Only half," I say.

"Half is enough."

"But Shizuka, the myobu—"

"Did she tell you not to become a fox?" Yukimi tugs her sweater over her head. "Or are you too afraid?"

"No." To both of her questions, actually. I take a deep breath and try to beat my anxiety. "But you saw me on the roof, that night before I ended up in the hospital."

"That's why I gave you the anburojia."

"But—"

"Tavian."

Hope darts through me like a bright bird. That's the first time she's called me that, in person, and not in a dream or some strange illusion. If I were a fox right now, I'd be dancing from paw to paw, my ears pricked, waiting for more.

"You can't wait any longer," she says.

Yukimi walks barefoot to me, wearing only jeans and a tank top in the winter air. Goose bumps dot her arms—she is vulnerable, after all. She places her hand in the middle of my chest, shuts her eyes, and pushes. Heat rushes outward to my fingers and toes, and I stagger back with a gasp. My skin is glowing, fading.

"What did you do?" I say.

She smiles, her teeth feral, and turns away. Her red pelt cloaks her skin as she shucks away the last of her clothes and slings them into the old sake cask. She stretches her arms, her fingers reaching as if she can claw the stars from the sky.

In a flash, Yukimi shrinks into the shape of a fox.

My breath comes ragged in my throat. A shudder ripples through me, and I drop to my hands and knees. My hands reshape into black paws, and my spine arches as it shifts. I grit my teeth and strain against the transformation.

Yukimi watches me, her head held low, her eyes burning.

I can't do this with my clothes on. I kick off my shoes and unzip my jacket and jeans—and I'm not going fast enough; I'm losing to my shifting body.

"I don't think I can—" My words choke off as my throat changes.

My pulse races until my heartbeats become uncountable. I black out, my thoughts erased by a blissful agony, a euphoria of pain. I scream—and it's the howl of a fox.

Slowly, the pain fades with every heartbeat. And my heartbeat, thudding a fast rhythm, isn't faltering. I crack open my eyes. I climb to my feet and look at myself.

I'm not dead. I'm a fox.

I leap to my feet and yip out of pure surprise. Yukimi trots to me and touches her nose to mine. She grins like only a vixen can, her tongue lolling. I shut my eyes and inhale her scent with a shuddering breath, my chest brimming with contentment. This is how it used to be. This is what I left behind—me and Okāsan, both of us foxes, with the night wide open before us. My legs feel light, like I can outrun the rising sun.

I point my muzzle to the wind and sniff. No hint of inugami.

Yukimi makes a little "quirk?" noise in the back of her throat. I glance at her eyes, and I know what question she's asking. We don't need words, the two of us.

I know how I want to reply.

With a leap into the air, I dart from the alley, my tail streaking behind me. See if you can catch me. She used to have longer legs than me, but I'll bet I'm faster than her now.

Behind me, I hear small paws drumming on the pavement.

I quicken my pace from an easy run to a headlong sprint, my blood humming in my veins, my legs pumping like a perfect machine. There's no room for fear or hesitation.

I hurtle down the dark street, starry sky spilling above me, reflected in the skyscrapers of Tokyo. We're on the outskirts, away from the heart of the hubbub. Out here, dark windows outnumber the light ones, and the streets are free of humans and cars. Mostly free—a man on a bicycle whirs past, then slows as he sees me. I keep pace beside him, glancing into his eyes.

"Hey!" he shouts, a silly grin on his face. "Kitsune!"

I could melt into the shadows, could make him think he saw no more than a mirage on a night when he was sleepy-drunk, but the temptation of mischief is too great.

I slow to a trot, then stand on the sidewalk, twitching my tail like a cat. The man brakes and hops off his bike in a wobbly way. He leans his bike against a trash can and creeps to me in a frog-legged crouch, one of his hands outstretched.

"Come here, little fox," he singsongs.

I glance at my surroundings, noting my escape routes, noting how Yukimi watches me from the shadows, waiting to see if I haven't forgotten how a wild fox behaves.

The man's breath stinks like cigarettes and beer. Judging by the red splotches on his cheeks, I'm surprised he could even stay upright long enough to bike this far. His glossy gaze stays on me as he sidles nearer. He reaches into his jacket pocket and pulls out a thin stick of something wrapped in paper.

"Here you go." The man holds it out to me.

I tiptoe nearer and sniff his offering. Minty. Gum? I curl my lip. Clearly this guy doesn't know any better. He gives me an empty, hopeful smile and shoves the gum closer.

Yukimi skulks a little closer, her eyes sharp with curiosity.

Oh, believe me, I won't disappoint. I haven't forgotten my old tricks, and I've learned some new ones.

I inch closer to the man's hand. I crane my neck forward until my whiskers brush the stick of gum, then grab a hunk of my magic and twist it into an illusion. I breathe onto the man's fingers. He watches me, his wet lips hanging open.

The stick of gum twitches in its silver wrapper. It wriggles and rears in his hand, shaping itself into a tiny serpent. The man's head jerks downward as he realizes the gum is moving, and the curiosity on his face twists into horrified fascination.

The serpent tastes the air with a gum-pink tongue, then hisses.

"Shit!"

The man flings the serpent-illusion away and keeps shaking his hand like it bit him. He leaps onto his bicycle, almost crashing onto the pavement, and starts pedaling hard. I trot alongside him, just to see the look on his face as he leaves.

I forgot how *entertaining* this could be.

Claws click on the sidewalk. Yukimi comes to stand behind me and rests her muzzle on my shoulder. I shut my eyes against the swell of pride overflowing from my heart, spilling through my ribs, spreading through my veins as bliss.

Yukimi pulls back to give me a look, her eyes challenging me to another race. The taste of anburojia lingering on my tongue, I follow my kitsune mother into the night.

There's something beautiful about forgetting, about letting your thoughts melt into a wordless blur of scents unwinding on the wind and paws skimming the ground and a belly full of a stolen bite of tofu, of a rice-flour candy given by the ragged woman in the park. In return for the candy, we gave her a blanket, an illusion strong enough to keep her warm through the snowy night.

We linger in the park, a scrap of green in the gray, a nearly forgotten memory of the forest. I can't help but feel a sharp craving in my stomach, a yearning for the aroma of clear air, of snow that contains no scents but its own wild coldness.

Then Yukimi nudges me with her nose, and we're running again.

We return to the alley near the Lair as dawn edges the bottom of the sky, gray leaking into black. Faced with the memory of the glittering nightlife of Tokyo, the grime of the alley looks that much grimier. I wait in my fox form, my eyes on the street, as Yukimi makes her transformation back to human.

"It's late," Yukimi says.

And by that she must mean early. Not the time for us to be running outside in our fur.

I sigh and squeeze my eyes shut. My pelt clings to my skin and my bones resist bending. I crawl out of my fox body and force myself to become a boy again.

As soon as my fur disappears, I'm dunked in glacial cold. My teeth start chattering like crazy, and I dig my fingernails into my arms like that will banish my goose bumps. I'm shaking from the inside out, but I'm not sure it's all because of the temperature. There's a scraping in my stomach, a craving in my gut.

"I think the anburojia is wearing off," I say.

Yukimi tosses me my jeans. "It will. You have to live with it."

Of course there would be withdrawal. Of course I would have to return to my human body and start thinking in words again, start remembering why I'm here.

I dress quickly, clumsily, my fingers numb. "That was…fun." I grimace at how lame it sounds. "That's not what I mean. It's been eleven years since we ran like that."

Yukimi rakes her hands through her feral hair and twists it back into a bun. "Yes."

"Why…" I study her face, but can see no hints of her mood. "Why did you wait so long?"

"You were gone," she says. "And then you were here."

I concentrate on lacing my shoes, so that I don't spook her by looking a little too interested in her replies. "So you could tell I was in Japan. From my dreams?"

Yukimi nods and stands there, finished dressing.

"Do you know where I went?" I say.

"No."

My fingers have become too stiff to tie my shoes. I bend over my feet, staring at the ground. "I lived in an orphanage, in Hokkaido, for about a year. Then a couple from America came and adopted me. They took me home with them, to Washington. The state, not the capitol. You know where that is?

"Yes."

I stand in one swift movement and look her in the eye. I catch a glimpse of emotion before she turns away, seemingly more interested in the street, but I know it's a lie.

"Mom and Dad—my parents—thought you were dead," I say.

"Understandable," Yukimi says.

"So did I."

A cone of light falls from a street lamp and she walks to its edge, the sharp planes of her face harshly illuminated. A convenient disguise for her expression.

"You will need a name," she says. "A true name."

I stand beside her, my heart thudding. "Shizuka was right? That's how I can survive?"

"All kitsune must be named to become adults."

I blow out my breath. "Yukimi." Her name tastes strange in my mouth. "You're very vague."

Her teeth flash in a grin. "Am I?"

"If you want to keep me safe," I say, "I need you to tell me the truth. About everything."

Her grin vanishes as quickly as it came. "I can't."

"Not everything, then." I'm so close that I could touch her, if I tried. "But at least about my father?"

Yukimi steps away from me, the distance between us filled with shadows so thick I'm not sure I can pass through them without pushing with my hands. Her face has become granite again, her eyes polished amber with emotions trapped inside.

"Your father was not a good man," she says.

"Was?"

"He doesn't belong in my life anymore. Or yours."

I hold my breath, afraid to say something that will silence her again, keep her from sharing her secrets. "But we need his name," I say, "and his blood. For me to be named."

Yukimi thins her lips. "That may be difficult."

"In what way?"

She looks at me as if she's about to say more, then shakes her head. "I will tell you at a time and place less dangerous than this. For now, we will return to the Lair."

thirteen

It's only when I'm lying on the floor of the bedroom I'd seen earlier, curled in blankets that smell like Yukimi, that the guilt catches up like a slow-moving sludge.

I've been running around as a fox with Yukimi—frolicking, damn it—and I'm not any closer to why I came here. I've been letting her control me, manipulate me into doing what she wants. I ate the anburojia, I shapeshifted for her, and I went to bed like a good little boy when I was done.

I'm chasing a memory. Okāsan doesn't exist anymore.

My throat clenches on a knife-sharp feeling. My

hands are still shaky, my forehead dotted with sweat, the lingering taste of anburojia sour on my tongue. This bedroom has no windows, but the darkness isn't helping me fall asleep, no matter how strongly fatigue tugs me down. I glance at my watch: 6:24 a.m.

Gwen. She's usually a night owl, waking up around noon on weekends, but the lure of Japan has been dragging her out of bed at ungodly early hours.

What is she going to do when she sees my empty bed? What is she going to do when she tries calling me, and my phone goes straight to voicemail?

I crawl out of my tangle of blankets. Now is no time for sleep.

My legs wobble beneath me, my kneecaps like Jell-O. My stomach growls, and the thought of anburojia makes my mouth water so hard it hurts. I shake my head. No addictive fruits for breakfast. No breakfast at all. Time to get up and go.

I'm halfway to the door when it creaks open. I see the silhouette of a woman.

"Yukimi?" I whisper.

"Oh, sorry." It's Aoi. "Did I wake you?"

"I wasn't sleeping."

Aoi shuts the door behind her and flicks on the light. I squint, my eyes aching. She leans on the wall by the door like she's guarding it. Did Yukimi send her to keep me in?

"I've been thinking," Aoi says, "about what you said."

I rub my forehead, trying to drag myself out of this

grogginess. "Have you decided I'm actually Yukimi's son? Or did she decide to tell you herself?"

Aoi twists her mouth. "That's the thing. I asked, and she didn't say no. But she wouldn't tell me any more."

I try not to hold my breath. "Any idea who my dad is?"

"I haven't known Yukimi for—how old did you say you were again?"

"Seventeen."

"I haven't known Yukimi for that long." Aoi tilts her head to one side and tucks her hair behind her ears. "And she's never been one to show much interest in men, if you know what I mean."

"I don't."

Aoi laughs, a cigarette-rasped sound. "She's never had a boyfriend for as long as I've known her. Not even a one-night stand, unless she's very secretive about it."

I raise my eyebrows. "So?"

Aoi shrugs and slips a pack of cigarettes from her jean pocket. "Do you smoke?"

"No."

Aoi hits the bottom of the pack to knock a cigarette out, then reaches for a lighter. "Yukimi was dating this lady maybe a year ago, but they split up. Hell, even farther back I thought Yukimi might be flirting with me—but she said she would never date one of the Sisters. She doesn't mix business with pleasure."

"Really." I stare at the ceiling. "Okay."

Yukimi never told me *that*. But why would she?

Aoi lifts her lighter to her cigarette, then hesitates. "Is the smoke going to bother you?"

I nod absently.

She heaves a big sigh and slips the cigarette back into the pack. "I figured. You look like somebody with virgin lungs, uncorrupted by nicotine."

I'd laugh at her joke if I were actually paying attention. "So how does my father fit into the picture? She told me that he was 'not a good man.' And that she would tell me more about him when it wasn't dangerous to do so."

"Dangerous?" Aoi arches her eyebrows. "Pretty much everybody in Yukimi's life is dangerous. Myself included."

"Sure," I deadpan.

She bares her fangs, a wicked light in her eyes. "Don't underestimate me, fox boy."

I hold my hands in the air. "Joking. Just joking."

Aoi crosses her arms, her gaze distant. "Well, there was that one guy…he had a particularly dangerous look to him."

"Who?"

"Oh, I never actually met him." Aoi tosses her hand. "But Yukimi keeps a photo. I found it one day by accident, when it fell out of a mirror of hers."

"What did he look like? Besides particularly dangerous?"

"He wasn't smiling. He was wearing a suit. I couldn't think of why Yukimi would keep a photo of him if he wasn't somebody important to her, maybe a brother."

Wearing a suit. That could be anybody, but...

The snow doesn't even touch his dark suit, just falls right through.

"You know," Aoi says, "she probably still keeps it there. I never brought it up, because I knew she would kill me if I said anything. Yukimi can be secretive, to say the least."

I square my shoulders. "Where is the mirror?"

"In her bedroom," Aoi says. "But she's sleeping there."

"Maybe if I asked her..."

Aoi frowns. "Oh, don't tell her I said anything to you. This whole conversation is top secret, okay?"

"Okay." But I'm walking to the door. "Which room is hers?"

Aoi sighs. "I'll show you."

We climb a rickety staircase with narrow, creaky steps. Upstairs, doors branch from a dimly lit hallway. Aoi stops at the first door on the left, and nods. I creep up to the door, which stands ajar, and raise my hand, ready to knock. Inside, I hear hushed breathing.

"I wouldn't wake her," Aoi whispers. "She's had a rough night."

"I won't," I whisper back.

Gently, I push open the door. Yukimi's room is a deep red, like the inside of a plum, with thick curtains draped over the window and four-poster bed. Yukimi lies with her body curled around a pillow, her face creased as she sleeps. She's still wearing everything she was outside, except for her boots.

"Over there," Aoi breathes into my ear. She points

to a silver hand-mirror, adorned with roses, lying on a battered dresser. "That's the mirror with the photo in it. But don't—!"

I slip past her and tiptoe to the mirror. It's cold and heavy in my hand and leaves my skin smelling sweetly metallic. Must be antique silver. Yukimi doesn't stir. Stolen mirror in hand, I sneak back out to Aoi and hand it to her.

"Show it to me," I say, my voice low.

Aoi glances into Yukimi's room, then wedges her fingernails between the mirror's glass and its ornate silver frame. She pries the circle of glass out, catches it in her other hand, and takes a wallet-sized photo from the hollow in the mirror.

"Take it," Aoi whispers, barely audible.

I pinch the paper between my fingers and hold it up to my eyes.

Is it the man from my dream? I stare at his strong jaw and sharply angled eyebrows. He's wearing a dark suit, but it's so generic—and how can I match a face to a faceless ghost? I turn the photo over, hoping for a name—

"Give it back," Aoi chants under her breath, "give it back."

There's no name. Nothing.

I hand the photo to Aoi, who slips it into the mirror's frame and clicks the glass back into place. She hands the mirror to me, then takes a step back into the shadows.

The door to the bedroom bangs open.

Yukimi stands there, her face perfectly calm but her eyes glowing like a fox's. "What did you take?"

Is she bluffing? Did she see us look at the photo?

"This mirror." I hold it out to her, and she snatches it from me.

"There's no need to steal from me," Yukimi says, her voice icy.

I plaster a hurt look on my face. "I wasn't. Aoi brought me to your bedroom because I asked, but I didn't want to wake you up."

"Don't touch my things." Yukimi steps into the hallway. "Aoi?"

Aoi leans against the wall and lights up another cigarette, puffing smoke into our faces. "He didn't break anything. The fox boy just wanted to see where you went."

Yukimi looks between us. "Well, I'm awake now."

"Sorry." I give her an attempt at a smile.

She sighs and puts her hand on her hip. "Aoi, stop breathing smoke in my face. Tavian, don't give me those hopeful, starving eyes. If you want breakfast, cook it yourself."

I mentally breathe a sigh of relief. "Breakfast sounds good."

Aoi saunters away, her cigarette smoke trailing behind her.

Yukimi glances down at her clothes. "I might as well show you the kitchen."

"Thanks," I say.

She heads for the stairs and I follow her. Every step I take, a thought thuds in my mind.

Do not speak to him.

Why would she not want me to speak to an anonymous ghost, one that had no connection to her, unless of course he knew her? Why would the ghost try so hard to keep me away from her? My father was not a good man. *Was.* Is that why she keeps his photo behind her mirror, so she can remember him every time she looks at her reflection?

"Tavian?" Yukimi looks back at me.

There must be something on my face, something betraying the terrible thoughts swarming in my head like a hive of wasps.

I shake my head. "I'm tired. Didn't sleep."

"Anburojia can do that to you," Yukimi says. "You need to eat."

She's actually caring about whether I starve or not, actually going into the kitchen and opening cupboards. Being something like a mother to me. Like Okāsan.

I stand at the threshold of the kitchen, my shoulders rigid.

"Can you cook?" she says, pulling out a bag of rice.

"I'm learning," I say.

Yukimi plugs in a rice cooker. "Come here, then. I'm not going to make breakfast for you." Despite her gruff talk, she pulls a carton of eggs from the fridge.

I stand by the stove as she sets a skillet there. I take

the oil from her and pour it onto the cold iron as it heats up, slowly, the oil starting to sizzle and pop.

What am I going to do? There has to be a way to say this right.

"Take the egg." Yukimi nudges my hand with its cool shell.

I crack it against the edge of the skillet, much too hard, and it explodes everywhere.

Yukimi growls under her breath. "What a mess. You have—"

"Tell me who he is," I say.

She grabs a roll of paper towels. "Who?"

"My father."

Yukimi rips off a paper towel, starts to mop up the egg, then shoves the roll at me. "Here. You clean it up."

I wipe the egg from the tile floor, but I keep my eyes on her.

I'm going to be the silent one now, to let the unspoken words blink into existence.

"Later," she says. She dumps some water into the rice cooker without measuring it, then grabs the rice.

"Then tell me who the noppera-bō is."

Yukimi stiffens, her hands gripping the edge of the counter. "Why?"

"Why not?" I straighten. "He's haunting me, isn't he?"

Yukimi closes the lid on the rice cooker and turns it on, still playing pretend. "You shouldn't listen to anything the noppera-bō tells you. He was a liar, and still is."

"So you knew him," I say.

"I did."

Finally, finally, she's answering my questions. Well, answer this.

"Was he my father?"

Her face stays serene, though I know now it's as fragile as eggshell. She opens the fridge again and pulls out a bundle of green onions, then takes a knife from a drawer, and a cutting board. She arranges them as delicately as if she's performing a traditional tea ceremony. Like this is a show.

"Yukimi," I say. "Tell me the truth."

She starts chopping the onions, her movements slow, careful.

"Okāsan."

Her hand speeds up, the onions springing off the counter.

"I know you keep his photo with you," I say quietly, no matter how loud the pain feels inside me. "I know you must still think about him. How did he die?"

Yukimi drives the knife an inch deep into the cutting board. "What photo?"

I wait for a moment, my heart thudding so fast in my chest I'm afraid of what might happen if I speak too soon, if she unleashes the barely restrained fury in her voice.

"The one behind the mirror."

Yukimi marches past me, aiming for the stairs. I follow her, but she breaks into a run and bounds up the steps. In her bedroom, she snatches the mirror from the dresser and yanks the glass out. The photo floats, see-sawing, to the ground. I lunge for it, but Yukimi blocks me with her arm and a fierce look.

"You will never see this again," she says.

And that's how I know I was right, and this was my father.

She grabs a lighter from the dresser. I strain to reach the photo, but it's too late. Fire crawls over the photo, shriveling the paper, devouring the man's face. Reflected flames dance in Yukimi's eyes as she drops it in a glass to burn.

"That will be forgotten," she says.

I watch the photo crumble to ashes. "Like you forgot me."

Yukimi looks at me, and her face twists, and I can tell she wants to tell me everything she doesn't know how to say. She grabs my arm, her grip bruising, but I yank away.

"Tavian," she says.

I walk out of the room.

My father is dead. My father is the noppera-bō.

The thoughts chase each other round and round my head until I'm dizzy, grabbing my hair in my fists. I stagger down the hallway and push open the door to a bathroom. I slam the door, twist the lock, and sit against the tub, pressing my spine against the cold porcelain, trying to borrow some of its solidity.

My father's voice echoes in my head. *You must learn my name.*

I lift my head, my gaze caught by the gleam of the mirror above the sink. I climb to my feet and stand before the mirror. I think of the way Yukimi kept his photo in her mirror, his face behind her own. My throat tightens until it's hard to breathe.

I lift my gaze to my reflection. Do I look like him?

My eyes blur and the mirror goes out of focus. I blink hard and lean with my hands on either side of the sink, breathing raggedly. I turn on the faucet and splash some water on my face. When I wipe the water droplets away, I can see again.

The noppera-bō steps beside me, inside the mirror.

The eggshell blankness of his skin melts, reforming into eyes, a nose, a mouth. He isn't faceless anymore; he has the face from the burnt photo. His pale, bluish lips part.

"Father?" I sound croaky. "Is that who you are?"

"Yes." He has a voice now, but it's faint, so faint. "Can't…her…"

I stare at him, unblinking, not even wanting to glance at myself in the mirror to see if we look the same.

"What does Yukimi know?" I say. "What is she—"

Footsteps rap down the hall. Yukimi pounds on the door so hard it rattles on its hinges.

"Tavian?" she calls.

I double-check the lock. "Go away."

"Tavian..." whispers my father. "Must..."

The reflected ghost melts into the silver sheen of the mirror. I press my palm flat against the glass, as if I can feel him, but there's nothing but cold beneath my skin. I watch him fade away, leaving me with a fierce hollowness in my chest.

"You're wrong." Yukimi's steely voice cuts right through the wall. "I never forgot you."

I wrench open the door.

She slides one foot into the room, then freezes, her weight poised on her toes. Her nostrils flare and her eyes darken. "He was here. You spoke with him."

I stare at her. "Why shouldn't I speak with my own father?"

Yukimi exhales her breath in a hiss and steps closer to me. "He will lie to you, say anything to lure you away from me. He will drop you in the hands of the enemies."

"My father is one of the enemies?"

She clenches her hands and lowers her gaze.

"Tell me," I say. "Just tell me. Why do you want to keep him a secret from me?"

Yukimi's eyelids flinch. "He's dead now."

I suck in a slow breath. "I didn't even get to look at his picture for more than a second. And now I'm afraid I'm going to forget his face—" My voice cracks.

Yukimi drags me into a crushing embrace. Her grip knocks the breath out of me and I don't know what to do with my arms—it's awkward and it's starting to hurt.

I fight her, trying pry myself out of her grasp, but she's an equal match.

"Let me go."

"No."

A hot tear slips from her cheek onto mine. The anger melts away inside me, and I let her hug me, because I don't know what else I should do right now, even though I have a terrible feeling I don't really know the woman I'm holding.

"I'm sorry," Yukimi says, "but I can't keep you safe."

fourteen

I take an uneven breath. "What do you mean?"
Yukimi untangles herself from me and steps back, her
head bowed, her hair shadowing her face. "I can't stop
your father's family from looking for you. And if they
find you …"

I lower my head, thinking. "Who are they?"

She plucks a tissue from a box and dabs her eyes.
"You have seen at least one of them."

"Who—what did they look like?"

She folds her tissue into smaller and smaller squares
on the bathroom counter. "You should avoid them. They
are your blood relatives, but they will not help you."

I sit on the edge of the tub, my elbows on my knees. "If I don't know what they look like," I say, "then I won't be able to avoid them. If I don't know my father's name…"

Her fingers clench, crumpling the tissue's careful folds. "True."

I wait, saying nothing, for her to speak.

"His name was Akira Matsuzawa."

I meet her gaze, and I can see raw hurt and fear in her eyes. She's not bothering to hide it, and that scares me more than anything. "That was his name?"

"Yes."

I lean my cheek on my hand. "Matsuzawa?"

Octavian. That was Zenjiro Matsuzawa.

I remember how Tsuyoshi spoke about the yakuza boss in a hushed, almost awed voice. What are the chances this is a coincidence?

I look at Yukimi, my stomach heavy with dread. "The same as Zenjiro Matsuzawa?"

"Yes. And you are Zenjiro's only grandson."

"Oh." I nearly fall backward into the tub, but catch myself in time. "That makes sense."

Yukimi clenches her fists, her knuckles white. "Even though you are half-kitsune, Zenjiro will want you. Maybe especially because you are half-kitsune. He might find it *useful*."

"For what?"

"We shouldn't talk too much more." She scans the room, sniffing the air. "I can feel Akira here, watching us. I'm worried that he might tell them where we are."

"You think the yakuza would use a ghost to spy on us?"

"Akira still has ties to his father." She squeezes her eyes shut and sucks in her breath slowly. "Akira has ties to me as well, but I have learned to shut him out. It's harder, though, keeping him from trying to talk with you."

A shudder passes over me. "So I'm actually a Matsuzawa."

"No," she says fiercely. "Your father has nothing to do with you."

But I think he has everything to do with me. And I'm beginning to realize why Yukimi left me in Hokkaido when I was nothing more than a six-year-old kit. The yakuza must have been hounding her relentlessly, trying to get at me…

She sits beside me on the tub and touches her fingertips to the back of my hand. "Are you still hungry?"

I blink, startled by the swerve in the conversation. "Maybe."

"Let's get out of here."

Ten minutes later, we're streaking through Tokyo on Yukimi's motorcycle, the icy wind stinging my eyes and erasing my thoughts. The sun shines crystal-bright from an eggshell blue sky, and the city glitters more than mere steel and glass can. The feeling of speed fills me with a temporary, fierce thrill.

We're in an area of Tokyo that must be part of the water trade, a series of concrete streets whose neon glitz pales in the stark daylight. The unlit lights look shabby and almost sad. Yukimi parks outside a hole-in-the-wall restaurant. As she chains her motorcycle to a lamp post, I try to peek through the paper-and-wood windows, but it's too dark inside for me to make anything out.

"What is this place?" I say.

"The Fat Oni," Yukimi says.

"That's an ... interesting name."

She grins. "Brace yourself for the best *yakitori* and sake around."

The thought of yakitori—skewers of chicken and other morsels, grilled over charcoal—brings a rush of saliva to my mouth. When Yukimi pushes open the door, the aroma breezing out makes my stomach growl thunderously.

"Knew you were hungry," Yukimi says.

I give her a thin smile and follow her in.

Cheap paper lanterns strung on wires dangle over tables and chairs wedged into a tiny space that looks more like an office break room than anything else. Despite it being so early, about half a dozen bleary-eyed customers huddle over their breakfasts.

A high counter curves around the open kitchen, and there's some muffled clattering and grumbling going on back there. Yukimi hops onto one of the stools.

"Ozuru?" she calls.

"What?" grumbles a raspy voice.

"I have a friend who would love to try your yakitori."

"Oh?"

Ozuru pokes his head out of the kitchen—and I take two steps back before I can stop myself. His skin glows an unnatural, poisonous-mushroom red, and antelope-horns poke from his matted hair. Ozuru sees me staring at him and grins, tusks jutting from his black lips, his snake-yellow eyes glinting.

Oh, shit. *Oni.*

Translation: ogre-demon, the man-eating brute of legends, though I don't know what they've been up to recently. Needless to say, you don't want to screw around with oni.

"This is your friend?" Ozuru says. "He's pretty little."

"You're pretty big," I mutter.

The oni growls, a sound like boulders grinding together. "You're with Yukimi, so I won't eat you, kit."

"I doubt I taste good," I say.

Ozuru laughs, which also sounds like boulders grinding together.

"Don't worry, Ozuru is harmless." Yukimi pats a stool next to her, inviting me to sit. "Harmless enough that I had to save his ass from the yakuza on more than one occasion."

Ozuru shrugs. "That was back before I became a chef."

"Chef!" Yukimi snorts. "You're hardly a cook."

"Want some spit with your yakitori?" His eyes twinkle and he almost looks like an evil-ogre Santa Claus.

"Actually," she says, "I'll have the *asuparabēkon.*"

"Of course." Ozuru looks to me. "You?"

"What's asuparabēkon?" I say.

Ozuru grins. "Yukimi's favorite yakitori. Watch out, she'll fight you for it."

Yukimi rolls her eyes. "It's bacon-wrapped asparagus."

"I'll stick with the chicken. Nothing weird, thanks."

"Sure, kit."

The oni turns to a freezer, yanks out some raw chicken, and impales it on a steel skewer.

I climb onto the stool next to Yukimi. "Now I *am* starving."

"Me too," she says.

We glance at each other, then look away. Watching the yakitori sizzle on the grill is easier than saying anything to each other, but it doesn't make this any less awkward.

"So!" Yukimi says.

"So?" I say.

"Why are you in Tokyo, anyway?" Her casual tone doesn't quite mask a sharper interest.

I clear my throat. "Visiting my grandparents. Adoptive, obviously, on my dad's side."

"What kind of family are they?"

"Successful." Not wanting them to sound mercenary, I add, "And they're good people. They were careful to explain everything to me when they brought me to America, in a way that a little kid would understand, and they taught me how to live there."

"I see," Yukimi says.

I glance at her. She's running her fingernail along a scar on the countertop, but I can see the crease between her eyebrows, the way her face looks older than it was a second ago.

"My dad works in the hotel business," I say. "Like his dad. My mom is a lawyer, and works mostly on contract law. They're pretty well-off. I don't have to worry about college."

"College?" Yukimi brightens. "What are you studying?"

"I'm not sure. Art, maybe, but my parents want me to study something more practical, like business." I swallow, my throat dry, and give her a lopsided smile. "Sorry, I know how awkward it is for me to be talking about my mom and dad."

Yukimi catches Ozuru's eyes. "The usual drink, please."

He slides a can of Kirin beer to her. She pops the top and takes a long swig, her eyes shut.

"How did you meet Akira, anyway?" I say.

Yukimi seems to have trouble swallowing. She sets down the can of beer and gives me a sideways stare. "I was young and stupid. He fell for me, and I let him. Is that enough?"

"You let him?" I say. "Even though you're ... you know."

Yukimi blinks, her face uncomprehending.

I draw in a breath, then hold the air tight in my lungs. "Aoi strongly implied you're a lesbian. So I didn't have a clear idea how you and Akira met, and all that ..."

Ozuru glances up from the grill. "Lesbian?" He laughs.

Yukimi gives him a death-glare. "Go back to cooking."

My face burns. "Is this not public knowledge?"

"It would be," Ozuru says, "if it were true."

Yukimi sighs, and the corner of her mouth twists. "I usually date women, but I have dated some men as well. Akira was one of the lucky few. Or unlucky few, I suppose."

Ozuru leans over the grill. "Akira? You mean that Matsuzawa guy?"

I sit up straighter. "You knew him?"

"Yeah, I met him." The oni slides bacon-wrapped asparagus off a skewer and onto a plate, then gives it to Yukimi. "Kind of liked him, before I knew better."

"Oh, really." I lean my elbows on the counter. "Tell me more."

Yukimi savagely tears a hunk of yakitori with her teeth, her eyes locked on Ozuru.

"Uh…" The oni scratches his chin. "I don't know much else."

I narrow my eyes. "You're not saying anything because Yukimi is glaring at you."

"The Matsuzawa family isn't chitchat material," Ozuru says darkly.

I hold my hands up in the air. "Fine. If you're too scared of a dead man to talk about him, I won't ask questions."

Ozuru's chest swells like that of a rooster faced with an enemy. "Listen, kit, I know you're trying to piss me off so I'll start blabbing about Akira, but that's something you should ask Yukimi about. She knew him better than anybody."

"I know," I say nonchalantly. "She knew him *really* well."

Ozuru lowers his voice, his gaze on Yukimi. "Out of curiosity, how much *did* you tell the kit?"

"Not much."

"Is he staying with you?" Ozuru says. "And your roommates?"

"Yes."

"The Sisters," I say, "I know."

Yukimi glances sharply at me. "How much did that myobu tell you about the Sisters, anyway?"

I take a plate of chicken yakitori from Ozuru. "Enough."

Yukimi growls, and I can't hide a grin. I can be just as evasive. Like mother, like son.

"You sure he's not spying on you guys?" Ozuru mumbles.

"He's my son," Yukimi says. "So no, I don't think he is."

Ozuru's mouth drops, his tusks on full display. "Your son? What the hell—are you pulling my leg?"

"No," she says.

"And is Akira—?"

"Yes."

I raise my eyebrows at Yukimi, my heartbeat thudding. "So have you decided to tell everybody?"

She gives me a look. "Like you haven't been."

I narrow my eyes. "Just Aoi."

"Well, Ozuru would have guessed sooner or later. I trust him to keep his mouth shut."

Ozuru manages to stop gawking. "So that's why you left."

Yukimi sips her beer. "I went to Hokkaido. Not too far away."

I take a bite of chicken, savoring its tender juiciness— but it's not as delicious as the information I'm hearing right now. I try to look as inconspicuous as possible.

Ozuru flips a row of skewers, steam hissing from the grill. "So I assume there was no sick grandma up in Hokkaido. And you were doing something else for six years."

Yukimi laughs harshly. "You thought I was so devoted? Of course there was no grandma."

"So you lied," I say. "To keep me a secret."

Her eyes glint dangerously. "You were better off a secret. If the Matsuzawa family knew you had been born, you would have been better off dead. I had to hide you."

Ozuru lowers his voice further. "But didn't Akira look for him?"

Yukimi shakes her head and tears off another hunk of yakitori.

"When did he die?" I say, with a hopeful look at the oni.

Ozuru shrugs.

Yukimi pats her mouth with a napkin. "Before Tavian was born."

"Tavian?" Ozuru arches his eyebrows. "That's his name? Why did you decide on that?"

"I didn't name him that," Yukimi says.

"You didn't name me anything," I say.

She sighs. "You weren't old enough." She sips more beer.

Ozuru lifts a skewer from the grill and gnaws on a sizzling piece of chicken, never mind that it's blazing hot. "I had no idea you and Akira were that close. Or that you two had a baby. Shit, Yukimi. I would've never guessed you're a *mom*."

"Me neither," I say dryly. "We parted ways when I was six."

"Oh?" Ozuru says.

Yukimi grabs my wrist, her claws pricking my skin. "Watch it."

I pry her fingers off me. "It's the truth."

"More beer?" Ozuru says, clearly trying to defuse the tension.

Yukimi drains her can and reaches for another. Frowning, I look away. I don't think alcohol is going to do anything useful. If anything, it will feed the anger coiled inside me.

I'm going to have to ask my father—Akira—for his version of events. It gives me a twisted feeling of satisfaction, a perverse thankfulness, to know that even when he's a ghost I can still talk to him. Do I want to know how he died? He must have been a yakuza, since he was a Matsuzawa, so it must have been violent.

Without his blood, you may use his bones.

I shudder and twist away from my food, my stomach

souring, and scan the restaurant. The breakfast crowd has thinned a bit—just a young couple in the corner, whispering and giggling over their food, a wrinkled old man devouring his yakitori, and a little girl with pink barrettes in her hair. No, she isn't a little girl. I know her.

The temple maiden from Ueno. Junko.

I slide off my stool. If anyone asks, I can say I'm looking for the bathroom. But in truth, I'm meandering toward Junko as casually as possible. She's not eating anything, just taking quick, nervous sips from a glass of water. When she sees me coming, her face turns beet red and she starts to stand.

"Wait," I whisper. "Junko, it's me."

"I know," she says, her voice so high-pitched it's almost squeaky. "But you're with *her*."

"It's all right," I say. "She—"

"Who's this?" Yukimi's voice sounds too loud in my ear. "Your girlfriend's come looking for you?"

Junko's face becomes a deeper beetlike shade.

"She's not," I say.

"Then who is she?" Yukimi looks sideways at me, her eyes shifting from black to amber.

"Someone I met earlier," I say with a shrug. "At a temple."

Junko nods and stands, bowing quickly toward Yukimi. "Excuse me, but I have to leave."

"Temple?" Yukimi's nose twitches as she samples the

air. "Interesting. I didn't think a myobu would dirty her paws by stepping into a restaurant like this."

Junko keeps her face downcast, but I see her eyes flash. "I know who you are, nogitsune."

"Oh, do you?" Yukimi blocks Junko's path. "Have a seat."

The miko sits, her shoulders stiff. She folds and refolds a napkin, her fingers twitchy.

Yukimi leans closer, her hands flat on the table. "Who are you?"

"Nobody," Junko says.

"Hey," I say, "let's not interrogate people over breakfast."

Yukimi ignores me, her gaze intense like she's scented prey and is just waiting for it to crawl back out of its burrow. Junko's fingers keep folding the napkin, creasing it, turning it over—origami. She's crafting an illusion. This should be interesting.

"We nogitsune are nicer than that," I say. "Right, Okāsan?"

Yukimi's gaze flinches toward me, like I knew it would. "Is this that myobu you talked about earlier? Shizuka, or whatever her name was, who knew so much about us?"

"What," I say, "you don't know her? She seems to know you."

Yukimi gives the myobu a cold glare. "She's clearly a spy."

Junko tugs on the corners of her napkin and it becomes square in shape. She brings it to her mouth and blows into it, inflating it into a perfect, tiny paper lantern.

"Oh, how clever," Yukimi says. "Is that a gift for—"

A glow sparks inside the lantern. Junko lifts the origami above her head, her eyes squeezed shut, and smashes it on the table—a blinding flash explodes.

A few people scream, and shouts go off like scattered aftershocks. I can't see anything but white, my eyes aching. I hear Yukimi swearing and a chair scraping on the floor. I blink fast, my vision returning in fragments: the chair—the man—the oni—the door. I stumble toward the door and shove it open.

Shoes slap on the road, growing fainter.

"Wait!" I shout. "Junko!"

The footsteps stop.

"Tell Shizuka!"

The footsteps start again, faster.

A hand latches onto my elbow. "Did you see which way the myobu went?" Yukimi says.

"No, I can't see anything," I say, which is mostly true.

"Damn," she growls. "I should have known better than to have fallen for such a simple trick—but it's so simple I wasn't thinking of it. That little myobu...how do you know her?"

"Like I said, I met her at a temple. She's not Shizuka."

"Don't hide anything from me," Yukimi says.

I take a deep breath and count to ten. I have the urge to tell her she's the master of hiding things. My eyesight comes back almost completely and I meet her gaze.

"She's just a scared miko," I say. "She probably thought she could win points by spying on us."

"On the Sisters," Yukimi says.

"Are you that paranoid about the myobu?"

"Yes." She stares down the road. "You have no idea."

"Well, fine. Be paranoid. But I'm going to finish my breakfast."

Yukimi glares at me, trying to hide a flicker of amusement in her eyes. "You can't eat if you're dead."

"I don't intend to die."

Ozuru marches from the restaurant. Out here, he's even more huge than he looked like inside. "What the *hell* happened back there?" he bellows, spit flecks flying.

"Then again," I mutter, "we might die right now."

Yukimi grins and claps the oni on the biceps. "Don't worry, Ozuru. We're fine. Just a myobu spy, but the mere sight of me scared her away. They're sending little girls now."

"That was a pretty big illusion for such a little girl," Ozuru says.

Yukimi's grin sours. "Maybe." She forces her mouth into a smile again. "Ozuru, now that we're out here, let me ask you a question. Do you happen to have any fruit on the menu?"

"Fruit?" Understanding dawns on the oni's face. "Oh, yeah, I do."

I arch my eyebrows. "Is this the fruit I think it is?"

Yukimi laughs, her eyes a bit wild.

fifteen

The back room in Ozuru's restaurant smells like decades of greasy cooking are baked into the walls. Cardboard boxes and crates stand in wobbly stacks. I hear a squeak and see a shadow that looks suspiciously like a rodent, but I say nothing.

"Still have rats?" Yukimi says.

"The little bastards have gotten smarter lately," Ozuru says. "Don't taste quite as good, either."

I try not to think about what might be sizzling on the grill right now.

Ozuru kicks aside some cardboard and unearths a small wooden box. He sets the box on a table and pries off the lid. Anburojia lies inside, each pale gold fruit individually nestled in tissue paper. The oni's huge fingers look like they would crush the anburojia, but he plucks one out with surprisingly delicacy and places it in Yukimi's hands.

"Only four?" she says.

"My supplier in Okinawa says it's been unusually cold."

"Hmm." Yukimi brings the fruit to her nose and inhales deeply. Her eyelids flutter shut. "I'll take them."

"Great." Ozuru fidgets, his eyes on the door. "Same price as usual."

Yukimi slips a wallet from her jacket pocket and peels away an obscenely large amount of cash. Ozuru flips through the bills, then nods and pushes the box of anburojia toward her.

"There's enough in there to cover the cost of our food, too," she says.

"Thanks. Good seeing you again, Yukimi." Ozuru glances at me. "And your son."

"Same to you," I say.

I sound so calm about this black market transaction.

We exit through the back door and Yukimi heads to her motorcycle. A trio of teen guys with cigarettes stand beside it, gawking—until their eyes slide over to Yukimi instead.

One of them whistles. "This your bike, lady? Hot."

My god, I can't believe my mother is getting cat-called. I seem to be invisible to these guys.

"Sure." Yukimi opens up a saddlebag and starts tucking fruits inside.

"Start her up," says a particularly delinquent-looking, zit-infested guy. "I'd love to see how fast you can go."

Yukimi buckles up the saddlebag, her back to them.

I roll my eyes and pick up a handful of pebbles. Let's see if I can pull this off. I bring the pebbles to my mouth and breathe on them, concentrating on a particular illusion. My heart beats faster but holds steady, and the pebbles start squirming in my hand.

"Hey!" I shout. "Look!"

All three glance my way, and I chuck the illusion in their faces. Black beetles cascade down on them, creeping into their hair, falling into their eyes, scuttling down their shirts.

Yukimi smiles as the guys shriek and swat at themselves. "Let's go."

We climb onto the motorcycle and zoom out of there, the engine purring like a big cat. Behind us, I hear the pebbles clatter on the ground as the illusion fades away.

"You should be careful doing that," Yukimi says, over the wind.

"Why?" I say. "It worked, didn't it?"

"For a small illusion, yes. But you still don't have full control over your foxfire yet. Not without a name."

"So when are we going to do this naming ceremony, anyway?" I say.

"Soon."

She accelerates, and the sound of speed erases my words.

Back at the Lair, the sound of snores greets us. I peek into the living room and see Aoi sprawled on the couch, her mouth open, the TV remote dangling from her hand. On the soundless TV, game-show contestants race down a slip-and-slide. Yukimi crosses the room to turn off the TV, and I follow behind her. There's a woman I don't recognize snoozing in the easy chair, and a vixen curled by her feet.

More of the Sisters, I guess. How many are there?

Something crunches beneath my foot. I glance down and see I've stepped on the smashed guts of my cell phone. And then it occurs to me that I don't need a cell phone to contact Gwen or my grandparents. All I need to do is enter their dreams while they're sleeping. I glance at my watch: 10:40 a.m. They have to be awake right now. But later...

Yukimi walks upstairs with the anburojia, and I follow her to her room.

"When are we going to eat those?" I say.

She tugs open a dresser drawer and tucks the fruits among sweaters. "After dark. For now, we sleep."

"But it's the middle of the morning!"

"And we've been awake all night." Yukimi arches an eyebrow at me. "Now isn't a good time to be running as a fox."

I stifle a yawn and try to pretend like I'm not swaying

on my feet. "What, the inugami have a day shift? Wait, I already know the answer to that question."

"Oh?" Yukimi says. "How many times have you run into them?"

I count off with my fingers. "Once in Harajuku. Again in Shinjuku Gyoen. And later, they attacked my grandmother and my girlfriend when they were coming home from shopping."

Yukimi's face darkens. "They know where your grandparents live?"

"I hope not, but probably—"

"Zenjiro won't let an opportunity like this pass."

I meet her eyes, keeping my voice calm. "If you think he's going to hold them hostage, why won't you let me call them? Then I can warn them, and tell them that I'm okay."

Yukimi tidies the anburojia, her gaze distant.

"Or would you not care," I say, "if an elderly couple got caught in your fight with the inugami?"

She shuts the drawer with a thump. "I'm not completely heartless."

Good to know.

"I was thinking of a pay phone," I say. "Far enough from here that it wouldn't give away the location of the Lair. We could take the metro so we're less conspicuous."

"We?" she says.

I smile. "Well, unless you want to let me go out there alone."

Yukimi's eyes flash. "Alone is bad."

"That's what I thought. So, when does the next metro leave?"

"Next metro? Nice try." She sits on the edge of her bed and kicks off her boots. "We'll do it tonight."

The hopeful smile on my face collapses like a house of cards. "Sure."

Yukimi slings off her jacket and falls flat on her bed, her hair fanning around her head like a dark halo. Shadows hide the fatigue on her face. She shuts her eyes.

"Go to sleep," she says.

"Of course." I try to sound upbeat. "Wouldn't want to drop dead."

She opens her eye a crack, then shoos me away.

I leave, shut the door behind me, and sigh. The sigh merges into a jaw-cracking yawn.

Damn it, I am tired.

I fill my cheeks with air and let it puff out slowly. My feet feel like anchors as I go downstairs. I head into the bedroom there and discover yet another strange woman sitting cross-legged on the blanket I'd had before. She's polishing a dagger with a rag and some oil. She looks bony, her face and her elbows sharp.

"Who are you?" says the woman. "Yukimi's?"

I hesitate in the doorway. "She told you?"

"Yeah." She holds the dagger to the light, her reflection glinting in the blade. "How long are you going to be here?"

"Not long."

The woman arches her eyebrows, then unfolds her

too-thin legs and stands. She sheathes the dagger in her belt and slips past me, leaning against the doorway so we don't touch.

"You don't belong here," she mutters as she passes.

"I already know that."

I close the door behind her, cutting off that nasty glint in her eyes, then grab a new blanket, one that doesn't have unknown fox fur on it. I spread the blanket in the cleanest corner and lie down, staring at the cracks and mildew on the ceiling, trying to find faces. As if the noppera-bō might actually return to me here. My father.

I shut my eyes.

It's dark in the room when I wake. My sleep was nothing more than time lost. I don't remember any of my dreams, if I had any, and fatigue still drapes me like a heavy blanket.

A shadowed woman stands over me, her eyes yellow.

I sniff the air, catching Yukimi's scent, and my muscles unclench. "What time is it?"

"You have a watch," she says.

So she's going to be cold again.

I look at my watch and hit a button to make it glow. 8:53 p.m.

"You overslept," Yukimi says. "Night fell hours ago."

"I was tired."

She walks out of the room, her boots clicking in the hall. "Let's go."

I climb to my feet and try to rub away the sleep clinging to my eyes.

"Are you hungry?" she says.

"Not particularly."

Yukimi slips a golden-white fruit from her pocket. The anburojia glimmers in the dim light, haloed in its own coat of fuzz. I suck in my breath, drinking in its exotic scent. I remember the last time I ate anburojia, and how craving-sick I felt afterward, but I can't help wanting to sink my teeth into the fruit.

"So we're running as foxes again?" I ask.

"Yes."

"After we call my grandparents," I say. "Remember?"

"We can stop at a pay phone along the way."

I scrutinize her face, but she's better at hiding her expressions than I am at reading them.

Yukimi rubs her thumb along the skin of the anburojia fruit. "You need to build your strength. It's no wonder you're so weak, living so long as a human among Americans."

I arch my eyebrows. "Am I not Japanese enough for you?"

"No."

Ouch.

She presses the anburojia into my hand. "Take it. Save it for later."

I close my fingers around the anburojia, the fruit's

flesh cool and soft against my skin, and tuck it into my jacket pocket. "How much later?"

But she's already walking away.

We leave the Lair on foot. A few stars try futilely to glimmer to life above, their glow outshone by the glare of Tokyo. Ragged clouds droop overhead, dripping slushy rain.

True to her word, Yukimi leads me to the nearest metro station. I duck into the porcelain-tiled underground, my heartbeat thumping, and look for a sign identifying our location. Shin-Nakano Station. On the Marunouchi Line. I don't remember where it goes, just vaguely recall it snaking like a red serpent across most of the map.

The sound of an approaching train echoes down the tunnel.

"Hurry," Yukimi says, her footsteps staccato on the tiles.

I jog after her. We're on the platform leading out of town, toward the edges of Tokyo. Away from Akasaka.

The train slides from the tunnel with a metallic whir. The brakes whistle and the doors chime open. We climb onto a car, our heads bent against the glow of fluorescent, too bright after the darkness. Yukimi slips on a pair of sunglasses and looks straight ahead. The passengers ignore us, and we them. We slip into the gloom of the tunnel.

In this place between places, I stare at my reflection. Bruises shadow my hollow eyes. My hair hasn't seen a comb for who knows how long and it spikes in every direction. I look like I could be a runaway, or homeless. I wonder what would happen if I managed to find a police officer. Would they even believe what I told them?

One stop. Two stops. Three.

I nudge Yukimi's arm. "Where are we going?"

"To the end of the line."

"We don't need to go that far for a pay phone."

"Yes, we do."

Judging by the hard line of her lips, she's not concerned about the pay-phone call. She's trying to find a place safe for foxes, far from the territory of the yakuza and their dogs.

The metro's brakes squeal. "The next station is Ogikubo."

I peer out the windows. We're above ground now, the tracks running past stores that aren't nearly as flashy as the ones downtown, the skyscrapers not reaching quite as high.

Yukimi touches my shoulder, nudging me from the metro. We cross the tracks and head down a narrow street bordered by stores selling ordinary things like eggplants and magazines and plastic trinkets. It doesn't feel like a dangerous part of town, but Yukimi still walks briskly, making eye contact with no one. She turns down a side street and walks in the shadows of patchwork houses stitched together.

I follow in her shadow, the slushy rain sticking in my hair. I already know that there's no pay phone out here, not where she's taking me. I can see trees ahead through the buildings, a place where we can shift into foxes and I can forget why I even came.

Or I could make my escape.

We reach a river, the water dark and glistening in its concrete constraints. Yukimi paces along its edge, the wind unwinding her scarf so it spirals behind her. I slip my hand into my pocket and tighten my fingers around the anburojia. As a fox, I can run faster. As a fox, I can slip into the night and lose Yukimi, then return to Akasaka.

"It's cold, isn't it?" Yukimi says. "My teeth are chattering."

"Well," I say, "at least we'll be warmer in our fur."

She laughs, giddy, as if she's already eaten the anburojia. It's easy to laugh back, to pretend like I'm also excited by the idea of slipping into my fox-skin and forgetting my humanity.

I walk a little faster. "Where are we going?"

"To a park farther down the river."

The bare branches of trees spiderweb the sky, and we leave the street behind for paths in a park. The river flows between artificial banks paved with cobblestones like fish scales. I find some stairs carved out of the stones and follow them to the water.

"I guess we don't care about clothes," I say.

Yukimi shrugs. "Hand them to me, and I'll hide them under that tree."

I'm not too thrilled by the idea of stripping naked by

the riverside when the air feels like it's well below freezing, and when my kitsune mother is watching me, waiting.

I slip the anburojia from my pocket. "Let's eat."

Yukimi raises her anburojia to the sky as if making a toast, then bites the fruit. Red juice dribbles down her chin, and in the starlight, it looks like blood. She watches me, her eyes already fox-like. I hold her gaze as I eat the anburojia, every bit of fruit, then lick my fingers clean. She smiles, her teeth curving downward into fangs.

I take off my clothes mechanically, like I'm going to shower in the locker room at school. I bunch my things together and hand them to Yukimi, not looking at her face, noticing out of the corner of my eye that she's already naked, already more fox than woman.

Ready, I stand over the river, looking down into my rippling reflection. My hair falls into my eyes, shadowing my face. I tilt my head to one side, and for a moment I look like Akira.

My mouth curls into a thin smile. "Here we go."

I shut my eyes and clench my jaw and tense all my muscles—and it happens in one swift rush, human to fox. I yawn, my tongue curling, and stretch leisurely, like I'm warming up for a little jaunt. Yukimi yips behind me, impatient, and I face her.

She's pacing at the top of the bank, her ears swiveled toward me.

I bound up to join her. She touches her nose to mine for a second, but I turn away, trying to make it look like it was an accident. I don't want her to touch me, don't want her to have power over me.

But the taste of anburojia still lingers in my mouth.

We trot along the river, weaving through the trees, dodging the puddles of light beneath street lamps. My nose twitches at the elixir of scents stirred by the night air—pines, rain, the slow-moving green wet smell of the river—and exhilaration dazzles my mind. My paws thud on the sodden grass, claws dig into the dirt, legs drive me onward.

Mice. There have to be some juicy little mice around here…

I trot farther from the river, lured by a promising scratching noise. There, between the roots of that tree. I cock my head, one paw raised. A whiskered nose peeks out from the hole. I pounce, my legs stiff, paws poised to trap the creature—but it darts underground.

Behind me, Yukimi makes a sniffing chirp. Laughing at me.

I turn to growl at her, and thinking about laughter—something so human—shakes my thoughts so they fall back into place. What the hell, Tavian? Mouse hunting? It's time to run.

The fur along Yukimi's spine spikes. She's looking straight in my eyes.

Does she know?

I let my mouth hang open, my tongue lolling, and pad toward her with a loose gait. Nothing to worry about. I nudge her shoulder with my nose, then leap away playfully.

And she falls for my lie.

Yukimi relaxes, and I bound away. She runs after me like this is a race and she can beat me. I let her pull ahead of me, but I focus on the gray speckling her muzzle, the way her left hind leg moves stiffly, like she cut her tendon once and it healed imperfectly.

I'm faster than her. She just doesn't know it.

I explode from a lope to a sprint. When I hurtle past her, I catch the look of surprise in her eyes. I'm leaving her behind, leaving the river behind, plunging into the dark maze of alleys. I skid to a halt in the middle of the street and glance back.

Three blocks behind, Yukimi runs after me, her breath steaming the air.

My chest tightens, and I don't know if it's from the exertion or from looking at her. I want to go back, to pretend like this was all a game, that I would never leave her…the way she left me.

She pauses, panting. She thinks I'm coming back.

I reveal nothing on my face as I turn away from her and keep running. My breath ragged, I push my burning muscles harder. I swerve between parked bikes, leap over hedges, squirm under fences. My legs quiver, their energy almost spent.

I duck under a parked car and look back.

She's gone.

I don't know which way I'm going, where I'm supposed to be. I point my nose in the direction I think is Akasaka, the direction I think is away from the Sisters—and most of all, Yukimi.

I'm free.

Then why does it feel like I'm wearing a straightjacket?

I need to breathe. I trot into an alley outside a bar, panting with my head down, my throat burning something fierce. Maybe I should change back, to hell with the nakedness, and find a pay phone—but I don't have any money, of course. Maybe Yukimi was actually going to help me, after we spent some time running as foxes, together.

God damn it. I squeeze my eyes shut, but of course foxes can't cry.

A drunk staggers out of the bar and unzips his pants, then sees me. "Hey, kitsune! Give me a kiss!"

He can't even tell I'm not a vixen? Well, male kitsune are rare—

The drunk lunges for me, stumbles on his loose pants, and almost falls on me. I leap nimbly out of the way. He swears loudly, then starts crying, big gulping sobs. Disgusted, I disappear into the shadows of the street. I could really screw that guy over if I wanted to. He should know better than to harass a fox. At least he wasn't an inugami.

I've got to get out of here. It's late; it isn't safe.

Did that drunk have tattoos? I wasn't looking, but there might have been something on his neck. I wonder

which territory around here belongs to the Kuro Inu—
and Zenjiro Matsuzawa.

And you are his only grandson.

I start moving again, trying to outrun that thought. I run along a main road, ignoring the way passersby stare and point, looking for some obvious landmark that will get me out of this maze.

There! That has to be a metro station. Which line?

I hover at the edge of the street, waiting for the traffic light. The light changes, and the wind shifts.

Bringing with it the unmistakable stink of dog.

sixteen

I freeze at the edge of the street. People leave the cross-walk to point at me, one of them snapping a flash photo. Shit, I have to *move*. I'm out in the open like a plate of meat on the sidewalk. It's almost hilarious, really, that the moment I leave Yukimi, bam, inugami.

Dread curdles my stomach.

The big gray mastiff, Ushio, is nosing around the corner of the street. Sniffing my trail. The brothers, Yuta and Katashi, follow him in human form, arguing with each other.

Illusions, illusions, think of something good, think—

Polished black shoes click on the pavement in front of me.

Akira? I look up.

The man wears a dark suit, his iron-gray hair sleek, his face every bit as wrinkled as Tsuyoshi's.

"Stop running," Zenjiro Matsuzawa says. "You look tired."

If this is a dream, now would be a very good time to wake up.

"What the fuck?" Katashi jabs his finger in my direction. "He's standing right in the fucking street!"

Ushio lunges, but Yuta yanks him back on his chain.

"I found him," Zenjiro says. "No thanks to you dogs."

Katashi shuts his mouth, but his face looks purple with fury. Yuta half-walks, half-slides toward me, dragged by Ushio. The mastiff growls and licks his chops, great ropes of drool swinging.

"Back," Zenjiro says.

He speaks in a gentle old voice, but the inugami instantly do as he says. Ushio even sits like an obedient dog, his droopy eyes hopeful. Yeah, hopeful he can rip out my guts.

Zenjiro bends to my level. "Do you know who I am?"

I nod.

"Good." He nods back. "Come with me."

A black BMW idles on the street. The driver opens the door for Zenjiro—for me, too. Like I'm going to jump in there, still as a fox, or maybe after changing back into a naked human.

Like I'm that stupid.

I bare my teeth at Zenjiro. I don't care if we're related by blood; he's unknown and untrustworthy. Toenails click on the sidewalk behind me, and I see Ushio fidgeting, itching to attack.

"I know who you are," Zenjiro murmurs. "Octavian Kimura."

Is that a threat?

My heartbeat pounds in my ears. I could attack him, fling an illusion at him that would make him scream. But the inugami would be on me in a second. Their teeth would drive past my pelt into my flesh. I don't even know if Zenjiro would stop them.

I meet Zenjiro's eyes, my face a mask. Then I walk past him toward the BMW, my head held low, my tail between my legs. He exhales in a puff of air. The driver's gaze flicks down at me, and I see a glimmer of disgust in his eyes. I pause, look over my shoulder.

Zenjiro waits patiently, ready to climb in after me. A wind whips down the street, driving sleet into our faces. He brings his arm up to cover his eyes, and the inugami squint against the cold.

Go.

I lunge under the car, skidding to the other side, reappearing in the middle of the street. A taxi barrels toward me, headlights blinding my eyes. The driver's eyes widen and he yanks the wheel. The taxi's side mirror screeches along the black gloss of the BMW. I leap out of the taxi's path, zigzag between bikes, cross the sidewalk.

Behind me, I hear Katashi shouting, "Let me at him!"

The blaring of a horn overpowers Zenjiro's reply.

I chance a backward glance and see traffic piling up, see Katashi ripping off his clothes and sprouting fur while Yuta grabs him by the shoulders and yells at Ushio, and Zenjiro…

He stands at the edge of the road, his head bowed.

I falter, and my paws skid on the icy road. No, I can't stop. I swing my head forward and point my muzzle downwind, letting the wind carry my scent away from the inugami. I dodge the reach of artificial lights, melting into the black night that pools in the cracks of the city. Silence swallows the pursuit of the inugami. I keep running.

Shinjuku Gyoen National Garden.

I disappear into the shadows of the trees as snow falls thick and erases the world around me. Adrenaline spent, I trudge through the snow, my muscles quivering. I make it to a pine and let my legs collapse beneath me. My breath clouds the air.

This is inugami territory. I have to get out of here, and soon.

I can't cover that much more ground as a fox; I should change back into a human and take the metro. Hopefully the slight change in my scent will confuse the inugami long enough for me to stay ahead. Hopefully the snow will bury my pawprints deep.

I drag myself to my feet and nudge my fox form, trying to push it out of the way, but it won't budge. Come on. I need to change back to human. They don't let foxes on the metro.

My rib cage creaks as it resists the transformation. Pain lances my heart, and I stagger. It feels like I never had a human form, like fox is all I've ever been and ever will be.

Shit. I force my eyes to stay open. The anburojia must be wearing off.

But this is the wrong body. Do I need to eat more anburojia before I'll find the strength to change back?

Yukimi has some. We only ate two of the fruits…

No. Not her. I need to find Gwen, and my grandparents, and warn them. I glance at a pay phone and sigh. Even if I managed to reach the receiver and fake some coins, what am I going to do, yip? Right now I'm as good as speechless. Unless…

With the last bit of my strength, I start digging. I claw away a little den in the snow where no one will see me, and crawl inside. Curled in a ball, I can almost pretend I'm not cold.

I shut my eyes. Time to sleep. To dream.

The river lounges among the trees, its silver skin shimmering with reflected summer leaves. I float face-up in a backwater pool, my eyes open toward the sky. A fly buzzes lazily around my eyelashes, then lands on my cheek. I feel its tiny feet crawling down.

Nasty itchy little creature.

I lift my arm to swat the fly, but my arm doesn't move. My fingers twitch in the pool, and they feel wrinkled, bloated, like I've been in the water for too long. The fly keeps crawling.

Footsteps crunch the gravel along the riverside.

Good. Maybe someone will come and swat this fly for me. I'm getting tired of drifting here alone.

The bushes rustle, and there's a flash of copper hair. Gwen.

A thought nibbles at the back of my mind. I need to tell her something, but I can't remember what. I'd frown if my face weren't paralyzed. And damn it, this fly is annoying.

Gwen scans the riverside, and her gaze falls on me.

"Oh my god." The color drains from her face, and even her freckles go invisible. "Zack! Come quick!"

Zack? Her ex-boyfriend? What's he doing here?

Gwen presses her hand to her mouth, her eyes watering, picking up some of the water's reflection. She inches her feet toward me until she's close enough to touch me, but she looks disgusted. Finally, the fly buzzes away from my face, and she gags.

What's wrong with her? What—

"Zack?" she calls. "Where are you?"

I try to open my mouth to talk to her, but my lips won't move. And then I realize why.

I'm dead.

In Gwen's dream, anyway. She told me about this: the first time she saw a dead body—two, actually—water sprites floating in a poisoned pool by the Stillaguamish River in Klikamuks. Back before I first met her, back at the beginning of the serial killings.

This is nothing more than a warped memory.

Gwen paces at the edge of the riverside. "Tavian," she says. "Tavian, what happened to you?"

I clear my throat, and water gurgles in my windpipe.

Gwen's eyes snap open wider. "Tavian?"

Choking, I struggle to stand upright, my arms and legs leaden. She wades into the pool and lunges for me, her fingers gripping my wrist. Under her touch, all the warmth floods back into my body. Half-dragged, half-crawling, I make it to solid ground.

"Breathe!" Gwen commands.

I hack up some tepid water, and she whacks me on the back. I take a few experimental breaths, the air whistling in my windpipe. I'm shaking all over. I know you can't die in dreams, but that doesn't mean I wasn't just scared shitless of drowning.

"Tavian, are you okay?" she says. "Answer me!"

"I'm okay," I rasp. I give her an approximation of a grin. "Don't worry."

The fear on her face warps into fury. "Don't *worry*? I thought you were dead! Was this some sort of—"

"Gwen," I say. "This is a dream. You're dreaming."

"A dream? But—" Her face twists. "Don't tell me you're actually dead."

"No! I entered your dream so I could talk to you."

Understanding dawns on her face. "Tavian, your grandparents have been looking for you—but the police haven't been able to find anything, and we all thought...where *are* you?"

"In Shinjuku Gyoen." I climb to my feet and take her shoulders in my hands. "Gwen, how fast can you get here?"

"It must be almost midnight, but I could catch the last metro and be there in maybe twenty minutes? Half an hour? I'm not sure." She stares into my eyes. "Are you safe there?"

"I'm hidden. I dug a little den for myself in the snow."

Her eyebrows descend. "You're a fox? But you haven't—"

"Long story." I shake my head. "Let's wake up and meet before the inugami catch up with me."

She nods, then snatches a kiss from me. "I'll be there."

I kiss her back, then blink myself awake.

I wait in my snow-cocoon with only my nose poking into the icy air. The sounds of the world above me are muffled, the roar of traffic no more than a distant humming. My eyelids droop, and I drift in and out of consciousness. The snow creaks under footsteps.

"Tavian! Are you here?"

My eyes snap open. I wriggle out of the den, clawing away snow, and poke my head into the air.

Gwen stands with her back to me, searching the darkness. Her curls fly behind her head, tangling with snow-clotted wind. I leap from the den and run to her. Shocks of pain jolt up my stiff legs. I bark and nip at her ankle, and she whirls to face me.

"Tavian!" Gwen falls to her knees. "I found you!"

It's all I can do not to bound into her arms like an excited kit-fox. I restrain myself and lick her hand. She dusts off the snow clumped on my pelt, her hands chapped and red.

"I took the last metro," she says. "But I have money for a taxi."

I nod and shake myself off, flinging her hand and the last of the snow away. I nudge her knee with my nose. Gwen slings a pack off her back and digs out some clothes. My clothes.

"Hurry and change back," she says. "I'll keep a look out."

I shake my head.

"It's not that cold. Come on, we need to hurry." Gwen narrows her eyes. "Can you not change back?"

I nod.

She swears under her breath. "Well, we're going anyway."

I bound ahead of her in the snow, my legs sinking deep. I still feel wobbly and woozy, but at least I'm awake. Gwen marches alongside me, shoves through a hedge, and steps onto the street. I glance around with my sharp eyes and nose, making sure we're safe.

Cars whoosh along the road, their tires spraying slush. A yellow taxi pulls around the corner, and I yip. Gwen darts to the edge of the road, jumping up and down and waving her arms. The taxi pulls up alongside us and the taxi driver stares at us.

"Akasaka," she says.

The taxi driver keeps staring. "Where in Akasaka?" he says.

In Japanese, of course—most taxi drivers don't speak English. But Gwen is prepared for this. She thrusts a piece of paper at the man, and I glimpse my grandparents' address written in Japanese. The taxi driver grunts and the back door swings open automatically. Gwen climbs inside and I slink in after her, hiding at her feet.

The taxi driver glances at the address, then pulls into traffic.

"Almost there," Gwen whispers to me.

The swerving and jolting of the taxi makes me car-sick, so I close my eyes until the taxi stops again. I crane my neck to see out the windows. The skyscraper where my grandparents live towers above us. Gwen pays the driver and he lets us out on the street. When I hop out, his eyes bug, and he accelerates faster than he should.

The doorman holds the door for me with no more than a frown. Maybe he already knows I'm a kitsune. It's bizarre padding across the marble floor of the lobby on paws. My fur bristles against people's stares. If only I knew an illusion for invisibility.

We climb into the waiting elevator. As soon as the doors click shut, Gwen turns to me. "I know you can't talk right now, but seriously, what happened? Did you just run off again without telling anyone? Or were you actually abducted this time?"

Obviously, she would be angry at me.

She exhales. "You can tell me later."

The elevator doors ding open. The thirty-eighth floor.

"Better be quiet," Gwen whispers. She fishes a key from her pocket. "I snuck out of here while your grandparents were still sleeping. They would go ballistic if they found me missing, too."

She opens the door and light spills into the hallway.

"Oh no," she mutters under her breath. "They woke up?"

My legs lock outside the doorway. I sniff the air, my nose twitching. No stink of dog—but the sweetness of jasmine tea.

"Is it safe?" Gwen whispers.

I'm not sure, but I step inside anyway.

The living room is empty. I creep along the wall and peer into the dining room. Michiko is pouring a cup of steaming tea for a stranger who kneels with his back to me. He murmurs his thanks and bends his head to sip. The light glints on his sleek iron-gray hair.

He beat me home.

Gwen slips off her shoes in the genkan and walks

ahead of me, her shoulders tense. She stands in the door-way of the dining room and clears her throat. "We have a guest?"

"Did we wake you?" Tsuyoshi leans into my view. He frowns at Gwen. "Why is there snow in your hair?"

"I ... went out," she says. "Who is he?"

But I already know. I don't need him to stand and gracefully bow to Gwen, to speak in that soft voice of his.

"Zenjiro Matsuzawa. And who do I have the plea-sure of meeting?"

She hesitates. "Gwen."

"We apologize for our guest's sudden arrival," Michiko says, and it's not clear whether she means Gwen or Zenjiro. "Please, everyone, sit and have some tea. It's a cold night."

Why is Zenjiro here? Why are they acting like it's okay?

Gwen steps into the dining room, and I duck back into the shadows. But it's too late. As the others return to the table, Zenjiro lingers, then strolls to the doorway and meets my eyes.

"Michiko," he says, "please pour another cup. Octa-vian is here."

seventeen

"Tavian?" Tsuyoshi clears his throat. "Are you certain?"

"Yes," Zenjiro says. "I would recognize him anywhere."

Before the yakuza boss can say anything to his advantage, I step into the room, feeling rather small as a fox. Michiko's hand shakes as she sets down her teacup. It tips over the edge of the table and shatters on the floor. She glares at the widening puddle as if it was the teacup's fault, then climbs to her feet and walks to me.

"I found him," Gwen says. "In Shinjuku Gyoen."

"As I suspected," Zenjiro says.

I bare my teeth. Oh, like this was all one big plan? Doubtful.

"But he's ..." Michiko squints at me. "He's a fox?"

"He's half-kitsune," Zenjiro says. "It's to be expected. Have you never seen him in his natural form?"

I glance at Zenjiro's face, and there's little more than mild surprise in his eyes. Isn't he disgusted that his only grandson is an animal right now? Isn't he going to sic his dogs on me?

Tsuyoshi stands behind Michiko, his hands resting protectively on her shoulders. "Change back, Octavian," he says, his voice deep and commanding—like that helps.

"He can't," Gwen says. "Not with everybody staring."

That's my cue to exit. I dart from the dining room and leap into my bedroom, shoving the door shut with my muzzle. The door opens again two seconds later, but it's Gwen.

She locks the door. "Okay. Some privacy."

Not for long. Not with Zenjiro out there.

Gwen sits on the floor next to me. "Are you really stuck?"

Even if I don't have anburojia in my blood, would it be impossible for me to make the change? I'm half-kitsune, half-human. I should be able to sidestep between my bodies easily.

I meet her gaze, then shut my eyes and push myself to transform. I can barely feel my humanity, like it's at the edge of my fingertips. I dig my toes into the carpet and arch my back. My heart drums a frantic beat. Pain rips through my spine, and I gasp.

"Tavian!" Gwen's voice is low, urgent. "Don't force it."

But I know I have to. I clench my jaw and claw my way out of my fox body, tearing my pelt away, shoving my fangs back where they belong. My skeleton grinds into a new shape. I groan and collapse on the floor. I wince when my raw skin rubs the carpet.

Skin. I'm human.

Gwen's hand grips my shoulder. "Are you okay?"

I pry open my eyes. "Yes."

It hurts to talk; it hurts to breathe. My ribs feel like they're squeezing my heart. I roll onto my back and try to massage away the pain. Gwen kneels beside me, her face pale.

"I think it's getting better," I say, which is only partway a lie.

Sourness rises in my mouth, and I swallow repeatedly. My stomach didn't seem to like the transformation. But then again, neither did the rest of my body. Wincing, I sit upright.

"What happened?" Gwen says. "Tell me what—"

I draw her into a tight embrace. She heaves a shuddering sigh and slides her hands over my back.

"I'm sorry," I say. "I tried to call you earlier and tell you where I was."

"Why didn't you?"

"My psycho kitsune mother smashed my cell phone and practically kept me hostage for my own safety."

Gwen withdraws, her face scrunched. "Seriously?"

I mirror her expression. "Yukimi can be overprotective."

"So you went to her."

"Yes." I keep my voice carefully even and unemotional. "I let her bring me to her hideout, and I tried to get as much information out of her as possible before I got away."

"Did she tell you how to shapeshift without hurting yourself?"

I hesitate. "She gave me something for the pain."

"Something." Gwen thins her lips. "Are we talking aspirin?"

"No."

"Okay. So this 'something' masks the pain you've been feeling?"

"Yes."

"What if you're hurting yourself without knowing?"

"That has occurred to me." I climb to my feet and my knees click unsettlingly. "Let me get dressed."

"Sure," Gwen says. "Not that I mind seeing you naked."

I roll my eyes at her. I'm rewarded with a sliver of a smile. She tosses me the clothes from her backpack and I start tugging them on. I'm still shaky, but I manage to hide it.

"Yukimi isn't our problem right now," I say. "Zenjiro is."

"Zenjiro?" Gwen says. "Do you know what he wants from us?"

My jaw tight, I finish buttoning my shirt. "From me."

"What do you—?"

Someone raps on the door and we freeze, staring at each other.

"May I come in?" Michiko says.

I blow out my breath and open the door a crack, just in case she's not alone. But there's nobody but my grandmother. I let her in, and she keeps her gaze latched on me, as if I might disappear.

"You're back," Michiko says, her eyes glistening.

"I am." I lock the door behind her and lean against it. "Obāsan, when did *he* get here?"

"Shortly before you arrived," Michiko says quietly, in case he might overhear. "He said he wanted to discuss something with us, but he hasn't yet arrived at the purpose of his visit."

"I know why he's here," I say.

"Oh?" Gwen's eyes glow. "Is that something else Yukimi told you?"

I breathe steadily to slow down my pulse. "Yes, actually. Zenjiro Matsuzawa is the father of Akira Matsuzawa." I glance at Michiko to see if this registers on her face, but I can't tell what her expression means. "My father."

Gwen stares at me, unblinking. "Zenjiro is your grandfather?"

"My biological grandfather, yes."

Michiko tugs a tissue from her cardigan and dabs her eyes. "It will not be easy for Tsuyoshi to learn this."

I touch her on the shoulder. "Did you know?"

"It occurred to me. You look like family."

My stomach flip-flops. "He isn't family," I say fiercely.

Michiko nods, but she won't meet my gaze.

I grab the doorknob. "Let's go out there. I have some questions to ask him."

"Octavian." Michiko catches my arm. "Be careful what you say."

"I will."

I march out into the hall and make my way to the dining room. Tsuyoshi and Zenjiro kneel opposite each other, the glow from the lamps throwing their faces into craggy relief. They sip their tea and say absolutely nothing, and yet their eyes say it all—they want to get down to business, even if etiquette says otherwise.

Michiko takes her place kneeling beside the teapot, her face a perfect mask of civility. "Please, sit." She pours two cups of tea. "You, too, Gwen. The tea will warm you up."

I kneel by Zenjiro, ignoring the soreness of my muscles.

"Tavian," he says. "It wasn't so long ago that we last met."

"It wasn't," I say airily. "Though this time you seem to have come without your dogs."

Zenjiro lifts his teacup to his lips and sips with relish. "You must understand that inugami are not always the most disciplined of men." His gaze slides to the bandage on Michiko's arm. "As much as we might wish otherwise."

"Discipline is the duty of their master," Tsuyoshi mutters.

Michiko's mouth hardens and she shoots Tsuyoshi a look. A second later, she's back to her calm face. "Would anyone like some refreshments to go along with their tea?"

I know she's probably looking for an excuse to escape to the kitchen. "Yes, please," I say. "Thank you."

Michiko bows slightly and shuffles from the room.

I clear my throat. "They bit her. Were you aware of that?"

"My sincerest apologies." Zenjiro hesitates. "Medical treatments can be so expensive these days."

Gwen's eyes glimmer golden, and I can tell she's itching to talk.

"They can," Tsuyoshi says.

Michiko returns with a plate of *mochi*, confections made of rice flour and sweet red bean paste. She offers them first to Zenjiro, who takes one delicately and thanks her politely.

Delicately and politely. It grates on my nerves.

"The cost of your injury will be compensated," Zenjiro says.

Michiko's eyebrows flick upward. "Thank you."

She's *thanking* him? Because he's paying her medical bills after *his* filthy dogs bit her?

Michiko offers me the plate of mochi. When I take one, it crumbles beneath my fingers. I force myself to relax, and clean up the crumbs with a napkin. But I can't take much more of this.

"It has been unseasonably cold," Zenjiro says, "this year."

"It has." Tsuyoshi relaxes, like he's on familiar territory. "I expect—"

"Why are you here?" I look Zenjiro in the eye. "My apologies, I don't mean to be rude, but I'm afraid I'm going to have to be."

The yakuza boss sighs ever so slightly. "Americans."

"I was born here," I say. "In Hokkaido. But of course you knew that."

Zenjiro pauses. "You were not born in Hokkaido."

"Please, enlighten me," I say.

"Octavian," Michiko says, her voice quavering. "Perhaps we should not discuss such topics at the table."

Zenjiro clears his throat. "Unfortunately, it appears we must." He turns to me. "You were born on the thirtieth of October, in Ueno, Tokyo. At the temple in Ueno Park, in fact, with the help of the myobu. But your mother fled soon after on the train to Hokkaido, taking you with her. You won't remember; you were only a baby."

A shiver crawls down my spine. "How do you know this?"

"I did not know all of this until after the fact," he says. "But at a later point, the myobu were quite forthcoming."

"The myobu would help a...help you?"

Zenjiro nods. "They are generous with their aid."

Generous. Most likely he wrote a check for the restoration of the temple, just like Tsuyoshi did.

"What else do you know?" I say.

Zenjiro shrugs. "Only that your mother vanished once she reached Hokkaido. Only that your father followed soon after, and vanished there with her." His eyes gleam like crow's feathers.

I grip the edge of the table. "I know who my father is. Was."

"Your father?" Tsuyoshi rumbles. "Your father is Kazuki Kimura."

My throat tightens. "I know that. Dad is … my dad. But my biological father was Akira Matsuzawa. Yukimi told me."

"Matsuzawa?" Tsuyoshi's head snaps toward Zenjiro.

Zenjiro meets his eyes and nods slowly, a trace of a smile on his lips, as if he's checkmated his opponent.

The color drains from Tsuyoshi's face. Michiko refills his cup of tea and whispers something in his ear. He drinks all the tea in one gulp and sits there, staring wordlessly at Zenjiro.

"So that makes you my biological grandfather," I tell Zenjiro.

"It does," he says.

My voice rises. "But it doesn't explain what you want from me. Or why you're sending your dogs after me, or knocking on Tsuyoshi and Michiko's door in the middle of the night for a cup of tea."

Zenjiro's tone is cutting. "You are my only biological grandson."

"I'm half-kitsune," I say.

Yukimi's voice echoes in my mind. *Even though you are half-kitsune, Zenjiro will want you. Maybe especially because you are half-kitsune. He might find it useful.*

Zenjiro looks at me with heavy-lidded eyes. "I am very aware of that."

Tsuyoshi sucks in some air and it sounds like he's having trouble staying calm. "Have you come to demand that Octavian return with you? Because you are his blood relative?"

"No demands are necessary," Zenjiro says gently. "But the myobu have brought it to my attention that you are chronically ill and will not live much longer without treatment."

"So much for doctor-patient confidentiality," I say.

But my sarcasm seems lost on Zenjiro. Maybe yakuza bosses never laugh. He slides his hand over the tabletop, as if he means to touch me, but my fingers curl into a fist.

"But there is a cure," Zenjiro says. "And I am willing to help."

I bite back a laugh. "Why?"

"That is obvious."

I force myself to smile. "I appreciate your offer to help, but no thanks."

Zenjiro arches one eyebrow. "So you will turn to Yukimi for help."

"Not with your dogs following me," I say.

He drains the last of his tea. "That won't be necessary. There are more subtle ways to determine someone's location."

"So you know where she lives?"

Zenjiro simply pops another mochi into his mouth and chews.

My blood freezes in my veins. Junko. She saw Yukimi and me in Ozuru's yakitori restaurant, not very far from the location of the Lair. And I told her to tell Shizuka, who's apparently in cahoots with the yakuza. How could I have trusted the myobu?

"Do you trust Yukimi?" Zenjiro says.

I sip my tea to stall for time. "Somewhat."

"I am sure it has occurred to you," he says, "what happened after your father followed your mother to Hokkaido."

I shake my head. "I was a baby. Like you said, I don't remember anything."

His gaze locks onto mine. "Akira never returned."

I force myself not to look away from his black eyes, even as cold sweat slicks my skin. My stomach tightens against the sick, sick feeling that I know the truth.

Tsuyoshi coughs quietly.

Zenjiro unfolds his long legs and stands. "I must go. Thank you."

"Nothing else to say?" I ask.

"It's late," he says. "I'm afraid I have already been too much of an imposition on your grandparents."

There's just the slightest emphasis on that last word.

"Goodnight," Zenjiro adds, his gaze on me. "Until we meet again."

Before the flood of inevitable questions, I speak first. "Let me explain."

We all return to the table, and with a lot of jasmine tea to wet my mouth, I tell them what happened: Yukimi, the inugami, the anburojia, the photo of my father, everything. Tsuyoshi and Michiko listen politely, nodding, not asking questions. But Gwen makes little noises of surprise or impatience, and I can tell she wants to talk.

"And then Gwen and I made it back here," I say.

"Your grandmother and I are glad that you are safe." Tsuyoshi's voice sounds scratchy. "It must be difficult to learn what you have. We understand if you don't wish to talk about it further."

I shrug. "I've barely had time to think about it, to be honest."

"Tavian." The word bursts out of Gwen. "What are you going to do? Zenjiro knows where Yukimi is."

My stomach lurches. "He could be bluffing."

"What if he isn't?"

Tsuyoshi interrupts. "Yukimi can take care of herself."

But she doesn't know the inugami are coming, and that the Lair is no longer safe. I rake my fingers through my hair and grab fistfuls of it, twisting until it hurts. I thought I needed to come here, to help my grandparents, but in fact Yukimi is in the most danger right now. What will the inugami do to her?

"I need to warn her," I say.

"Do you have her phone number?" Michiko says.

"No, of course not."

"Email address?"

I glance at my grandmother and see the challenging look in her eyes. "I know you don't want me to go back there, but I can't let them hurt her."

"Yukimi can take care of herself," Tsuyoshi repeats.

"She doesn't know they're coming!" I'm shouting, I don't mean to, and I take a deep breath. "Sorry."

"Tavian," Gwen says. "Can't you enter her dreams?"

"You think she's sleeping right now? I ran away from her in the middle of the city. She must be looking for me."

"Then let her find you," Michiko says, folding her hands on the table.

I grit my teeth. "Zenjiro is watching this place."

"Octavian." Tsuyoshi stands from the table. "I will call Kazuki and your mother and let them know you are safe."

I wince. "You told them already?"

Tsuyoshi's face darkens. "You were missing for a

night and a day. And most of this night. They deserve to know."

"All right." I rise to my feet. "Let me talk to them."

He hands me the phone, and I retreat to my bedroom.

Gwen lingers in the doorway. "What are you going to tell them?" she says in a low voice.

I rub my face with my hands. "I don't know, Gwen. I just got back here after running like hell, and now I find out I was running the wrong way."

She shuts the door behind her. "You can't go back out there."

"What else am I going to do?"

"You think shapeshifting back into a fox is a good idea?"

I make a noise between a growl and a sigh, then slump on the floor against the bed. Gwen sits by me and I wrap my arm around her shoulders. Some of the tension melts from my muscles. I kiss her, softly at first, then harder, until she sighs against my lips.

"Don't leave," she says, "without taking me."

I look into her eyes, see how they glimmer from hazel to gold. "So you do want to go?"

"Not without a plan."

"Of course." I squint. "You're actually being less reckless than I am? This astounds me."

She bites back a smile. "Stop it. You're too tired to be sarcastic."

"Maybe." I stare at the phone in my hand. I know

the numbers I need to press, but I don't want to. "Wait a minute…"

"What?"

I run over to my luggage and unpack the little blue netbook my dad insisted that I bring, even though I told him I'd be more likely sketching than Photoshopping on this trip.

"There's wifi in here, right?" I ask Gwen.

She shrugs. "I think so."

I boot the netbook and sit on the edge of my bed, joggling my leg as I wait for it to load. "Come on…"

Gwen peers over my shoulder. "What's your brilliant idea?"

"I don't have Yukimi's phone number, but I can get somebody else's. Think about it. Who's known Yukimi for a long time, trusts her with his life, and also runs a restaurant?"

She only has to think about it for a second. "The oni. Ozuru."

"Bingo." I type as fast as I can on the miniature keyboard. "I remember the name of the place…the Fat Oni. Let's see if I can pinpoint an address and phone number."

"Do you think they're still open?"

"It's a yakitori bar kind of thing." I click on links for food reviews, directories, maps, until— "There!"

Gwen hands me back the phone and I punch in the number.

It rings, rings, then picks up. "The Fat Oni, how may I help you tonight?" A woman's voice.

"Is Ozuru there?" I say.

"Ozuru?" The woman hesitates. "He's busy right now. Can I take a message for you?"

"It's urgent. Please, I need to talk to him."

"And your name is?"

"Tavian."

I hear nothing but the background din of conversation and the sizzling of yakitori on the grill. Then, the sound of the phone changing hands. "Hey, this is Ozuru, who am I talking to?"

"Tavian. Yukimi's son."

A long pause. "How did you get this number?"

"Google."

"Kit, it's one in the morning." Ozuru sounds gruff. "What are you calling for? Does your mother know about this?"

"No, she doesn't." I talk quickly before he can cut me off. "You need to find her, Ozuru. You need to tell her that the inugami are coming for her, and that the Lair isn't safe anymore."

"What the hell are you talking about?"

I blow out my breath. "Zenjiro Matsuzawa tracked me down. And he strongly implied he knows where the Sisters are."

"God damn it." Ozuru sighs. "I'll go find her. Thanks for the tip."

"And tell her I'm safe right now," I add. "With my grandparents."

"Will do."

He hangs up, and I set down the phone.

"So he's going?" Gwen says, who was eavesdropping.

I nod. "Hopefully he'll find her in time." I stare at the phone in my lap. "Now I need to call my parents."

eighteen

Alone in my bedroom, I sit on my bed, my back against the wall, and stare out the window at the city. The phone rings once. Twice. Three times. Maybe it will go straight to voicemail, and I won't have to—

"Hello? Do you have news about Tavian?"

It's Mom.

A lump forms in my throat. I swallow hard. "It's me, Mom."

"Tavian! Are you all right? Where are you? Let me get your father, he was just heading out to work…"

It must be early morning there. I shut my eyes and try to imagine my dad chugging down coffee and blundering into things while reading a book with breakfast, and my mom opening all the blinds to let the gray overcast light of morning inside.

There's a click and scuffling sound. "Tavian?" It's Dad.

"I'm here," I say. "I'm back with Tsuyoshi and Michiko. I'm safe."

"What happened to you?" Dad says. "Where did you run off to?"

"I didn't run off," I say. "I found Yukimi."

Dead silence. I use this opportunity to tell them everything I told my grandparents. It's bizarre describing my biological mother to Mom, or telling Dad that my biological father was yakuza. I hear a little intake of breath from both of my parents when I tell them that Zenjiro Matsuzawa has been hounding me.

"I don't know what Zenjiro wants." I laugh bleakly. "To adopt me?"

"That's ridiculous," Mom says.

"I mean, I'm his grandson," I say. "His only grandson. But I'm also the son of a nogitsune they've been hunting for years. Yukimi told me that Zenjiro might find me 'useful.'"

"That's how yakuza operate," Dad says, his tone thick with cynicism. "I don't know much about Zenjiro in particular, but he likely wants to use you as leverage against Yukimi and kitsune in general."

Mom exhales in a hiss. "I don't care who Zenjiro thinks he is," she says, getting all fierce. "I have an attorney friend or two who can sue him into submission. Hell, I'll even do it myself."

"Mom!" I groan. "Don't sue anybody."

"Zenjiro can't be trusted," Dad says.

"Obviously," I say.

Dad clears his throat. "Even if he's your grandfather by blood."

I grimace. "I know."

"It's too dangerous there," Mom says. "Tavian, you're coming home. Don't worry, we can change your ticket so you can fly home before New Year's; you'll be safer back in the U.S."

A flock of anxieties flutters through my stomach. "I can't. Not without the naming ceremony. I need Yukimi's blood, and her true name. And since I can't have the blood of Akira, I need one of his bones."

"So a little bit of DNA and some mumbo-jumbo is going to cure you?" Dad says, not even bothering to disguise the skepticism in his voice. "Sounds like modern medicine to me."

I grit my teeth. "Maybe I'm a mumbo-jumbo kind of person."

"Tavian, ignore your father," Mom says. "Could you explain the naming ceremony again, for me?"

"Well, Shizuka would perform a ritual, and grant me my true name. With my true name, I should be able to control my kitsune magic and stop it from killing me. I know, it sounds frustratingly mystical. Shizuka didn't exactly give away any trade secrets."

"Okay," Mom says.

"I know you're not totally convinced," I say. "I'm not, either. But this is my only shot."

"We don't know that," Dad says. "We've been in touch with a doctor—"

"Dad!" I fight the urge to shout. "Let me try this."

Another long silence.

"I promise I'll keep in touch," I say. "And I'll try not to drop off the face of the earth. But I need to do this."

"Kazuki," Mom says, "he's old enough to make his own decisions."

Dad grumbles something that sounds like a tectonic plate moving.

"Please?" I say.

"Don't do anything stupid," Dad says.

I lower my head and sigh. "I won't. Thank you."

"Text me," Mom says. "Oh, your phone is broken, I remember. Well, buy a new phone and text me."

"I'll try to keep this one intact," I say dryly.

"We'd better go," Mom says. "We're going to be late to work soon. Good night, Tavian."

"Good night," I say. "Or rather, good morning."

Mom laughs a tired little laugh. "Love you!"

"Love you, too."

Dad grunts, his version of *love you*.

I hang up, then drop the phone. Exhaustion overtakes me, turning my bones to lead and my muscles to mush. I fall back onto my bed, spread-eagle, and exhale in a rush.

"Tavian?" Gwen whispers.

I pry open my eyes a crack. She's standing over me in her pajamas, wearing a blanket like a poncho.

"I heard some of that," she says. "You were talking kind of loud."

"Sorry," I say. "I'm done now. You can sleep."

"It's too cold." With that as her excuse, Gwen crawls into bed next to me. "Let me steal some of your warmth."

I wriggle out of my jeans and toss them over the edge of the bed. The two of us snuggle together under the blankets and I tug her closer, feeling the length of her body against mine.

"How are you feeling?" Gwen says.

I think for a moment. "Bad?"

"That's not really what I meant."

I sigh. "Like an impostor."

Gwen props herself on one elbow to look at my face in the dim light. "What do you mean?"

"Like I shouldn't be here, with Michiko and Tsuyoshi."

"Why?"

I swallow back the bitterness. "I'm not really their grandson."

"That's not true. They adopted you."

"It doesn't matter who adopted me. I'm the son of a nogitsune and a yakuza. I might as well paint a big red target on my forehead and go stand out in the middle of the street."

"Hey. No being melodramatic," Gwen says.

"If I knew this was going to be such a melodrama, I don't think I would have ever set foot in Japan again."

"You aren't glad you found Yukimi? Or learned about your father?"

I stare heavenward, my eyes tracing patterns in the darkness. "Not glad," I say. "But I needed to know."

Gwen snakes her arms around me and squeezes me. "You're going to get your true name. And then we're going to go home, and this will all be a story we can tell people together."

My eyes sting, my throat burns. "I hope so," I whisper.

Seconds slip into minutes. Gwen's breathing deepens and her arms slide away from me, limp with sleep. I close my eyes and will my breathing to slow, but I can't fall asleep.

I'm afraid of my own dreams.

I hunch over the bathroom sink and cough so hard my ribs ache. The taste of iron lingers on my tongue. I swish water in my mouth, then spit. Red swirls on the ivory porcelain.

I freeze, my hands gripping either side of the counter. Blood?

There's a soft rap on the door. "Tavian?" It's Gwen.

"I'll be out in a minute," I say.

I open my mouth wide to see if maybe I bit my

tongue, but I can't see any wounds. The tickle in my throat starts scratching again, and I gulp another cup of water to try to drown it.

"Are you okay?" Gwen says. "I heard you coughing."

"Sorry," I say. "I didn't want to wake you up."

I wipe my mouth on a tissue and throw away the evidence, then open the door and try to look okay for Gwen's benefit. She doesn't seem convinced, her face pale enough to lose her freckles again.

"You don't look okay," she says.

There's no point in lying, is there?

"It's the anburojia," I say. "You were right, it was masking the pain of shapeshifting."

She comes into the bathroom and shuts the door behind her. "Tavian?"

"What?"

"How sick are you?"

My hands tremble as I fill my glass for another drink of water. I sip slowly, then start coughing halfway through, sputtering into the sink. Blood, unconcealable evidence of my body failing.

Gwen's eyes grow huge. "That's not good."

I wipe my mouth off on another tissue. "You think I should wake up my grandparents? I don't want to go back to that useless hospital. Those doctors didn't know anything about kitsune."

"I don't know. Do you want to wake them up, or should I do it?"

"You? Please?"

She sighs, then stalks out of the bathroom.

When my grandparents arrive, I get the same huge eyes.

"Come on," Michiko says. "Lie down in bed. Tsuyoshi, help him."

I shake my head. I'm not about to lean on my elderly grandfather for support. I can hobble to the bedroom myself. My head feels like a balloon on a string, floating high above my body. I lie down on my bed and watch the room spin like a demented merry-go-round.

"What happened to him?" Tsuyoshi asks Gwen.

"I don't know," she says. "I woke up when he started coughing, and then I saw him coughing blood—"

"Coughing blood?" Michiko's face looks ashy. "How much?"

"Not very much," I say hoarsely. "And by the way, I can still talk. I'm not a total invalid, you know."

Tsuyoshi glowers at me like too much sarcasm is bad for my health.

"We think it was the fruit," Gwen says. "The anburojia."

Michiko looks to Tsuyoshi. "We should call the myobu. See if Shizuka will come this early in the morning."

Tsuyoshi glances at his watch. "It's nearly dawn. She will come."

With another hefty donation to the temple, of course she will.

"We trust Shizuka?" I say. "We know she's working with Zenjiro."

Tsuyoshi doesn't even answer, just leaves the room.

Michiko sits beside me and pats my hand. "Sometimes," she says gently, "the best way to fight the yakuza is to not fight them at all. Shizuka will be able to help you with your sickness."

I stare at her. "So you're saying if we give up, we win?"

"You misunderstand me," Michiko says.

Clearly.

"The more you struggle," she says, "the more it will hurt."

I stare at her. "Are you saying that I should give myself up? Let the myobu hand me over to the yakuza? I don't know what Zenjiro wants from me, but I don't think it's good."

"If we believed Shizuka would betray you," Michiko says, her eyes sharp, "we wouldn't call her here."

"For enough of a price, she will," I point out.

Tsuyoshi returns, telephone in hand. "She will be here shortly."

Shortly turns out to be about twenty minutes. I spend that time hunched over in bed, wracked by another coughing fit, and try not to panic at the blood-speckled tissues in my hand. Gwen sits beside me, handing me tissues, her mouth set in a grim line.

Shizuka appears in the doorway to the bedroom. She's dressed in a storm-gray kimono—not a twelve-layered one, though—and has snowflakes in her tightly-pinned hair. Her eyes glint amber as she looks at me, so like Yuki-mi's that my heartbeat stutters. Then again, my heartbeat has been stuttering on its own lately.

"What can you do to help him?" Michiko says.

"Let me determine that." Shizuka's voice sounds as silky as ever. "Please, some privacy."

Michiko and Tsuyoshi bow—too low, if you ask me—and exit the room.

As Gwen walks past Shizuka, she looks at the woman with guarded fascination. But of course Gwen's never seen a myobu before, and she's always fascinated by new Others.

No matter how untrustworthy they might be.

As soon as we're alone, I swing my legs over the edge of the bed and sit up—a little too quickly. Darkness constricts my vision. I fight it, refusing to show any weakness on my face.

"You have worsened quicker than I expected," she says.

"Shizuka," I say, "I already know what's wrong. I ate some anburojia and shapeshifted when I shouldn't have."

"Anburojia?" Shizuka arches a delicate eyebrow.

"You know, the golden fruit that tastes bitter to humans but sweet to people like us, and enhances our magic."

"Supposedly," she says. "I believe the substance should be illegal."

"Illegal? Well, that's not really a surprise."

"Anburojia acts as a powerful stimulant to the mind,"

Shizuka says, "and possesses the ability to numb the body. In your case, it would merely mask the negative effects of your condition. Did Yukimi explain this to you before giving you the anburojia?"

"No." My face heats. "She said it would help me."

"And did she explain to you the nature of foxfire?"

"Foxfire? No." I pause. "And you never really did, either."

A thin smile touches Shizuka's lips. "True."

A cough claws its way up my throat, and I hurriedly swallow another glass of water. "I remember"—I gulp some air—"that you said foxfire was the same as a kitsune's magic."

"Yes. Or rather, foxfire is the expression of a kitsune's magic. Just as intelligence is the expression of your mind, and strength the expression of your muscles. All kitsune possess this talent, to varying degrees. But for a half-kitsune such as yourself, the physical limitations of your weaker body obstruct the expression of foxfire."

I frown. "Wouldn't that stop me from doing any magic?"

"You aren't human enough for that." Shizuka's eyes soften, until she's looking at me with something revoltingly similar to pity. "Your body is being eroded by the foxfire, like a rock too soft to channel the flow of a river. The river slows as its path becomes more and more winding, but it never stops until the rock has completely worn away."

"Okay." My stomach plummets. "So the anburojia was helping with…the eroding. Making me worse."

"Yes. Unfortunately."

I inhale deeply, ignoring how my ribs ache. "I still don't have anything for the ritual."

Shizuka takes a pouch of evening blue silk from her kimono. "Yukimi would not tell you her true name? Or give you her blood?" She tugs on the drawstrings of the pouch, and pulls out a vial of black liquid.

I rub the bridge of my nose. "I need to find her again."

"The ritual requires it."

"I know. I'm working on it." My stomach tightens into a knot. "Don't take this the wrong way, but I'm not sure I want you naming me."

Shizuka holds the vial of black liquid to her eyes, and shakes it. "Oh?"

"I want to name myself."

She meets my gaze. "That's unconventional."

"Is it impossible?"

Shizuka's eyes look like embers. "Do you know yourself?"

"Yes? Yes. I'm Octavian Kimura. I'm half-human, half-kitsune, and I'm going to die unless I can get my shit together."

"True," she says, "but not the whole truth."

"That's evasive."

"There is more to you than Octavian Kimura." Shizuka takes the empty glass from my bed stand. "Please wait while I fill this with water."

I squint at the vial of black liquid. "To dilute that?"

"It has a rather disagreeable flavor," she says. "The water will help."

I nod, and she slips from the room in a rustle of silk. She left the vial on my bed stand. I pinch it between my two trembling fingers and stare at it. The liquid inside looks like honey the color of midnight. I'm tempted to twist off the cap, but I return the vial.

Shizuka reappears with the glass of water. "A drop to help you sleep."

"I'm curious," I say. "A drop of what?"

"Medicine," she says.

I glance into her eyes, but I can't see a trace of a lie. "Were you there? At the temple, when I was born?"

Shizuka's gaze flickers to my face. "Yukimi told you?"

"No," I say. "Zenjiro did."

"Ah." Her face tightens, ever so slightly. "I was no more than a miko then, and you a newborn. Of course we would not recognize each other, now, but it is remarkable that we are reunited."

"Did you talk to Yukimi? Do you remember if she said anything?"

"No," Shizuka murmurs. "She was in a great deal of pain, and it was a long time ago."

I realize how overeager I sound, and I clench my jaw. She twists the cap from the vial, then presses the open vial into my palm. Her slender fingers feel cool against mine.

"It will help you sleep a dreamless sleep," she says.

Dreamless. The word sounds like a whispered promise. I can lie back and let the pain disappear.

I curl my fingers around the vial. "How much?"

"One drop," she says. "Any more, and it will be difficult to wake."

I open my mouth, tilt back my head, and shake a single drop onto my tongue. It tastes like burnt rose petals and the way rain smells on sizzling pavement in the middle of summer. It ripples down my throat and sets my head spinning, dizzying me.

"Rest," Shizuka says, "before you chase Yukimi again."

"Sure thing," I mumble, and my voice sounds slurred.

One moment, Shizuka is there, and the next, gone. Gwen takes her place. She looks down at me, her face blurry, rippling like the reflection of the moon in a black pond.

"You're pretty," I say.

"Thanks," she says. "Shizuka didn't skimp on the medicine, did she?"

I shake my head, my thoughts sloshing around in my skull. "I'm sleepy."

Gwen sighs. "You're not uncomfortable sleeping in your jeans?"

I close my eyes. She crawls into bed beside me, and I feel the warmth of her body mingling with mine. She says something, but I'm already too far away. Emptiness laps at the edge of my consciousness. If this is what death feels like, maybe death isn't so bad.

When I wake, it's a lighter sort of darkness. Evening, not night.

I drift in a pleasant daze as I stare out the window, admiring the fading gleam of the sun on the skyscrapers of Tokyo. Lights glimmer in the darkness like thousands of fireflies. A white veil of cloud drifts past the window, blocking my view. I frown. Hopefully the wind will pick up speed. But the cloud lingers, shifting as it hangs.

A face appears from the mist. Not Akira, but Yukimi.

Her lips move, and I hear her voice in my head. *Tavian.*

I sit bolt upright, black out, and almost fall back down again. My vision returns, and I see the translucent image of Yukimi hanging like a ghost outside the window. Like a ghost. Is she …?

I will wait for you to come to me, she whispers soundlessly.

nineteen

My dry tongue sticks to the roof of my mouth and I swallow, trying to summon up some spit. "Okay."

She can't be a ghost. That's an illusion, right? An illusion.

"What's okay?"

Gwen's voice startles me. She's standing in the doorway, her paranormal studies textbook tucked under one arm. She's staring right at me, but doesn't seem to see the cloud-Yukimi floating outside the window, behind my head.

"Finally awake?" Gwen says.

I don't know if I'm totally awake, to be honest. Maybe

I'm still dreaming—but of course I had a dreamless sleep, a sleep where Yukimi couldn't reach me or talk to me…

I turn back to the window, but the cloud-Yukimi is gone.

"Tavian…?" Gwen says slowly. "You seem kind of jumpy."

"She was there." My voice is ridiculously scratchy, so I clear my throat. "Yukimi, outside my window."

"Can she fly?"

Gwen's sarcasm wakes me up like a cold splash of water. I must sound like a raving lunatic, still under the effects of the medicine—the sleeping potion, whatever—that Shizuka gave me.

"Of course not," I say. "She sent an illusion."

I swing my legs over the edge of my bed and experimentally put some weight onto my feet. My muscles feel like noodles, but they don't seem to be collapsing out from under me at this point.

"An illusion of what?" Gwen says, her hands on her hips.

"Herself. She wants me to go outside," I say. "She's waiting."

Her eyes flare. "How do you know this isn't a trap?"

"Who else could craft an illusion like that?"

"I don't know, Shizuka working for the yakuza? Or maybe Yukimi being tortured into helping them?"

"Point taken."

Gwen grabs her coat. "I'm going with you. Backup."

"Thanks, super ninja pooka."

She sighs in exasperation. "Don't you ever get tired of cracking terrible jokes? Even when you look like an invalid?"

A smile creeps onto my face. "No."

"You do realize it's six o'clock," Gwen says. "Michiko will be back any minute. She just went to the grocery store to grab a few things for dinner, and Tsuyoshi insisted on driving her."

My smile wilts. "They're still out there? Alone?"

"Tavian, I bet your grandparents are tougher than you think." She coils a scarf around her neck. "Besides, if Zenjiro is trying to play nice now, I doubt he's going to hurt them. He's after you."

"That makes me feel so much better," I say.

"Let's hurry," she says, "and come back before they do."

I nod, and we both leave the condo. On the elevator ride down, I keep glancing at my reflection.

"I *do* look like an invalid," I mutter. "With the hollows under my eyes, and the whole pasty-skin look."

"Don't worry," Gwen says, "it won't last forever."

I can tell she's trying to cheer me up, but I'm not sure it's going to work. If I don't find Yukimi, I'm history. Not to mention I have no idea where Akira lies buried.

The elevator doors ding open and we hurry through the lobby.

"Did she say where to meet?" Gwen asks.

I shake my head.

But then, from the corner of my eye, I see a wisp of fog curling into a beckoning finger. It wants me to go into an alley across the street. I grab Gwen's hand and dart through the crosswalk.

At the end of the alley, a dark figure huddles.

"This looks suspicious," Gwen hisses, her eyes glowing.

"Yukimi?" I call.

"Who's with you?" It sounds like Yukimi.

I waver at the entrance of the alleyway. "Gwen. My girlfriend."

"You were supposed to come alone."

I walk nearer to her, my night vision adjusting. She's wrapping a bandage over her left calf muscle. Blood seeps through the gauze and she hisses with pain, baring feral teeth.

Acid rises in my throat. "You got bitten."

She nods. "Damn thing won't stop bleeding."

"Did you get bitten as a fox?" Gwen says, her eyes sharp with curiosity. "I'm also a shapeshifter, actually."

Yukimi glances at Gwen as if seeing her for the first time. "Really."

"She is," I say. "You never asked."

"Yes," Yukimi says, "I got bitten as a fox. Those dogs must be getting faster, because I doubt I'm slowing down."

I don't bother to point out how fatigue adds years to her face.

"We can help you," I say, "if you come inside—"

"No." Yukimi's eyes burn with a feverish light, like those of a cornered animal. "It's safer outside. I barely escaped from the Lair after Ozuru warned us the inu-gami were coming."

"Then why did you come here?" I say.

She knots the bandage with a savage yank, then scoops up a handful of snow and cleans the blood off her fingers. "I don't have much longer before they catch me and punish me."

"Punish you?"

She reaches into the pocket of her leather jacket and pulls out two tickets. "The night train from Ueno to Sapporo leaves at seven o'clock. We need to move now if we want to catch it."

Sapporo, Hokkaido. My childhood home. The heart of my memories.

I stare at the tickets, then take a deep breath. "Tonight?"

"Yes." Gingerly, Yukimi rolls her jeans down over the bandage.

"I don't see how we can go back to hiding in Hok-kaido."

"No." She fixes me with her gaze. "This is for your true name. You will need at least one of Akira's bones for the ritual."

I feel like I might throw up. "Right. We're going to dig them up?"

"Of course," she says. "They are buried, after all."

I sway on my feet and Gwen grips my wrist. "Tavian," she says. "This is what you need, to get better."

I stare at her. "You think this is a good idea?"

Gwen thins her lips. "Not a good idea, but necessary."

Yukimi walks to me and touches the back of my hand, gently, like the brush of a bird's wing. Her amber eyes look deeper than I've ever seen them before. "My time on the run is almost up. I would rather know that you are not nameless and doomed to die."

A shudder passes over my spine, and I take a ticket from her.

"There are only two tickets," Yukimi says, with a glance at Gwen.

Gwen looks at her with a challenging glint in her eyes, then takes a deep breath and nods. Yukimi retreats further into the alley, and I notice her motorcycle parked in the shadows.

"Tavian," Gwen says.

She steps into my arms, and we kiss. When she pulls back, she looks into my eyes and mouths some words.

I'll follow you.

I nod, very slightly, so that Yukimi doesn't see.

Of course Gwen wouldn't be content waiting around in Tokyo while I go on what might be the most important journey of my life. Knowing her, she'll probably shapeshift into a bird and fly overhead.

"Take this." Gwen presses her cellphone into my hand. "Since you don't have one."

Text me, Mom said. Maybe I will.

I slip it into my pocket. "Thanks. Might be useful."

The motorcycle rumbles to life, and Yukimi climbs on. "Let's go."

I climb on behind her, and we rumble from the alley.

Gwen pretends to wave goodbye, but she doesn't look nearly as sad as she should. I keep my face blank. I glance at the main road, then back at Gwen, and she's already gone.

Yukimi tears through the streets of Tokyo, only braking so she doesn't run red lights—I'm sure police on our tail would slow us down. Above us, I glimpse a gray-winged bird soaring overhead, swerving between the rooftops: a great horned owl. Not the most subtle thing on Earth, Gwen. But Yukimi never looks away from the road.

We park outside Ueno Station as the sky lingers in that shade between blue and black. I hop off the motorcycle and stumble, still a bit wobbly, and Yukimi grimaces as she steps onto her wounded leg.

"We both should really be in a hospital," I say.

"No time for that," Yukimi says briskly. She chains her motorcycle to a lamppost, muttering, "If anyone tries to steal this while I'm gone, I'll kill them when I come back. If I come back."

"When," I say.

We descend into the fluorescent-lit underground of Ueno Station, threading our way through the crowd. A small cluster of people wait on a platform at one end of the station.

"We're taking the sleeper train," Yukimi says. "The Hokutosei."

I vaguely remember "Hokutosei" as the name of a constellation. The Big Dipper, I think. How poetic.

A shrieking whistle echoes down the tunnel. People lug their luggage closer to the edge of the platform. I glance around, looking for Gwen the owl, but I don't see any animals down here.

"We don't have much stuff," I say. "Compared to everybody else."

Yukimi's hair fans in the coming wind. "We won't stay long."

A midnight blue train with gold stripes coasts into the station, wheels singing like a wet finger on a wineglass. It has a sort of boxy charm about it, the kind of thing Gwen would think is cute if we were actually on vacation like we're supposed to be. Where *is* Gwen?

The doors to the Hokutosei open. People start climbing onto the train. Yukimi nudges my elbow, then leads me to one of the cars. We file along the narrow hallway, brushing past rows of curtained windows. Yukimi slides open the door to an immaculate but tiny room with twin beds. Sheets lie in neatly folded squares at the foot of each bed, and blue-and-white *yukata* pajamas lie on our pillows.

I hesitate in the doorway of the room. "Looks nice."

Gwen must be coming. Maybe she already made it onto the train—but how will she know which room is ours?

Yukimi slides the door shut behind me and slings off her backpack. The Hokutosei shudders gently, then begins to accelerate. A conductor raps on the door, bows politely, and checks our tickets.

Over his shoulder, through the open door, a tiny tan moth flutters in. I hold my breath and try to look causal. The moth darts overhead and lands on the curtains, blending in perfectly. Damn, Gwen's been getting better with the whole shapeshifting thing lately.

The conductor bows, and Yukimi locks the door behind him.

"We're safe for the next sixteen hours," she says. "I didn't smell any inugami while boarding. Did you?"

I shake my head, trying not to look directly at Gwen the moth.

Yukimi sighs. "This could have been a nice trip to Hokkaido."

"Have you been back?" I say. "Since we…separated?"

"Separated" being the nicest way to say it.

"No," she says.

Yukimi's face is the color of ivory yellowed by age. She limps over to her bed, kicks off her boots, and grabs her wounded leg to help swing it onto the bed. Her eyes tighten with pain.

I perch on the edge of my bed. "Do you need help?"

"No."

She rolls up the left leg of her jeans. Blood blooms like a ragged red flower on her bandage. She swears and starts to unwind it. Fresh blood leaks through the gauze.

"You shouldn't do that," I say, "or it will keep bleeding—"

"I know what I'm doing," she snaps.

"Fine. You don't want my help."

She meets my gaze, her eyes burning. "You're sicker than I am. Lie down. Get some sleep."

I ignore her, and keep staring as she takes the bandage off.

A crescent of torn skin glistens red on her calf. Blood seeps from the wound, trickling down her ankle. She yanks open her backpack and pulls out a wrapped bandage and a tube of medicine.

"I'm going to kill Katashi," she says through clenched teeth.

"Katashi did that to you?"

"That dog has been after me ever since I took his wife from him."

I nod. "I remember." My face heats. "In your dream."

She concentrates on squeezing a thick white cream onto her forefinger, then daubing it directly onto the wound. "You surprised me," she says. "When you entered my dream."

"By accident," I point out.

"Still." Her toes curl as she rubs the cream in. "You have potential."

"Thanks," I say.

Yukimi tears open the bandage wrapper with her teeth, then starts wrapping it around her leg. When she's done, she lies back against the bed, her eyes shut, her face ashy.

"Are you all right?"

"Yes," she says.

After a moment, she opens her eyes. "I'm going to

wash this gunk off my hands. The bathroom is just down the hall. I won't be gone long." She gives me a don't-go-anywhere look.

As soon as she's gone, I peel off my clothes and slip on the yukata. It's comfortable cotton, and it's making me sleepy. I crawl under the sheets and flick off the light by my bed.

I yawn. "Shizuka's medicine probably hasn't worn off yet."

Gwen the moth flutters over to the curtain by my bed.

"Are you okay staying a moth for sixteen hours?" I say. "That's how long it's going to take to get to Hokkaido."

She flexes her wings upward. I'll take that as a yes?

Yukimi returns, flicks off her light, and collapses into bed without even undressing. She feels the yukata under her head and chucks it to the foot of the bed. Clearly pajamas don't suit life on the run.

"Good night," she mutters.

"Night," I say.

I wait until Yukimi's breathing deepens into soft snoring, then grab my jeans from the floor, find the borrowed cellphone, and shield its glow from Yukimi with my hand. When I hit a button, it beeps, and I muffle the phone under my pillow. I've never used this phone before, but I figure out how to bring up the text message menu quickly enough.

Slowly, I type out a text.

Safe on train to hokkaido with yukimi, love Tavian.

I don't want to risk waking Yukimi with unnecessary beeps from punctuation and capitalization. That's good enough. I punch in Mom's number and hit send, then hide the phone under my pillow.

Yukimi whispers so softly it takes me a moment to piece it into words.

"I'm sorry."

I stare at the shape of her in the darkness, my spine rigid, too afraid to ask her what she should be sorry for.

After a small eternity, I whisper, "Yukimi?"

She says nothing.

I know she can't hear me, but I say it anyway. "I'm sorry, too."

Gwen flutters from the curtain and lands on my cheek like a soft kiss. I close my eyes, sinking toward unconsciousness.

Blood red leaves drip into frostbitten air. Brittle grass crunches beneath my feet. I walk along a gravel path lined with wild chrysanthemums—white chrysanthemums, for the dead.

The trees hiss in my ears. *What is your name?*

"Tavian," I say.

What is your name?

I try again. "Octavian Kimura."

Your name? Your name? Your name?

My ears ache from all this echoing, and I cover them with my hands. There's something wrong with this forest…it feels empty, when I know there should be someone here.

"Where are you?" I call.

A gust of leaves swirls through the trees and coalesces into the shape of Shizuka in a crimson kimono. She glides to me, her eyes glowing amber, the wind stirring the fur of her tail.

"You are not ready," she says.

I shake my head. "I am."

"You should not be here."

Frowning, I advance on her and touch her arm. It crumbles into leaves, and Shizuka disappears into the wind. I back away, staring at my hands, not knowing what I did wrong.

Farther into the trees, I hear a familiar man's voice.

"Where is it?"

I push deeper into the forest, my footsteps nearly silent.

"Nowhere," a woman says. Yukimi.

Ahead, a thicket of dry grass sways in the wind, taller than my head. I drop down and press myself low to the ground. Beyond the crosshatching of grass, ragged black hair flies in the wind. I crawl nearer on my hands and knees, my hands crunching dead leaves.

Yukimi and Akira stand opposite each other. Her

face looks creased by exhaustion—but not the permanent creases of age, and no white streaks her hair. He wears a mud-flecked suit and his shoulders sag with fatigue, but his black-eyed stare never leaves her eyes.

"I know you hid it," Akira says, his voice taut. "It. A boy or a girl?"

Yukimi stares at him with a perfectly blank face. "A boy."

"Let me see him."

"No."

Akira lunges toward her, and in one swift motion grabs her wrists. "You can't hide him from me forever. You thought you could come here to Hokkaido, and I wouldn't follow—"

"I knew you would follow," she says calmly. "Let go of me."

"Tell me where you've hidden him. Yukimi, it's freezing out here. You can't leave a little baby outside in this weather."

"Let go of me." Her eyes glisten. "You're hurting me."

Akira's grip tightens around her wrists. "No."

Her eyes flash orange, and she clenches her hands. White light seeps between her fingers. Foxfire.

"Stop." He shakes her so hard her head jerks back. "Not on me."

"I will," she says through fangs, "unless you *let go of me.*"

Slowly, deliberately, Akira peels his fingers from her wrists. Even from here, I can see the red marks on her skin. My heartbeat pounds in my ears, and I feel the urge to hurt him.

"I know he's here. I know my son is here." Akira's voice cracks.

"You want to take him back to Tokyo," Yukimi says, and it isn't a question. "Back to Zenjiro."

"Zenjiro is his grandfather," Akira says. "He will be safe with his family."

"And I'm not his family?" she says, a mild expression on her face.

Akira's nostrils flare. "You aren't fit to be a mother."

"And you're fit to be a father?" She laughs, harshly. "Delusional."

He slaps her, knocking her head to the side. "Don't mock me."

Wind blows Yukimi's hair slantwise across her face, hiding her expression. "I wish things didn't have to end this way, Akira. I wish you could remember how we used to be together."

"Where is he?" He steps so close they almost touch.

"I will never tell you," she says.

Akira's face twists into something ugly, and he lunges. She seizes him in an embrace, her lips meeting his, and kisses him so fiercely he freezes in his tracks. Tension dissolves from the muscles in his shoulders, and he leans into her arms—slumps into her arms.

Yukimi steps to the side, and Akira falls to his knees.

My breath snags in my throat. I creep nearer to see what happened—but Yukimi's eyes glitter with wildness, and I don't want to get too close to her, or the bloody blade in her hand.

Akira speaks in a strangled voice. "You…bitch."

She looks down at him. "Don't let those be your last words."

He falls onto his side, then rolls onto his back, clutching the wound between his ribs. Tears slide from his eyes and cling to the curve of his jaw before dropping onto the leaves.

"You…" He gasps. "You broke my heart."

"I know," she says.

Akira tries to reply, but he coughs, blood bubbling from the corner of his mouth. He's shuddering violently now.

Yukimi kneels beside him. "I loved you," she says, "Akira."

He reaches for her, his fingers bloody, and she slides her fingers into his and holds his hand until his arm falls, limp, beside his side—and he must be gone, because he's not blinking anymore. She sits beside him, silent tears creeping down her face.

"Goodbye," she whispers.

Then, with her hands still covered in his blood, she climbs to her feet and walks into the grass. I stalk after her, my heart beating so fast I'm not sure it's beating at all. Yukimi crouches over a thin rivulet of a stream and washes the blood from her hands.

There's a whimper in the grass.

She bends, paws away a tangle of leaves, and picks

up a tiny gray-furred kit too small to open its eyes. It paws blindly at the air, squirming, and she holds it close to her breast.

"We're safe now." She kisses the kit. "Kogitsune."

A choked cry escapes my throat.

Yukimi looks up, and I scramble away backwards.

I can't let her see me. I can't let her know what I've seen. That I know the truth. That she killed my father.

twenty

"You're unusually quiet," Yukimi says.

It's half past six. We're sitting in the dining car of the Hokutosei, eating a breakfast of omelets and fish.

I shrug and take another chopstick-full of food. "Nervous."

"Understandable." Yukimi dabs her mouth with a napkin.

My stomach feels like worms have taken up residence. I'm not the least bit hungry. I stare out the window. Tokyo was getting a little salt-shaker snow, but Hokkaido is blanketed in white.

Hokkaido. A thrill zips down my spine.

I'm finally back in my childhood home. Although that phrase sounds much too cozy and nostalgic for the way I feel about it.

"We're getting off at Mori," Yukimi says. "Do you remember Mori?"

I shrug. "Probably. Where are we going from there?"

"Into the forest."

Do Akira's bones lie buried in the forest of her dream, mingled with twisted old tree roots in the dirt?

I shudder, then lower my voice. "How's your leg?"

Her face closes off again, like I knew it would. "Not now."

We finish our breakfast in silence.

"I'm going to take a shower," Yukimi says.

I perk up. "They have showers?"

"You needed to make a reservation last night."

"Oh." I poke at my omelet some more. "Okay."

Yukimi sighs. "But you can have my reservation."

I meet her eyes for the tiniest of glances. "Thank you."

When I head into the shower with a borrowed towel, I make sure to hide the little moth on the towel's underside. I lock the door to the changing room and start pulling off my clothes.

"The door's locked," I say.

The moth shivers, beating its wings rapidly, then flutters to the floor. It grows and grows into a giant moth, then blinks into the shape of a human—Gwen. She gasps and climbs to her feet.

"That was *bizarre*, Tavian," she says.

"Not too loud," I say in a low voice.

"I don't think I've ever shapeshifted for so long," she whispers. "My brain was starting to get all mothy."

I nod. It's distracting to stand so close to her in such a tiny space. She's totally naked, of course, and brushing against me in a way that would be more than welcome at any other time.

"We're getting off the train soon," I say. "At Mori."

"What's in Mori?"

I stare at the pattern of tiles on the floor. "My father's grave."

"That's not what I—Tavian, are you okay?"

I shuck off the rest of my clothes, then step into the shower and hit the button for hot water. Eyes closed, I tilt my face toward the spray and let it wash away the tears I know must be on my face.

Gwen slips in after me and hugs me.

"She killed him," I whisper. "My mother killed my father."

"How do you know?" Gwen's voice sounds odd, like she's already suspected this, or thinks it's obvious.

"I slipped into her dream last night."

She withdraws from me and smoothes her wet hair from her face. "So you aren't sure if it was a memory."

I scrub my face, hard. "It has to be."

"Well." Gwen takes a deep breath. "You'll have to ask her yourself."

She looks so miserable for me that I draw her into a tight embrace. I bury my face in her wet curls and concentrate on the realness of her skin against mine. She sighs, and I kiss her neck, her cheek, her lips. We stand together, wordless, beneath the water.

And it's almost a moment where I can forget.

I recognize the trees, even beneath their draperies of snow. And even if I didn't, the look of deep-buried sorrow in Yukimi's eyes would betray her. She walks by my side, limping through the snow.

"We're almost there," she says.

Above us, a crow glides over the frosted trees. Gwen managed to shapeshift again after eating smuggled food, though I'm still amazed at her endurance. Myself, I feel like lying down.

Yukimi's nostrils flare. She sniffs the wind, circles beneath the bare-branched trees. I could tell her that yes, this looks like the place in her dream. But I don't have the guts to do it.

"Here," she says.

"The ground is frozen," I say, stalling for time. "Obviously."

"And obviously, I brought a shovel and a strong young man with me."

I narrow my eyes. "Thanks, but no thanks."

Yukimi laughs, and I've never heard a more empty laugh. She drops to her knees and starts pawing the snow away with her bare hands, even though it must be at least three feet deep. I sigh and kneel beside her, scooping handfuls of snow out of the way.

My fingernails scrape dirt, and I stop digging. "Yukimi?"

She slings her backpack off, grabs a small shovel, and attacks the frozen earth. Acid rises in my throat. I can't look, I won't look—a crow caws hoarsely above me. I glance up, and I see a black comet streaking against the overwhelming whiteness. Gwen? She lands with a thump in the snow and struts toward me in that jerky sort of crow walk.

"What does she want?" Yukimi says.

"She?" I stare at her. "You know—?"

"It was obvious. She said she was a shapeshifter. And that crow doesn't smell like an ordinary crow."

Well, obviously my sense of smell isn't that good.

Gwen nips at my sleeve and tugs. I frown, and she hops back and shapeshifts. She huddles there naked, nothing left of her crow body except the imprint of her wings in the snow.

"Tavian," she says, her teeth chattering. "The inugami."

Yukimi straightens, the shovel clenched in her hand. "Where?"

"I saw them coming." Gwen hugs herself tight. "A pack of dogs."

I peel off my jacket and hand it to Gwen. "Here."

She shakes her head. "I'm changing back." Squeezing her eyes shut, she shrinks into the black body of the crow again. She pumps her wings, whirling snow around her, and takes flight. In a few minutes, she's gone again.

"We have to get out of here," I say to Yukimi.

"Wait." Yukimi bends over the ground—the grave—again. "Almost."

I swallow back the returning acid in my throat. I walk away from her and stand near a tree, scanning the snow for any sign of the advancing inugami. Wind whisks clouds away from the face of the sun, and the diamond glittering of the snow dazzles me.

"Tavian!"

I turn and see Yukimi kicking clods of frozen dirt and snow back onto the shallow grave. I hurry to help her. I'm not going to leave my father's bones out in the open for animals to gnaw on. No matter what kind of man he was. Was that a bone under my foot? I recoil with instinctive revulsion, before I can stop myself.

"You can go," Yukimi says. "Leave here while I distract them."

I meet her gaze. Sunlight shines sideways through her amber eyes.

"Forget it," I say. "I don't abandon people in the snow."

"I can't run quickly like this," she says, "and you can't create any illusions like that. You go. I'll stay."

I smooth the last of the snow over the grave, my hands numb. "No."

Yukimi growls. "I didn't do this just so those dogs could get you."

"Neither did I."

In the distance, cawing ricochets off the trees.

"They're coming." I grab Yukimi's arm and drag her after me. "Run!"

We struggle through the deep snow, our feet sinking deep, our breath clouding the air. Both of us are weak, like foxes who have run far too long already. But the dogs are coming.

"Let me stay," she says.

"I know why you want to stay," I say, my tone mocking, my throat tight. "You think everything will be better if you make your last stand by Akira's grave and die where he did."

She twists her hand from my grasp, her fangs bared. "That isn't true."

She's angry. Good. That will goad her into going faster.

"Then let's get out of here," I say.

A chorus of baying and barking rises above the trees. The sound injects adrenaline straight into my blood, and I break into a sprint. Yukimi keeps pace, but she's limping badly now.

"Wait," she gasps.

I turn back to see Yukimi bending double. In the forest ahead, the first of the inugami burst into the open. Katashi. His breath steams the frigid air; his tongue lolls from his mouth like he's craving another taste of Yukimi's blood. Yukimi grabs fistfuls of snow. Inky darkness seeps from her fingers into it. She tosses the black snow high into the air, and it blurs into a twisting thicket of brambles that hits the ground and grows into a wall of thorns impossible to run through.

Yukimi smiles thinly, her lips white. "Now we run."

We plunge onward while the dogs yelp and bark behind the brambles. I wonder how long the illusion will hold. I'm panting hard, my lungs and legs burning. We dart down a ravine, and I skid and fall. The barking sounds distant now, so I sit for a second to catch my breath. Yukimi drops down next to me, clutching her wounded leg.

Blood seeps through her jeans and stains her hand.

"We need to hide," I say. "Maybe as foxes—"

"No," she says. "It's too dangerous for you."

"I can't keep running."

Yukimi exhales in a puff of white. She reaches into the pocket of her jacket and hands me a scrap of white fabric knotted around a small, hard object—a bone. One of Akira's finger bones.

My mouth instantly turns sandstone dry. "Why are you—?"

"Shhh." She takes a switchblade from her belt, rolls up her sleeve, and slides the blade along her arm. "Damn it, where did I put that?" Bleeding, she fumbles in her jacket pocket.

"We can do this later," I say, my voice unsteady.

She shakes her head, then pulls out a tiny bottle and lets her blood drip inside. "You need this now."

"But—"

Yukimi presses the bottle into my hands. "Don't lose this."

She's leaving me. Again.

"No." My voice cracks. "You can't."

"I have to." She sighs. "And I have to tell you…"

That she killed Akira. But I already know.

Yukimi slips her hand behind my head and draws me closer, her breath hot in my ear. "My name is Kazahana."

My heart stops beating for a moment.

And then she's withdrawing from me, shedding her clothes and the last shreds of her humanity, disappearing into the shape of a fox. She comes to me, not limping so badly on four legs, and licks one of the tears from my face. Then she bounds into the forest.

Straight toward the inugami.

"Wait!" I say.

Yukimi runs as if she doesn't hear me. I scramble after her, but she's a red streak across the snow. I'm losing her.

"Okāsan!" I shout.

She doesn't stop.

I run, stumble, climb to my feet again. My throat's so tight it's choking me. Between the trees ahead, I see Katashi and Ushio and the rest of the dogs swerve in their tracks. They circle around the fox, trap her, fling themselves on her and drive her down.

A root sends me sprawling. I strain to lift my head.

I can't see her anymore. I can only see the dogs, and bloody snow.

I struggle to my feet and start limping forward. A black horse gallops from the trees. Gwen.

"They have Yukimi," I say. "We have to help her."

Gwen shakes her head, then tosses her mane and trots to me. She nudges me with her nose, away from the inugami and the blood. I try to sidestep, but she fixes me with a stare from her golden eyes, like a true pooka. *Ride.*

The fight slips from my muscles, and I climb onto her back, clinging to her with fistfuls of mane.

I look back. All I see is a little scrap of red on the snow.

On the last night of the year, I stand silently in a secret temple room while all of Tokyo celebrates Shōgatsu. I want to be out there with my grandparents and Gwen, listening for the temple bells, eating mochi and sipping tea together, but of course I can't. Instead I stand here, wearing a coarse cotton robe, and watch as Shizuka grinds my father's bone to dust. The silver embroidery on her smoke-gray kimono shimmers by the light of the candles. She purses her lips.

"Is it going to work?" I say.

Shizuka nods, and pours the bone-dust into a bowl of polished granite on the table. She trickles my mother's blood over the bone, then whispers a few words too old for me to understand.

"Your mother's name?" she says.

When I close my eyes, I can still see the way Yukimi looked at me that one last time. I try to speak, but my mouth is too dry, and the word comes out as a puff of air. I try again.

"Kazahana."

"A lovely name," Shizuka says quietly. "Do you understand it?"

I shake my head.

"A winter wind bringing snow." She tilts her head to one side. "Not that unlike the meaning of the name Yukimi."

Snow beauty.

A tiny smile tugs at my mouth. So she did always share a shadow of her true name—but I never knew it until now.

"And your father's name?"

My face goes blank again. "Akira Matsuzawa."

Nothing special about that. But he was who he was. I can't let myself think too much about it, not yet.

Shizuka lifts the bowl from the table. My heart starts pounding in my chest, and I force myself to take deep breaths. I already know what's going to happen, but I don't think I'm ready.

"Son of Kazahana and Akira, what is your name?"

I stare at the glinting flecks of granite in the bowl. I stare at the dark potion within, the essence of blood and bone blended with magic. I stare at Shizuka's eyes, looking for hints, for help.

I swallow hard. "I'm not sure who I am."

Shizuka remains motionless and silent.

"But I know who I want to be. I want to be someone who understands his past, but isn't defined by it. Someone who can make his own future." I pause, thinking. "And is good at art."

A corner of Shizuka's mouth twitches. "Taste it first."

I lift the bowl from her hands and tilt it at my lips. The potion fills my mouth with a bitterness richer and darker than any chocolate, paradoxically sparkling on my tongue like champagne.

I swallow. "It tastes like … lights in the darkness."

"Then that is your name. Hotarugari."

"Hotarugari?" The name resonates in my bones. "What does it mean?"

"Catching fireflies."

Bells start to ring in the nearby Buddhist temples. It must be midnight. I know the bells will ring one hundred and eight times, once for each of the worldly sins. Afterward, these sins will be cleansed from the people of Tokyo, and the New Year can begin in peace.

I drain the rest of the potion, then open my eyes. "Hotarugari."

twenty-one

Heat.

Sweet, perfume-drenched heat, the kind that soaks your skin and touches your bones. Eyes closed, I drink in the fragrance of infinite flowers. When I open my eyes, I still can't believe I'm not dreaming, and I'm here.

Sunshine pours onto the lavender fields of Hokkaido, rows upon rows of purple that stretch to the startlingly blue horizon. In the distance, a stand of cheerfully spiky pines waves to the clouds wisping across the sky.

I'm home. But it's not my home anymore.

A lovely sadness lingering in my chest, I look back at the watercolor I'm working on—a painting of the way the wind sends shimmering ripples through the flowers. The illusion I've crafted mimics this movement on paper. I'm a better artist with colored pencils, but watercolors seem to suit foxfire better.

"This," I say, "is the Hokkaido I remember."

Gwen leans over my shoulder to look. "I think it needs more squigglies."

"Squiggly isn't a technical artistic term," I say dryly.

She rolls her eyes. "You know what I mean. Those things." She points at the way the lavender sways in the illusory wind.

I sigh. "They aren't easy."

It's the summer after my freshmen year at Humboldt State University. I've spent my first two semesters getting my artistic butt kicked by rich-kid faeries who've been crafting glamours since they were toddlers. But I'm learning.

I smile evilly at Gwen. "Or I could always paint you."

"No!" She laughs. "No portraits."

I study her face. Freckles pepper her cheeks—I like to think of them as Gwen's happiness barometer, since she adores the sun. Hokkaido has plenty of sun in the summertime. We're staying in the center of the island, close to where I ran as a kit-fox, and far away from Yukimi and Akira.

I swallow hard. I don't know when that will ever stop hurting.

I pick up my paintbrush again, since art says what I can't find words for. There's a single pink lavender flower growing nearby that I want to paint in the foreground, but I'm not sure about the colors. From the corner of my eye, I see a flash of red on purple.

I blink. The sun must be getting to me.

"I'm going to go read," Gwen says, "back on the infinitely more comfortable grass. Okay?"

"Okay," I say, sounding absent-minded in a perfectly calculated way.

Gwen hikes away, a book under one arm, and I keep fiddling with my watercolors. I pretend not to notice how the vixen creeps from the lavender and stares at me.

It can't be her...unless her death was no more than an illusion.

"Kazahana?" I whisper.

The vixen flicks her ears back, then trots to me as if she can't help herself. I meet her eyes, and I know it's her.

We don't say anything; we don't need to. A giddy feeling spirals through me. She tricked the yakuza, and lived.

I keep my voice low, as if I might spook her. "It is you."

Kazahana—Yukimi—Okāsan—touches her nose to the back of my hand, her whiskers tickling my skin, then bounds back into the field and disappears, like a drop of red in a pool of purple.

"Tavian!" Gwen calls. "Come here!"

My heart thuds harder and I feel a twinge of pain. It could be the yakuza and their dogs, back to finish the job. Taking a steadying breath, I look back and see Gwen standing on the crest of a hill. Her curls fly behind her in the wind, glinting in the sun.

"I found a gorgeous flower for you to paint," she says.

I smile.

Karen Kincy

About the Author

Karen Kincy (Redmond, Washington) lives among countless trees, some of which—her pet kumquats and oranges—have lovingly invaded her apartment. Luckily, her life is free of faceless ghosts and vicious dog-spirits. Karen has a BA in Linguistics and Literature from The Evergreen State College, and is studying toward a Master's in Computational Linguistics. Visit her online at www.karenkincy.com.